infinity

JUS ACCARDO

Entangled Publishing, LLC
2614 South Timberline Road
Suite 109
Fort Collins, CO 80525

Entangled Teen is an imprint of Entangled Publishing, LLC.

Visit our website at www.entangledpublishing.com.

Edited by Liz Pelletier
Cover design by LJ Anderson
Interior design by Toni Kerr

ISBN 9781633754973
Ebook ISBN 9781633754966

Manufactured in the United States of America

First Edition November 2016

10 9 8 7 6 5 4 3 2 1

To the Thursday morning crew…
Every time my cell phone moos, we think of you.

Chapter One

"It's a miracle I haven't been caught yet..."

Sure, I was technically talking to myself. And yes, in some circles that might fall strictly under the *someone get Kori Anderson a white jacket with pretty silver buckles and rubber room, stat* category. But this thing was freaking huge—and no one had a clue I was the culprit. I was pretty damn proud.

I'd heard chatter around town, and even at school. It was thrilling to hear them talk. An even mix of opinions ranging from pure vandalism to unequivocal talent. Some nights I wondered what they'd do to me if my identity were discovered. An award or scholarship to a prestigious art school? A slap on the wrist or a short stint in the pokey to *teach me a lesson*? No matter what, it would have all been worth it.

The spray can fizzled and spit until nothing but air came out. "Damn." I set it down, resisting the urge to send it flying across the grass. Along with my thick chestnut-colored hair and dark brown eyes, I'd inherited a good portion of Mom's hair-trigger temper. Running out of midnight blue was going to cost me time I didn't have.

I'd started the mural less than five hours after my mother died. Dad was on a mission at the time, but I was there. I'd been right beside her when she slipped away. Funny how even when you can see something like death coming from miles away, it always seems to take you by surprise. A sucker punch to the tender parts that shreds your insides good and proper.

I sat there for hours, shocked despite the inevitability of it all, with my cheek pressed against hers, until her skin had cooled and my entire body went numb. The memory was still so clear, her last words, *Promise me that you'll live your life in vivid color*, still haunted my every move. Sometimes at night, when I lingered at the halfway point—not awake, yet not really asleep—I'd find myself transported back two years, to that hospital room. The sound of the machines filling the painful silence. The sharp scent of disinfectant and medicine, along with her unnatural stillness. I would never forget the look of her skin missing that subtle vibrancy that came with life.

When I finally found the strength to leave her behind and walk from the building, it was almost midnight. There were men from the army base waiting to take me home. Dad's subordinates were all nice, but I'd wanted to be alone. Needed it. I gave them the slip and wandered around the city for an hour, finally ending up on the edge of Clifton Park. That's when I found it. The wall.

I ran my fingers over the uneven brick. When I pulled them away, there was the smallest trace of blue on the tips. I'd gotten the night sky done, and most of the stars. They'd been the hardest. Partially because eight feet of the wall was night sky, and also because of the subtle shape I'd arranged them in. The only things left were the silhouette of a woman, a few finishing touches, and the words. *Love from here to infinity*.

It's what had been etched into my parents' wedding bands. What I would insist be etched into mine, should I ever find a guy willing to put up with my array of irritating habits and low tolerance temper. It's what mom said to me each night before I drifted to sleep... Real love, she always said, knew no bounds. It wasn't hindered by space or time. It couldn't be weakened by death. Real love started in your heart and went straight through to infinity.

I set the empty spray-paint can down and grinned at my masterpiece. Pulling the clip from the edge of my shirt, I twisted my long hair and secured it atop my head. If all went well—and I managed to bring the right supplies—a few weeks and I'd be finished. I would have to be careful, though. Getting caught would be disastrous at this point.

Something crackled behind me. The kind of sound a shoe made as it stomped down on twigs, or leaves... I whirled around, heart hammering, and saw...nothing. It was just me, the trees, and the wall.

The wall... It had become something of an urban legend in the area. I'd done so many over the years. Everything from jungle scenes loaded with exotic animals stalking their prey, to panoramic landscapes of treetops and epic mountain ranges. Whatever my mind deemed peaceful at the time. Each time we moved I'd pick an out-of-the-way spot, something dank and depressing, and work my magic. Turning garbage to gold, I liked to think of it. The previous ones hadn't been easy. Living on base made nighttime forays into the city impossible. I'd had to be crafty. Pick low traffic areas I could work on during the day when it wouldn't look suspicious leaving the base.

This last one was different, though. Much more personal than the others and, obviously, far more visible. I'd chosen the inside section of the wall around the park, about a hundred feet from the lake. Unlike the other ones, this needed to be seen. Proper tribute needed to be paid. But my choice in location had come with a price.

For months after I'd started, the police patrolled the park looking for the vandal—aka me. The whole thing pissed me off. Here I was adding a little culture and class to an otherwise dreary area and they wanted to punish me for it? Once I'd even had to start again. Seven months in, the mayor had city workers paint over my work to prove that *vandalism wouldn't be tolerated*. Because the grime-covered wall with its chipped bricks and scattered profanity were so much better than actual art? I'd been crushed at the time, but a few weeks of crying and a whole lot of peach frozen yogurt later, and I came back with a vengeance, determined to show the world my tribute to an amazing woman.

The wind kicked up, and I heard it again. Definitely not my imagination. And this time when I turned, I saw that I wasn't alone. "Oh my God!"

"Not quite," the guy said.

He was tall—probably just over six feet—with a long face and dark hair. He took a single step forward. The move brought him into the full beam of the park light, revealing brown eyes and a somewhat crooked nose. He'd broken it at one point, I guessed. But the injury gave his face depth. Personality. As an artist, I lived for the imperfections. The small details that made things unique. Perfection was boring. Give me complication and bumpy roads and I was a happy girl.

I glanced at the wall, then turned back to him. "I, uh…" Yeah. What was I supposed to say here? I was standing in front of the wall, paint cans all over the ground at my feet, covered in blue. There wasn't any way to talk myself out of this.

He snickered, but said nothing.

"This isn't what it looks like?" I tried.

Still, nothing. All he did was stare—which was starting to freak me out a little.

"Are you okay?" He didn't look homeless, but maybe he'd been in an accident? "Do you need help?"

More staring.

"Oookay then," I said, taking a step back. "Well, if you speak English, do me a favor and don't rat me out."

He laughed again, and took a single step toward me. "You have bigger things to worry about." Then, without another word, he turned and started to walk away.

"I think that's it for tonight," I said to myself as he faded into the night.

I wiped both hands down the sides of my jeans. My uniform. Every color of the rainbow streaked the lovingly worn denim, making the jeans a piece of unique artwork themselves. I'd had them for years; they were stretched and frayed, and Mom used to joke that when I was a famous artist, she'd frame them and hang them in the hallway.

A quick check of my cell told me I was in trouble. It was almost one in the morning. I hadn't meant to stay this late. Dad was traveling to Washington in a few hours, and that meant he'd be up at half past a rooster's ass. If I wanted to get back into the house without being caught, I needed to move fast. Besides, I didn't want to be around if creepy guy came back around.

I tugged down the sleeves of my oversized sweater and grabbed my bag, stuffing supplies inside. Several colors of spray paint, a few brushes, and a tube of white. A car passed on the road just beyond the back gate of the park, slowing suspiciously. I held my breath and pressed myself flush against the wall, waiting. But it was fine. The headlights faded and the car didn't double back.

Snatching up my jacket, I zipped the pack closed and started for the gate. The town of Wells, New York was small, consisting of barely two thousand people, most of which lived on the Fort Hannity Army Base. We lived off base, in a small cul-de-sac about five blocks away, and I thanked God for that every day. Base life was like living under a microscope. No privacy, stomping boots and gunfire at all hours of the day and night, not to mention more green than a Seattle forest. No thank you. This was the first place Dad had been stationed that we hadn't lived on post. The freedom was intoxicating, and I'd admittedly gone a little nuts with it.

I picked up the pace. The wind howled, sending a shiver down my spine, more from the sound it made — like a woman screaming bloody murder — than the chill, though I wasn't a fan of that, either. Fall. I hated this time of year. Everything was in the process of dying. The smell of leaves that fell from the trees and rotted on the ground turned my stomach. I'd been born on an army base in Hawaii and was convinced my body simply wasn't made for the lower temperatures. Anything below eighty was just too damn cold. And the snow? For the polar bears and elves. If God wanted humans to trudge around in all that white crap, he would have given us fur-covered bodies and skis instead of feet.

The leaves beneath my sneakers crunched and crackled, and about three blocks from home, I heard another noise. Not the howling wind. No. This was softer. Muted and more controlled. Slowing my pace, I took a deep breath and listened. *Thud. Thud. Thud.* Faint, but unmistakable. Footsteps. Had that creepy guy from the park followed me?

I stopped walking for a second and peered over my shoulder. A row of nondescript shadows stretched along the buildings, cast from the streetlamps overhead. Several mailboxes. Dark storefronts. The bench I'd puked on last year after drinking too much blueberry vodka at the one and only party I'd ever gone to... All typical roadside denizens.

Nope. Nothing to see here...

Adjusting the pack on my shoulder, I gripped the strap just a little bit tighter. It was heavy enough to be used as a weapon if necessary. Dad made sure I knew at an early age that good soldiers were always prepared. One never knew when danger would come knocking. You had to be prepared to knock back. Hard.

I took a deep breath and was about to start forward

again, but something in the distance clattered. A loud sound that echoed through the empty streets and sent my heartbeat thumping double-time. A second later, the *danger* walked into the light.

Well, danger if you counted destruction at the paws of a stray dog.

It looked like a collie mix and trotted into the light of the streetlamp from the alley to my left, and I let go of a breath. It paused momentarily, staring me down with clinical interest. Once it assessed that I was no threat, it continued on its way without so much as a second glance.

Convinced it was safe, I resumed my pace, but half a block farther I heard it again. Footsteps. Much closer than last time. Okay. Not the dog. It was that guy. It *had* to be. I readied my bag and sucked in a deep breath. When I whirled around, I lost my balance, nearly tumbling to the ground.

"A little late for a young woman to be out on the streets, don't you think?"

Instead of the weird guy from the park, a man in a dark uniform with broad shoulders and a bushy moustache towered over me. He was vaguely familiar. Officer Hennas or Hensley, or something. He'd almost caught me at the mural a few times. I tried to get out here at least once every week. Last week I'd had to scrunch myself up inside a bunch of pricker bushes a few yards from the lake to avoid detection. It'd taken hours to get all the tiny needles out. I was still convinced I'd missed a few.

He folded his arms and began tapping his elbow with his ring finger. *Tap. Tap. Tap.* "Mind if I ask what you're doing out here?"

"I, uh—" Something told me *out for a midnight stroll* wasn't going to cut it here. Suddenly the guy's cryptic warning made sense. He'd either seen the officer in the area, or had scampered off and tattled. Either way, I was screwed. "Studying at a friend's house. Didn't realize the time."

His gaze dropped to my pack, and suspicion erupted across his face. "I'm sure you won't mind opening your bag for me. Show me your books?"

I didn't move.

"What were you studying?" he tried again. He held out his hand, wiggling his fingers and giving me no choice. I handed over the bag.

As he unzipped the main compartment and peered inside, I held my breath. Time seemed to stand still for several moments. When his gaze finally lifted to meet mine, I saw the understanding spark there. The subtle hint of triumph.

I swallowed back the acid bubbling up in my belly. "Um, art?"

Yep. I was so screwed.

Chapter Two

*A*fter calling Dad, the *nice* officer—whose name was actually Henley—escorted me back to the mural to wait. Dad didn't rush—probably letting me stew in it for a bit. By the time he arrived, I was freezing my toes off and had to pee like never before.

Officer Henley nodded as Dad extracted himself from our red SUV. "Sorry to wake you, sir, but..." He inclined his head in my direction. "This belongs to you?"

Dad looked from Henley to me, lips pressed in a super thin line, then rounded the corner to glare at the wall. I hated it when he got quiet like this. It'd be fine if he raised his voice. Yelled and screamed and sent me to my room like a normal parent. But Dad wasn't normal. He was twenty plus years of restraint and perfection rolled into the body of a U.S. army general.

"Technically I should take her into the station," Henley continued with a frown. "I'm sure you're aware that this thing's been a sore subject for the mayor for a while now. However, I'm going to let you take her home instead."

"I appreciate that," Dad said. He took my bag from the officer, then handed it back to me. I almost didn't take it. That thing had sealed my fate, and that didn't put us on the best of terms.

"The mayor—all of us—have the greatest respect for you Fort Hannity boys. I'm sure he'll be willing to work something out about the wall."

Again, Dad nodded. The only hint of his anger with me was the smallest twitch of his right thumb. When that thumb flicked, you knew you were in for it. "I'm leaving for Washington in a few hours. I will contact him as soon as I get back to town if that's satisfactory."

Henley eyed me.

"Don't worry." Dad clapped a hand down on my shoulder, giving a firm shake. "I've already arranged for supervision while I'm away. You won't have any more trouble from her. Isn't that right, Kori?"

"Yes sir," I answered, standing a little bit straighter. He hated when I slouched.

"Thank you, General Anderson." Officer Henley tipped the rim of his hat. "Have a safe trip, and Godspeed."

We watched him make his way toward the gate and back to his squad car, and I waited, breath held, for the lecture to begin.

Dad turned from me to face the wall. He traced one of the lines of stars with his finger, then sighed. "Do you really think she would approve of this?"

She. *Mom*. It was the first time he'd brought her up in a long while. It was an unspoken rule, we didn't talk about her, and I hated it. She'd died, but he treated it like she'd never existed. Like merely the mention of her name might bring an end to the world in a shower of hellfire and brimstone. "I think she'd understand."

His brows rose. "She would understand defacing public property?"

This time I didn't answer. Mom used to tell me stories about her wild-child youth, but he was right. She wouldn't have approved. This had nothing to do with simple teenaged rebellion, though, and deep down I think he knew that. But slapping a vandalism label on it was easier to face than the truth. Two whole years and Mom's loss was still a raw, open wound. It'd changed both of us. She'd been the glue that held things together. The light in our now dark house. And we each had our own way of dealing. Mine was art and, um, freedom of expression.

His was denial.

"I'll be gone a few days." He gripped my shoulders and turned me toward the truck with a nudge. "When I get back, we'll deal with this."

I cringed. This wasn't going to be pretty, but at least I had a few days to prepare.

Dad was gone more than he was home. I used to hate it, but since Mom died, I found myself thankful. Not because I wanted him gone. I loved him. He loved me, too. I knew that—even if we'd never fully understood each other. But we didn't know how to deal with each other anymore. We didn't know how to talk.

He'd lost a part of himself when we lost her, and what was left belonged to Uncle Sam. He'd made a choice to live each day entrenched in service to our country rather than face life without her. Never mind that I was still here... Never mind that I missed our Sunday horror movie marathons complete with caramel-covered popcorn, and the yearly trip he and I took to the Great Lakes.

But there were moments he believed himself alone—moments he thought the rest of the world wasn't looking—that little bits of the old him bled through. Like right before he traveled. It had become a weird tradition between us. I crept down the stairs, tucked myself around the corner, and watched him go.

Suitcase packed, he would gather his keys and papers and head for the door. Halfway across the room he would pause, like it was something spur of the moment, then lean in and plant the softest kiss on the picture of Mom and me that hung above the end table. He pretended not to notice me there, but you don't get to be a general by coasting along, unobservant. I liked to think he did it to let me know he still cared. To prove that he was still in there even if he couldn't find the right ways to communicate with me. I wanted to believe it was his way of saying *I love you*.

Following that same routine, Dad pushed off just after four in the morning, and I'd crawled back into bed for a few hours to catch up on my z's. By the time ten a.m. rolled around, it was obvious that he'd made good on his promise to Officer Henley. I was spending this trip under strict supervision. My babysitter was on the front steps, pounding on the door.

I squared my shoulders and pulled open the door, hoping for Bentley, one of Dad's more clueless subordinates. He'd watched me before and tended to distract easily. All it took was a little cable TV and some powdered doughnuts. At least with him, I'd have a chance to sneak out and get a picture of the mural before they painted over the thing. The mayor wouldn't waste any time, and I refused to let all that work go without some kind of reminder. Unfortunately, it wasn't Private Bentley on my doorstep. It was someone else.

Two someone elses.

"General Anderson sent us," the one in the front said. He was tall, with what looked like dark hair. It was hard to tell. He was wearing a black skullcap and had the collar of his leather jacket flipped up, assumedly to shield him from the chilly breeze.

"Really?" I cracked open the door and wedged one of my sneakers behind it. This babysitting thing wasn't something new. Dad had done it before. My penchant for trouble was near legendary around town—though, as rumors went, it was greatly exaggerated. I had a reputation of not playing well with others—my own personal middle finger to society for moving Dad's post all over creation more than twelve times in my life alone. That led to stories of inflated debauchery and rebellious behavior, only a quarter of which I was actually guilty of. My biggest crime to date was hardcore tagging. Not the cheesy *write your handle all over the wall* kind, but quickie works of art that, in my opinion, improved the scenery. Splashes of color that breathed new life into dead things.

All the other times Dad arranged babysitting detail,

he'd sent uniformed soldiers complete with the formal stick shoved up their asses and the expressions wiped from their faces. I couldn't see the other guy, he was standing behind hat-boy, but this one oozed attitude. I might have actually liked him on sight—in a *might be cool to hang with* kind of way—if he hadn't been a greenie. "You're telling me that you're soldiers?"

"Is that something people lie about around here?" His blue jeans were worn, pulled over battered black combat boots. The sole of the left one was peeling away from the shoe. Did he think he could slack because Dad wasn't here? That no one would see him and report back? Even if they had permission to be in civies, there were strict standards. While off duty, a soldier had to maintain a neat, well-groomed appearance. This was more an outfit worthy of a high school rebel, which, honestly, this guy didn't look much older than.

The one in the back pushed him aside and came forward. Black hair fell just below his ears and had a slight wave to it. It was fuller than normally allowed, not even close to regulation. On some of our previous bases, hair standards weren't strictly enforced. But at Hannity, they were sticklers. High and tight. Those were the rules.

Like the other guy, he had on a leather jacket with black fatigue pants tucked into slightly worn combat boots. Unlike the first, though, this one had seen some trouble in his day. There was a thin scar on the left side of his face. It went from just above his eyebrow, down across his eye and to the tip of his chin.

My pulse spiked a little as his gaze raked over me. Down and up, then up and down, lips parting slightly. I didn't go for greenies, but this one sent the butterflies in my stomach tripping crazy. It was the scar. It added character to his angular face, suggesting that maybe there was more than meets the eye. Or possibly it was the way he was looking at me. With a spark of hunger and something close to wonder in his expression. I'd never had anyone look at me that way. Like I was something mythical and rare. A creature that shouldn't exist. I twisted, shifting so that the door obscured just a little more of me from his view.

He hesitated, focus still trained on me, and for a moment I thought he might poke me to be sure I was real. Clearing his throat, he finally said, "I'm Private First Class Cade Granger, and this is…" He paused to glance over his shoulder. "Recruit Noah Emeal."

"A private and a fuzzy? *Really?*" I wasn't sure if I should be pleased or insulted. I mean, why bother sending supervision at all if you were going to scrape the bottom of the barrel?

"I promise you'll be safe with us, Miss Anderson."

Miss Anderson. Huh. Maybe there wasn't more to this guy. He sounded just like the rest of them. Formal and uptight. "That right? So you're here to save me from myself?" Because, really, that was the problem, right? I couldn't be trusted to keep myself out of trouble.

"I'm not sure I understand." He tilted his head to the left, confused, but didn't take his eyes off me. In fact, if anything, his gaze grew more intense. It was like he and I were the only ones in the room. In the world…

"I'd really appreciate it if you could stop staring." I snapped. "I can't tell if you're mentally trying to strip me, or contemplating which way to cook my skin for Sunday dinner. Either way, it's creeping me the hell out."

His mouth fell open, but he recovered quickly, squaring his shoulders. A dark gray T-shirt peeked out from beneath his leather jacket. There was a logo on the front—something that looked kind of like a man with a wand—but I couldn't see the words.

I sighed. Really, what was the point? Maybe Dad sent chaperones he thought I'd be able to identify with. Maybe this was his weird way of extending an olive branch. "Identification?"

"Of course." Cade nodded and dug into his back pocket, producing a small badge. Obediently, he held it out to me.

"Private First Class Cade Granger," I read aloud. In the picture, his hair was short and tapered to contour his head as per regulation. It looked much better grown out. Then again, I was a sucker for long hair. I sighed and stepped aside. "Suppose I should let you in."

"Thank you." He stepped inside, followed by Noah.

I led them down the hall and into the living room, and pointed to the long couch against the wall. "That one pulls out into a bed." Then, to the one on the other side of the room. "And the other is strictly a *what you see is what you get* deal. Fight it out between yourselves."

"Thank you," Cade said again. He gestured to the couch. "May I?"

"Go for it." I sank into the chair across from him. Noah was still standing in the doorway like at any moment he might make a run for it. Where Cade stared, he was doing his best to avoid looking. He scanned the room, gaze bouncing off everything except me. I wasn't sure which I preferred. Cade's scrutiny was on the unnerving side, but his partner's complete lack of interest kind of freaked me out, too. "So what's the deal here? Lay it out for me."

"Deal?"

I rolled my eyes. "The rules. Guessing the general gave you a list of do's and don'ts? That's his usual play. Just wanna know what I'm in for."

"Oh," Cade said. "We're here—"

"Go about your daily routine," Noah interrupted. "Do whatever it is you normally do on a Saturday."

Joking. He was joking. I hitched a thumb toward the door. "So…I can leave?"

"No," Cade said vehemently, while at the same time Noah supplied a semi-cheerful, "Sure." They glared at each other, a silent argument flaring to life.

"Well, which is it?"

"No," Cade answered with an air of authority. His expression softened. "I'd rather you stayed here."

"Rather?" I challenged. "So, then I *can* leave."

He shook his head and pinned his partner with a stern expression. Noah looked ready to explode. "I suppose it would be all right."

Victory!

I couldn't help grinning, and immediately started for the door to claim my prize.

"Of course, we'd have to go with you," he added, and I froze. Just one foot from freedom! "I'm sorry."

Sorry? He didn't sound very sorry. In fact, he seemed kind of smug. But that was okay. Because apparently he'd never gotten the memo on teenage girls. Telling us not to do something was the fastest way to nudge us toward doing it.

Chapter Three

I killed the day in my room, venturing downstairs only to use the bathroom, or when the munchies struck—which wasn't often. Dad was a health food nut. It almost made me happy when he went away. I took advantage of the opportunity to eat junk food and load up on carbs, and ordered a pizza for dinner. When it arrived, I snagged a slice, then retreated back to my hole to pass my sentence in peace, away from prying eyes.

Because it was unsettling. Each time I went downstairs, there was more staring. This must be how zoo animals felt. No wonder so many were ornery. Either they were taking Dad's *watch her* orders just a little too seriously, or I'd grown a set of horns and a third boob I wasn't aware of.

At about two in the morning, I pushed off the covers and threw my legs over the edge of the bed, frustrated and unable to sleep. I couldn't get the mural out of my mind. It was silly, but I felt close to Mom in the countless hours I'd spent painting. Like she had been there with me for each brush stroke. Had supervised every spritz of color. I imagined her standing over my shoulder, wild chestnut hair fluttering in the breeze, and humming softly.

I sighed and kicked at the air. The moment I'd gotten caught, the town of Wells had gotten a little bit smaller. My long leash of semi-freedom tightened. This time when they painted over it, there would be no starting again. Anywhere. They'd know it was me.

I had to see it one last time. I *had* to say good-bye.

As quietly as I could, I dressed and slipped both feet into my sneakers, then crept across the room. The boards creaked and I cringed, freezing. I held my breath and listened for a moment, convinced I'd hear at least someone stirring. But there was nothing.

So far so good.

I took it as a sign and kept moving. One foot in front of the other, I ventured into the hallway and paused again to listen for movement. It was dark and the lights were all off downstairs except for one. It looked like the lamp on the coffee table in the living room.

"What did the general say?" Cade asked in a hushed voice.

Noah sighed. "He checked into the names we gave him. Only one is a soldier on base. Miles Hann. Penny Bloom runs an animal hospital in town, and Odette Ferguson works at some advertising firm. All three are unaccounted for already."

"Dylan's moving fast this time for some reason," Cade growled. "He's been here only twenty-four hours and they're all gone."

Unaccounted for?

People were missing? I could see the interest in the Miles guy. Military took that kind of thing seriously. But what about the two civilians they'd mentioned? Why involve the Hannity boys? Wouldn't that have been a local police issue?

"He's worried about her." Noah continued. The venom in his voice when he said *her* made me twitch. I assumed he meant me. Apparently he wasn't a fan—which made no sense. Usually people needed more than five minutes to decide if they loved or hated me.

"Jesus, man. You can't even say her name, can you?"

Noah mumbled something too low for me to hear—which drove me nuts—then added, "In the meantime, we're not supposed to let her out of our sight."

"Hadn't planned on it. We're her shadows until the general does what he needs to."

"This isn't what we're here for," Noah complained. The springs on the couch squeaked.

"This is exactly what we're here for! How the hell can you even say that? The entire plan—"

"The plan," Noah said with a snort. More squeaking from the couch. "Is a roundabout way for you to—"

"Do *not* finish that sentence, Noah."

"Whatever, man. You know I'm right. And on some level I don't blame you. This whole thing has you messed up."

"And you're not, right? This is all so easy for you?"

"You know that it's not."

They continued to argue, but the heat kicked on, making the rest of the conversation impossible to hear. Bad for snooping—all that *plan* talk had me crazy curious—but good for escaping. I gave up on it and eased down the stairs, one at a time, then pressed myself close to the wall. Slow, but steady. Twenty steps and I made it through the hallway and around the corner of the kitchen.

The conversation had died, but they'd turned on the television. The faint sound of sitcom laughter was just what I needed to cover the slight squeak of the backdoor hinge and the click of the lock as it closed behind me.

One last look. That's all I wanted. I would be there and back before they even knew I was gone. I'd snuck out to the wall a thousand times. What could go wrong?

*I*t took me forty minutes to get into town. It would have taken less time if I'd been able to cut through the Harper farm like I'd planned, but the lights were on up at the barn, and the faint sounds of chatter drifted through the field. I'd been forced to go the long way.

I hit the main drag and pulled out my cell. Almost three a.m. and I was still four blocks from the park. I stuffed both hands into my pockets and picked up the pace. I was about a half block away when someone called out.

"Hey again."

I froze, terrified to turn around. They couldn't nail me for doing anything wrong. Technically. There was no curfew in Wells, and I had nothing on me that would be considered vandal friendly. I was just a girl out for a stroll. In the middle of the night.

Nope. Nothing suspicious about that.

"Kori Anderson, right?"

This time, I turned, expecting to see a police officer, or possibly someone familiar from the base. Instead, I saw the ass from earlier. "You!" I jabbed a finger in his general direction. "You ratted me out. And how do you even know my name?"

He took a single step forward, but didn't answer. Great. So we were back to the mute thing again?

It was more than that, though. Something stirred in my belly. An unfamiliar feeling that made goose bumps spring to life across my skin and spawned an itching sensation in my legs. It took me a minute to place it, but I realized it was fear. I wanted to back away. It was the way he was looking at me. If I had to put his expression to words, the only ones that would come to mind were *sizing me up.* Debating how easily I'd go down. I held my ground, but my heart thumped triple time.

Show no fear…

He gave a dark laugh, sending a nervous shiver up my spine. He hitched a thumb over his shoulder and tilted his head to the left. "I gotta thank you. You made this really easy."

"Plan on tattling again? Because, technically I wasn't doing anything wrong…"

He laughed again. For some reason, he found this whole thing funny? Odd, but I could probably work with it. Funny was better than crazy. "You're not in trouble, Kori."

I let out a breath.

"With the base, anyway," he finished, taking another

step forward. This one was different. Menacing. It matched the viperous gleam in his eyes and, as he moved closer, I was reminded of a documentary I'd seen on the Discovery Channel last week. How tigers stalked their prey.

Because that's how I felt in that moment. Like prey. I backed away and surveyed the area without being too obvious. I could scream, but there was no one around at three in the morning to hear me. Why? Because normal people—*smart people*—were tucked away in bed and not wandering the streets.

"Going somewhere?" He tilted his head to the left, shadows consuming half his face and giving it an eerie quality. His grin was wide, loaded with a wicked confidence that made the hairs on the back of my neck jump to attention.

"Home," I answered as calmly as possible.

Show no fear. Show no fear.

I turned and started moving, in no particular hurry, hoping it conveyed that I wasn't afraid—which, honestly? I wasn't.

I was terrified.

I was having trouble remembering a time in my life that I'd ever been *this* terrified of anything. Acid churned in my belly and bile crept up my throat. It burned a scorching trail as I swallowed it back and struggled not to choke.

I got four steps—maybe five—before his hand closed around my arm. The air caught in my throat.

What would a soldier do? What would Dad *do?*

In that moment, I felt every beat of my heart as if it were a heavy metal drum solo going to town against my ribs. Panic, raw and unfiltered, washed through me. I'd been taught to defend myself. As the daughter of a U.S. general, you didn't attend the ballet or weekly tea parties in Mom's makeup with stuffed animals and oversized high heeled shoes. And up until that very moment, if you'd asked me if I was confident I could hold my own with an attacker, I would have answered a resounding *hell, yes*. But that was mainly because I'd never been tested. Now that reality was staring down my nose, heralded by broad shoulders and an angry twitch, I wasn't so confident.

He pulled back, and I went with him.

Fight. Use what you have.

I followed through and jerked my elbow upward with all my strength. It connected with him—I had no clue where, and didn't much care. As long as I'd made contact. He cursed and stumbled away, letting go of my arm. That was my window. I ran like hell.

Behind me, his laughter echoed through the empty street. An eerie battle cry tinged with excitement. "Well, this is new," he called. A second later, his footsteps clapped against the ground and he let out an enthusiastic hoot. "I like it!"

I ran, tipping over whatever I could get my hands on. Garbage cans, sidewalk signs, traffic cones. Anything that might be a hindrance. Might slow him down. I also pounded my fists against every surface that might make noise. The blows echoed off glass storefronts and doors, a nightmarish thunder against the night's silence. There was a slim chance someone else could be lurking around, and I knew a few of the old-timers had apartment spaces above their shops. All I needed was to piss someone off enough to call the cops.

But no one surfaced. I was alone. A quick check of my cell told me outside help wasn't an option, either. No service. I veered to the left at the end of the block, ducking around the side of Jarvis's Deli. This guy was probably stronger, but I was faster. I'd gained some ground, and if I was lucky, I could lose him in the courtyard maze.

It was what people called restaurant alley. A web of eateries, most with backyard tables and gardens. They were all connected by a series of small rock walls that made the whole thing resemble a maze. It was pretty; they kept it strung year-round with thousands of white Christmas lights—which under normal circumstances I loved. Unfortunately, now the tiny bulbs illuminated my every move, creating a telltale shadow that made it impossible to hide.

I raced through the maze, looking over my shoulder just once. I had no idea who this guy was, or what he wanted, but I had no intention of finding out.

"I just wanna talk to you, Kori," he yelled, followed by a knowing snicker. "But, if you don't wanna talk to me… Well, we can go another route."

Talk my ass. You didn't chase down a girl to chat her up. You approached her in the daytime. Asked her name. Tossed a few compliments. Got her digits… Excessive force and stalking? Grabby hands and thinly veiled threats? Not the way to go.

I ducked down and scrunched myself under a cluster of thick bushes. Just in time, too. The guy entered the courtyard and slowly made his way toward me. I thought about pulling out my cell again. It could have picked up a signal. But he was too close. He'd hear me just as soon as I opened my mouth, and help would never get here in time.

Despite a heavy military presence, Wells was just like any other town. Hell, I'd heard stories about violence on the base. No place on Earth was truly *safe*. This guy could just be some wack job looking to stash me away in his windowless basement for the next fifty or so years. Except that he'd mentioned the base. This was the second time tonight I'd seen him, and he knew me by name. There was nothing random about this.

I was targeted…

"Come on," he said in a singsong voice. "I just need to ask you a few questions. I promise I won't hurt you." A soft snicker. "Much…"

He'd almost passed and it looked like I was in the clear. I said a silent prayer of thanks and leaned forward on my heels, ready to dash off the second I was sure he was gone. Of course, that's the moment one of the game apps on my phone started going off…

Chapter Four

"Shit!" I fumbled with the cell, trying to silence the thing, but it was too late. He turned and was already on his way. I rocked back on my heels, ready to bolt, but he was on me in a flash.

Unyielding fingers wrapping around a large chunk of my long hair, he dragged me out from the brush and growled, "You're a lot more trouble than the others."

"The others, who?" I struggled against his grasp. Did he make a habit of this? Attacking girls on the street? Not that I cared. Right now the only thing I wanted was for him to let go. But his grip was like iron, unforgiving and unrelenting. No amount of squirming gave me leeway.

Without answering, he made his way across the courtyard, dragging me behind him like a child's toy. My eyes watered and my nose itched. That tickle that comes right before you sneeze. I wasn't a crier, good soldiers sucked it up and pushed onward through the worst of times, even though this situation certainly would have warranted a breakdown.

We headed for the darkness of the alley. Four feet. Three feet.

No.

I sucked in as much air as I could and screamed. The sound tore from my throat, ripping free like ten thousand tiny shards of glass.

With a curse, he jerked me backward and slapped his hand down across my mouth.

Or at least, that's what he tried to do. I threw myself sideways to send him off-balance. Whatever it was he wanted, I wasn't about to give in without one hell of a fight. "Someone," I bellowed as he made another swipe. His hand caught the corner of my face, jarring my head sideways with a violent jerk. "Help me! Please, I'm—"

He was successful on the third try. His meaty hand covered my mouth. The pressure of his fingers digging craters into the sides of my face brought involuntary tears to my eyes as my heart hammered out an uneven, erratic beat. "Do it again and I promise that you'll live just long enough to regret it."

He removed his hand and spun my body around, pitching me backward into the building. I tried to scream again—his threats were nothing compared to the colorful imagery my imagination cooked up—but my forehead smashed against the brick and everything swam out of focus. When it cleared, he had his left hand around my neck and the right braced against the wall beside my head. He leaned close and the scent of cigarettes filled the air around me. I almost gagged. "Make a sound and I'll break your neck."

Fight or flight kicked in. Hard. Technically, they were one and the same at that moment. If I wanted flight, then I had to fight. Adrenaline surged through my system like rocket fuel, and I brought my right knee up, as hard as I could, but he was smart. He blocked the blow and shimmied sideways, free and clear of my assault.

Shaking his head, he clucked his tongue. "Bad idea, Kori. Behave. Please. This will go much faster if you simply tell me what I want to know," he whispered against my ear.

His breath, fetid and hot, induced a violent wave of nausea, and for an ill-timed and insane minute, I was worried I might vomit on him. That would probably do less to endear him to me than the screaming. Nobody liked puke. "If this is about my dad, you're out of luck." I turned my face away and swallowed back the bile creeping up my throat. "I'm not involved with anything. I don't *know* anything."

He growled, a dark, dangerous sound that made the acid churn in my belly. "We'll see about that." His fingers tightened around my neck, and with a smile that could only be described as joyous, he began to squeeze.

No. This is not happening...

I clawed at his hand, desperate for air. My nails dug deep, drawing blood—I felt it, warm and slick—but it didn't make him loosen his hold.

He grinned, as if pleased I was fighting back and, as I kicked out blindly with both legs, he laughed out loud. "Where is Ava?"

I tried to tell him that I had no idea who the hell he was talking about, but the lack of oxygen was becoming an issue. Surely if he wanted an answer—not that I had one—he'd have to let me breathe.

"Ava Harris," he barked. "She's not in Wells. I can't find her. Tell me where she is!"

He pushed me around to face him and shoved something under my nose. A picture. In it was a petite, raven-haired girl with a heart-shaped face and mischievous grin. The photograph had seen better days. It was creased down the middle with frayed edges and faded colors. Whoever she was, I'd never seen her before.

When I didn't answer, he squeezed my neck. The edges of my vision clouded, becoming watery and vague. Another scream built in my throat, but died without the oxygen needed to release it into the world. My mind was jumbled. Panic and regret and sadness over all the things I'd never get to do. Dad knew I loved him, right? We were like oil and vinegar most times, but he knew... If I'd only listened. Stayed home and done what I was supposed to...

I was seconds from blacking out when a blurry shape rocketed into the alley from the right. Whatever it was hit us with horrible force and sent both me and my attacker to the ground. I stumbled away, determined to use this new turn of events to my advantage, and put distance between us while choking on the fresh rush of glorious air.

A series of muted blows and grunts filled the alley. I used the wall as a crutch, trying to get to my feet so I could see what was going on, but it was no use. I made it only halfway before the ground dipped and swayed and gravity made me its bitch.

This time I stayed down. I might not be able to get

up and run, but I could sure as hell try crawling. You worked with what you had. Adapted and made due. I could see now that the blur was actually another guy— two of them. Cade and Noah. They must have followed me and been lagging behind, or they would have intervened sooner. Either way, I'd never been so happy about being tailed.

They stood with their backs to me, a welcome barrier between me and my new not-so-friend. I wasn't the kind of girl who normally needed saving, but even I could admit when I was in over my head. Granted I'd put myself there, but, hey…semantics.

"We all know how this goes," the guy said. His gaze found mine and he winked. "What makes you think this time will be any different?"

"We found you, didn't we?" Noah quipped.

"Come on now, Noah." My attacker's grin widened. "We've been here before. How many times now—ten? Eleven? You always say the same thing."

"This time is different, Dylan," Cade interjected. He stood stiff, arms ridged at his sides with both fists clenched tight.

I managed to climb to my feet. This time? So it *had* happened before. I wasn't the first. Was it a military thing? I'd heard stories of soldiers getting reprimanded for bad behavior, but this took it to an entirely new level.

Dylan snorted. "I can honestly say that this time I'll actually regret it. She's nothing like the others." He leveled his gaze at Cade, then winked. "I'm doing you a solid, bro. Usually they're so docile. Boring and sweet— just your speed. But she's a new breed. Way too much fire for you to handle."

Noah lunged forward. Dylan, almost like he'd anticipated the move, danced to the right. "Be seeing you again soon, princess," he called as he took off for the maze. Noah followed without hesitating.

When they were out of sight, Cade turned to me. I expected to see concern in his eyes, maybe distress in his expression. Possibly even fear. You *misplace* your superior's daughter and it's kind of a thing. What I didn't anticipate was fury.

"How could you be so damn stupid?" He stalked toward me and stopped a few feet away. "Coming out here? *Alone?*"

"I—"

"You didn't think anything would happen, right?"

I'd just been attacked, questioned, then nearly choked to death. I wanted to do nothing more than run back home and hide under the covers until tonight was nothing but a bad, distant memory.

Keep it together, Anderson.

I'd been wrong. Had made a mistake by sneaking out. But berating me for it? At least let the shaking stop first. Let me catch my breath and calm down.

"That's the problem though, isn't it?" he continued, oblivious to the fact that I was on the verge of an epic breakdown. "As far as you're concerned, everything is sunshine and roses, right?"

Okay. Whoa. "What are you talking about? *Sunshine and roses?*" I managed once I found my voice. "You don't know anything about me. And for your information, I'm well aware of the ass ratchets that inhabit this city. This world! There's no such thing as sunshine and roses, so spare me the lecture, asshole."

His eyes went wide, and for a moment, I thought he might actually pass out. Maybe he wasn't used to people talking back to him like that? I found a lot of these army guys had something of a God complex. "You—" He took a deep breath, and his expression softened. The tension faded from his body like someone had popped a pinhole in an overinflated balloon. He took a step away. "You're right. I'm sorry. Are you all right?"

All right? No. I was the farthest possible thing from *all right*. But I wasn't about to let him in on the secret. Especially not after he spazzed like that. "That guy asked about someone." Ask, being an extremely polite way of putting it. "Ava Harris?"

Cade kept his expression neutral. "What did you tell him?"

"Everything." I folded my arms and flashed him a severe frown. "I spilled just as soon as he said pretty, pretty please."

He paled.

Jeez. You'd think I just confessed to national defense secrets…

I sighed. "Kidding, relax. I have no idea who Ava Harris is, so, no. I didn't tell him anything."

"Did he say anything else? Ask anything else?"

Before I could respond, Noah trotted back into the alley looking like someone had peed in his Cheerios. "He got away." He stopped a few feet from us and kicked at the wall. After a moment, he did it again, harder. The guy definitely had some anger issues. "I fucking lost him."

"We'll get him," Cade said.

"Damn right we will." Jabbing a finger in my direction, he added, "And *she's* the ticket."

Noah's eyes met mine, and I fought a shiver. Where Cade's gaze made me feel like I was some kind of one in a million gemstone, rare and unfathomable, Noah's made me feel like, well…steak. It was like he was seeing an opportunity to use me to feed the entire world.

Cade's eyes rounded like baseballs. He cast a nervous glance my way, then turned on Noah, furious. "Are you insane?"

Noah shrugged, stuffing both hands into his pockets. There was challenge in his eyes. "If it gets the job done, why not?"

Cade's face bloomed scarlet. He positioned himself in front of me. It was all very caveman, and maybe under different circumstances, I might have found it charming in some weird way. At the moment, though, my patience level was absolute zero, and it was daunting. "How can you—"

I whistled. The sound of it echoed in the alley and stopped both boys dead in their tracks. Like bobble dolls, their heads swiveled in my direction. Good. Now I had their attention. These were two of the strangest soldiers I'd ever come across. Nothing about them was the norm, from their clothing and cursing, right down to general attitude. Normally I would have been relieved. In my opinion, America's finest needed to yank the stick from their asses. But this had gone too far, and really, I had no idea if I was any safer with them than I was with that Dylan guy.

Dylan.

Holy crap! That's the name I'd overheard Cade say back at the house. When they were talking about missing people. *Dylan's already started.* That's what he'd said.

Then there was all that talk about plans... Something was going on. "How about you two tell me the truth."

Noah folded his arms and pinned me with an uninterested glare. "Truth?"

"What was up with that guy who attacked me—Dylan, was it? And who the hell is Ava Harris? I heard what you guys were saying at the house about people having gone missing. A plan? If this has something to do with my dad, then I deserve to know."

Cade's expression, from the slight tilt of his head to the confused twist of his lips, screamed perplexed. "Three people—"

"It's all classified," Noah responded coolly. "And not your concern."

I bit my tongue. I could see if I'd done something to the guy—insulted his granny or accidentally stepped on his junk—but we'd just met. He had no reason to dislike me so much. Recruit or not, you knew the score when you enlisted. What was expected of you. A soldier was a walking, talking representation of the United States. Respectful and polite. Brave and strong. Nowhere did it say you should act like a dick under any circumstance.

"Begging to differ, pal. That asshole just dragged me into the dark and assaulted me. That makes it my concern. If you don't start talking, I might consider stuffing a paintbrush up your ass sideways to help loosen things up."

They both stared at me. Noah's jaw fell open, but Cade just sort of smiled. He reached for my arm, and I didn't think. I balled my fist and struck. In part, it was leftover adrenalin from the chaos of the night, but also reflex. Mom always joked I had my Dad's *soldierness*—

his determination and drive, as well as his *take no crap* attitude. Act first, think later. That's why from the time I could walk, she'd tried—in vain—to interest me in anything and everything that didn't revolve around the military.

Glitter and ponies. Dollhouses and tea parties. All things sweet little girls traditionally loved. Dad never approved. He felt like that was too close to babying. To making me soft and weak. But Mom was determined. She didn't want me following in his footsteps. She shouldn't have worried, though. The military held as much appeal to me as slug tartar. I hadn't had the heart to tell her I felt the same way about all the lace and pink frills. From as far back as I could remember, it was always art. First, crayons. Then, as I got older, watercolor and oil paints. Then, my ultimate love, pencils.

The blow connected with his jaw, the force reverberating through my hand and sending a parade of sharp prickles up my arm. There was a muffled grunt, and Cade's head rocked back. He didn't topple, but I'd gotten him good. You didn't grow up on army bases without knowing how to toss a punch.

He brought a hand to his jaw. "You *hit* me."

"You *grabbed* me." After the night I'd had, he really should have known better.

"Apologies." He let go of his jaw and stood a little straighter. A glint of admiration flashed in his eyes. "Let's get you back to the base."

"Okay—wait. The base?"

Cade frowned. He looked as enthusiastic about the idea of heading to Fort Hannity as I felt. Probably because he was going to have to admit they screwed up. Guard duty meant ensuring nothing bad happened to your charge. Letting me slip through his fingers and go traipsing around town, then to top it off, get attacked, probably wasn't going to win him any medals. "Because the incident involved a family member of a soldier, this needs to be reported. It will be the commander's decision where to go from there."

"We could keep it between us." The last thing I wanted was to march in there and admit I'd snuck out of the house. Because as much trouble as Cade would land in, mine would be worse. This, added to the mural debacle, was going to destroy any and all the freedom I'd enjoyed since coming to Wells, not to mention bring a shitstorm of scrutiny down on Dad's head.

Stupidity, thy name is Kori...

Noah looked like he was just fine with a cover-up, but Cade shook his head. "I'm sorry. It needs to be reported. Those are the rules."

The look of determination on his face told me arguing was pointless. In the short time since I'd met him, I got the distinct feeling that Cade was a by-the-book kind of guy. A shame, really, because this was going to suck.

I was having a really crappy week.

Chapter Five

They'd been in the Red Room—aka Commander Simmons's office—for almost an hour now. It was going on five in the morning, and keeping my eyes open had become more than a challenge. The only thing that made clinging to the waking world possible was the need for an explanation. I refused to leave without one.

I leaned closer to the bathroom mirror to get a better look at the damage. There was a small cut above my left eyebrow and some minor scrapes on the left cheek from where my skin had kissed the brick wall. The lighting inside the small room was horrible, but I could still make out the faintest shadow of a bruise beginning to bloom across my neck. It was sore, and in a few hours it would probably be ten times worse. My shoulder, too. I'd jarred it pretty good when Noah crashed into us in the alley. And, of course, there was the steady thumping in the back of my head that made me seriously reconsider my no-pain-meds stance. It threatened to split my skull in half, causing my eyes to water and my stomach to roil.

If I wasn't alone, I'd probably joke that the colors would be wicked once the bruises came through. Dub myself a walking piece of *art*. I'd shrug it off and make light of the whole thing, possibly proclaiming it as my first war wound. But, without an audience, I was free to acknowledge the fact that, if things had gone differently, I might not be standing there.

Gingerly, I placed my hand over the mark at my throat, letting my fingers hover just above the skin where Dylan's fingers had been, as a tremor ran through me. How close had he come to snuffing me out? To leaving my dad all alone in the world? Would he have lost it? Taken the news with stoic acceptance, then thrown himself even deeper into his service? He was always telling me I never thought things through. That I was too impulsive and foolhardy for my own good... It wasn't until tonight that I had started to believe him. Would he blame me for what happened? Stay angry at my memory until the day he died?

The thoughts brought on a wave of fresh panic, and I had to hold my breath and count to ten in order to tamp it down. A single tear spilled over and ran down my cheek, but I swiped it away and brushed my hand down the leg of my jeans. No time for a meltdown. Not now.

Time to get answers...

I washed my hands and face and stepped from the bathroom. The timing was perfect. Cade and Noah were just exiting the office, followed by Commander Simmons.

Simmons smoothed out his shirt and pinned me with a stern gaze.

Here we go.

I cringed, prepping for assault. Dad never raised his voice—which didn't make him any less intimidating—but other people didn't have the same restraint. Simmons had caught me behaving in a manner *unbefitting* of a general's daughter on multiple occasions. Most of the time I found it secretly funny. The poor guy was wound even tighter than Dad. His eyes would bulge, and the vein on the right side of his neck would protrude and throb. If he wasn't careful, there'd be a heart attack in his future.

He folded both arms, glaring down at me from someplace around an imposing six foot five. "You're sure you're okay, Kori?"

I nodded, surprised by the lack of screeching. "Yes, sir."

He returned the nod, then gestured to Cade. "Private Granger will escort you home. In addition to that, I'm putting several armed guards outside your house." With a glance in Noah's direction, he added, "Recruit Emeal, I'd like you to debrief the team on what happened tonight."

He wasn't going to keep me here? I had no desire to stay on base, but at least here I was protected. What place was safer than fortified, fenced-in acreage patrolled by soldiers? No one had told me a thing about this Dylan guy yet. Who he was. What he wanted. Why he'd targeted me. I had a hard time believing it was all over and done with.

Was this a plot designed to go after the families of soldiers? If so, why would a lowly recruit know so much about it? Is that who Ava Harris was? A terrorist? Why would Dylan think I knew her? This whole thing was like a jigsaw puzzle with huge missing pieces, and a small part of me wanted Simmons to find a way to contact Dad. To insist he report home immediately so I knew he was safe.

So I could feel safe…

I eyed the commander and tamped down my urge to argue. If he didn't think me staying here was necessary, then I was okay, right? He would never let me walk out the door if I was in any real danger. I could be a pain in everyone's ass, but we looked out for our own. That's the way it worked.

I still didn't know what was going on, though, and all good soldiers were prepared. Unfortunately, pumping him for information was the quickest way to get none. I decided Cade was my best option and kept my mouth closed until I could get him alone.

The commander leaned in close and narrowed his eyes at me the way he'd done a thousand times before. *I pegged you as trouble the moment I saw you*, he'd jokingly told me once. "And don't try sneaking out again. We can't protect you if you go gallivanting by yourself at all hours of the night."

Protect me…

This wasn't like getting caught with the mural. I wasn't in trouble for sneaking out. This was serious. I was starting to think that Dylan hadn't told the cop where to find me. That had been pure bad luck. This whole night could have been potentially life altering. Fatal. Whoever this guy was, whatever his *deal* was, he had the commander on alert—and that made me nervous. Simmons wasn't the kind of guy you got on the ropes.

I nodded and silently followed Cade out into the cool morning air. I couldn't help pausing just outside the building to enjoy the silence. I kept my distance from the base whenever possible, but on the occasion it couldn't be avoided, I usually left with a headache. Between the gunfire during combat drills, the almost competitive cadence calls of rival units, and the sharp, barking instruction from the drill sergeants, it was enough to drive a girl mad. All hours of the day, and sometimes, the night. It wasn't uncommon for soldiers to be torn from sleep by the call of an unscheduled nighttime drill.

Cade had the keys to the commander's jeep and rushed ahead to open the door for me. Just in time, too. A quick glance at my cell told me it was almost wake-up time. Soon this place would be a bustle of earsplitting activity, and after the night I'd had, I didn't want to hang around.

"Aren't you the lucky one getting stuck with babysitting duty? Bet this wasn't what you hoped for when you enlisted," I said, slipping into the vehicle. Noah was nowhere to be seen, and I wondered if that was why he disliked me so much. Guard duty probably wasn't his definition of *be all that you can be.* "You should probably thank me for making it interesting."

The corner of his lip tipped up. "I get the feeling any time spent with you could be considered an adventure."

There went the temperature. It was that global warming. That was my story and damn it, I was sticking to it. I'd had *things* with a few of the braver guys at some of my schools. Most of the time it consisted of me approaching them, spewing something to the tune of:

Hey, I like you. Let's hang. There'd be some kissing, and an occasional gropefest, and it pretty much ended at that. But flirting? I didn't do flirting. Yet the words inexplicably tumbled out. "Pretty sure you couldn't handle my brand of adventure."

"Don't be too sure." His lip twitched again, the smallest hint of a smile, and he closed the door.

Oh my God. Had that just happened? Was I flirting with one of these guys? Witty banter and coy smiles. Yep. That was flirting. What the hell was next? Hair tossing? Dropping things and bending to pick them up just so I could wiggle my ass at him?

Bad Kori. Bad!

He shifted in the driver's seat, eyes traveling the length of my body, lingering much longer than they should have. If he was really my dad's subordinate, then there would be no way he'd be sneaking peeks like that, right? Unless he was suicidal.

But he didn't look away. Then again, I wasn't one to judge, because neither did I. This could all be chalked up to leftover adrenalin. The lingering effects of the night had warped my brain, making everything feel more electric. So much more intense.

After a moment he cleared his throat and turned. The jeep lurched forward. "He talks about you often," he said as we came to the front gate. Cade stopped the jeep. The gate guard nodded, and a moment later the fence rolled open with a squeal. No doubt Simmons had called ahead to let him know we'd be coming. "Tells us all how proud he is of you."

"Oh?" I knew he loved me, but I was pretty sure Dad never said that. To Mom's relief, I made it clear at an early age that a military career wasn't for me. I knew that came as a disappointment to him. Much like most things I did. Hell, I'd been disappointing him, literally, from day one. From the moment I arrived in this world, a girl rather than the predicted bouncing baby boy. I'd seen pictures. For the first year of my life the nursery was done in a sickening blue cutesy-camo theme.

"I've seen your work," he added with the smallest hint of a smile. "It's amazing. You have a lot of talent."

If I'd been standing, I would have fallen on my ass. "My *work*?"

"Your art?" There was a smidgen of fear in his voice. Like maybe he'd said too much. The car slowed to make the right turn onto Broadway. Before accelerating, his fingers tightened around the wheel and he snuck a peek at me from the corner of his eye.

"Oh," was all I could say. It surprised me that Dad had spoken about it. He didn't think it was an appropriate means to earn a living. Playing with finger paints and crayons, he always groused. Such a waste of a healthy young life.

After a few minutes of uncomfortable silence, Cade sighed. "You know what you did was stupid, right? Why did you sneak out? If you wanted to go someplace, I would have taken you."

What I meant to say was that I had no idea there was someone out there gunning for me. Instead, what came out was something far more personal. "I didn't want an escort. I wanted to be alone. It's complicated." I wanted to stop there, but for some reason, the words just kept coming. Verbal diarrhea at its best. "There's this painting in town—"

He nodded and turned the jeep onto Fisher Avenue. "The mural."

"*The mural?*" I squeaked, and twitched in my seat. "Did he take out an advertisement? It was the middle of the night for crap's sake. How did he even have time to tell people?"

"I don't understand." He pressed down on the gas to bring the jeep up to the newly bumped forty-five mile an hour speed limit. The fact that he was keeping it on the nose was driving me nuts. "Me knowing about the mural is bad?"

"*Anyone* knowing about the mural is bad. Defacing a public building *is* bad! I got busted. They're going to hand my ass to me on a silver platter, then pass it around at the buffet..." I let out a whistle. "Good-bye freedom, hello snoozefest of regimented after school activities."

"You're not at all what I expected. Cursing, destruction of public property, sneaking out...violence."

I shrugged it off, but secretly, I was thrilled. I liked surprising people. They all had this rigid preconceived notion when meeting me. I took pride in turning it on its ass. "It's true. The daughter of the great General Anderson is something of a delinquent. Sorry to disappoint."

He tilted his head and peeked at me again from the corner of his eye. He needed to stop doing that. It did funny things to my insides. "I didn't say I was disappointed."

Huh. Good thing it was dark or soldier boy probably would have seen me blush. I didn't go for these guys, but Cade seemed somehow different from the rest. Not nearly as rigid as the norm. Kind of funny in a weird, stiff way. I imagined getting him to open up would be all sorts of fun. I had a brief image of the two of us walking into a store and me convincing him to rip the tag off a mattress and run. I wasn't sure he could do it without his head exploding. "So, you gonna tell me what that guy was all about? Who the mysterious Ava Harris is?"

"Nope," he replied, turning onto my street. The smile slipped from his face, replaced by that same annoying resolve I saw my dad wear all the time. Carrying the weight of the world on his shoulders. Toting top secret, world-saving information. All crap if you asked me. "I'm not cleared to share that."

"Shouldn't I know what's going on? What if he attacks me again?" Granted, I was fishing for information, but the question was valid—and a real concern. Being blind to a threat was dangerous. Any good solider would tell you that.

He paused and took a deep breath, his gaze meeting mine. "He can try, but I won't let him within a hundred yards of you, Kori. *No matter what.*"

A shudder rippled through me. The ferocity in his voice was one part promise and three parts threat. For whatever insane reason, I actually believed him. And his eyes? I'd never seen such conviction. There was the smallest hint of madness, and I got the feeling that anyone—or anything—that tried to come at me would end up shredded. I swallowed. "Well, I'll give you this— you're confident."

My eyes fell to the house at the end of the road. Home. White with dark red shutters and a blue flamingo in the middle of the lawn. Mom named him Elvis. Elvis used to have two friends. Paul and Ringo. Alas, they met their demise at the business end of a lawnmower several years back, leaving Elvis all alone in the world.

She'd been so happy when they couldn't find room for us on the base. Most places had all these stupid rules. What size table you could have in your yard, how high the bushes could grow—prejudices against families of plastic blue flamingos... In Wells, Elvis was allowed to live free, guarding the house against unseen intruders. In the nights following her death, I'd sit on the lawn, the dew-wet grass soaking through my flannel pajama pants, and talk to him. All the things I'd wanted to say to her and never had time. He was a good listener, Elvis. I owed him a large portion of my sanity.

Cade swung the jeep into the driveway and killed the engine. He slid out, rushing around to pull open the door before I even got my seat belt unfastened. It was equal parts sweet and irritating. I was all for a gentleman, but we weren't on a date or anything. He was my warden, and I was his prisoner.

Keeping a respectable distance, he followed me up the walk, then reached around to pull open the screen door.

"You want something to eat? Drink?" I asked, unlocking the door. The sun was just coming up, and even though I was dead tired, pancakes didn't sound half bad. Stepping inside, I moved and gestured him forward. The words tumbled out before I could think and I was taken aback by my hospitality. I had always made it a mission to make sure Dad's watchdogs felt as unwelcome as they were. Now I was offering breakfast? Obviously the night's activities had hit me harder than I thought.

"I'm fine. Thank you."

"Okay." I was relieved. Forget food. My brain wasn't firing right. The last few hours had officially caught up to me. Sleep. That was the best thing I could do. I took a step toward the stairs, and moving my feet was like trying to dance with cement shoes on. "Well, then I'm gonna crash for a few hours. Been up all night, ya know?"

He nodded. "You'll be safe. I'll be right down here. On the couch."

Ten thousand replies bubbled to the surface, and I had to bite down hard on the inside of my lip to keep them from spilling out. He was cuter than I'd thought earlier. The scar on his face didn't detract from that, either. In fact, it added to his appeal. Broad shoulders and well-muscled arms. His brown eyes were deep set and always moving. Scanning for danger. Surveying the field. He was alert and ready. Yet there was something about him that screamed unconventional. And not just his hair and civilian duds, either. Maybe it was the way he carried himself. Not with the self-discipline of a true soldier, but with caution. Like he was afraid to say and do the wrong thing. Like the entire world was resting on the hinges of a mistake just waiting to be made. It was those small cracks in his soldier armor that enabled me to look at him like a normal person.

My intention was to say goodnight and turn away, but a wave of boldness overcame me. "Thank you for helping me out tonight." He was technically just doing his job, but I was grateful despite that. I leaned in and kissed his cheek. Or, that's what I'd aimed to do. He turned his head at exactly the wrong moment.

Or, depending on how you looked at it, exactly the right one...

Our lips met. Warm and soft with the smallest jolt of something that stirred the butterflies in my belly into a frenzy. "Wow," I whispered, pulling away just a little. A nervous giggle spilled from my lips. "Not exactly what I meant to do."

I expected him to move back. To be surprised. Maybe apologize for moving his head. Good soldiers don't suck face wih the general's daughter. *Really.* It was an official rule.

What I didn't expect was for him to grab the sides of my face and kiss me again.

If you could call it a kiss…

I'd had my share of stolen smooches under the bleachers in grade school, then as I got older, a few scorchers from the boys brave enough to tempt my dad's wrath. There'd been a few butt-grabs and exactly two under-the-shirt-over-the-bra breaches. But compared to all that, despite the fact that this was a kiss, this was some serious next-level shit.

Cade's lips moved fervently over mine as his fingers skimmed upward and tangled into my hair. It sent every nerve into hyper drive, and in response, I rose onto my toes to deepen the kiss. The butterflies in my stomach turned to falcons, frenzied and trying to break free from a lifetime of oppression. Falling. I felt like I was falling. That dizzy, dropping sensation that came when balanced at the top of a rollercoaster, just before taking the final, daring plunge into what you hope isn't oblivion.

No. This wasn't a kiss. This was something cosmic.

When he finally pulled away, I was breathless. My pulse hammered beneath my skin, a wildly thumping, erratic rhythm that I was afraid he'd hear. "You are so *not* like any other soldier I've ever met…"

He took a step back. When I finally worked up the nerve to look him in the eye, I saw he was pale. Pale, and horrified. "Kori… I didn't—"

"Oh man, don't freak."

And please, for the love of God, don't say you regret that!

I threw up my hands and took a step back. "I'm not gonna tell my dad or anything." My heart still pounded, and remnants of an all-over tingle lingered, making me a little lightheaded. Damn. If he didn't seem ready to have a coronary, I probably would have considered doing it again. "I mean, I totally instigated it." Which wasn't technically true. The kiss had been a result of timing. Or, cosmic intervention, my mom would say.

"You should get some rest." His breath was quickened and his gaze lingered on my lips for a moment before he turned his back on me.

Ouch. Okay. I could spot a brush-off. Maybe I was that bad a kisser… Or maybe he was ashamed he'd taken it so far. Afraid someone would find out. Either way, I was beat. Pride a little raw, I let it go and made my way upstairs without another word.

A shower was too much trouble. The pillow had been calling my name since my butt hit the chair outside the Red Room. I didn't even bother peeling off my jeans. I managed to kick off my shoes and shrug out of my sweater, leaving the tank top on, and decided it would have to be enough. I crashed into bed with a groan. Even the blankets were too much trouble to fight with. Leaden and suffocating, I ignored them and snuggled into my pillow. Oblivion was what I needed. That heavy weightlessness that came with sleep and could wipe away the remnants of the last twenty-four hours—even if only for a little while.

I tilted my head and checked the clock above the door. The hands were made from real paintbrushes. Mom had given it to me the Christmas before she died. I smiled and let my eyes drift closed.

The last thing I remembered was thinking to myself, *Dad's gone. That means I can have a Klondike Crunch bar for dinner.* The next thing I knew, it was hard to breathe.

I opened my eyes, and for the second time in less than twenty-four hours, everything swam. I panicked and tried to take a deep breath, but there was a heavy weight on top of me. Solid and large. Terror chased away the last remnants of sleep, and I screamed, except the sound didn't carry. It came out muffled and low—probably due to the fact that a warm and callused object was clamped across my lips.

"Shh," a male voice whispered. "Like I said earlier, this will be much easier if you just go with it."

I kicked and thrashed. That voice. I knew it. I'd heard it only hours ago.

The weight on my body shifted, and a second later, the light on my nightstand beside the bed flicked on. Dylan had me pinned down and was wearing a wicked grin. "This sucks, I know, and you're probably confused by the whole thing."

His hand still spread across my face, pushing down with so much pressure that I couldn't even nod.

"Here's the truth," he whispered, leaning closer. The spark of anger in his eyes chilled me to the core. My heart pounded. Cade and Noah were downstairs. I just had to find a way to get them up here. I struggled, trying to lift my body to jar him, to loosen his hold, but it was no use. His grip was unrelenting, and he weighed what felt like a metric ton. "You got a raw deal, Kori. Over and over, you're stuck paying for someone else's mistake, and I'm truly sorry about that... In the end, though, you have to die. You *always* have to die."

Chapter Six

I tried to scream, but it came out garbled and low. A muffled sound that came close to mimicking an irritated cat.

"This is nothing personal," he continued as though we were chatting calmly about the weather. "I like you. Always have."

Always have?

Forget terrorist. They needed to toss this guy in the nut house and throw the key out to sea. I squirmed again, shaking the bed. The headboard rattled, knocking into the nightstand. As a result of the commotion, the lamp clattered as it wobbled a bit.

Bingo!

I struggled again, doing my best to cause as much movement as possible. Dylan laughed. I assumed he thought I was trying to escape. But when the bed whacked the nightstand hard enough to send the lamp crashing to the floor, his grin faded.

"Bitch," he spat, wrapping his fingers around my neck. Downstairs, someone called my name—it sounded like Cade. When I didn't answer, he started up the stairs. I could tell because the first, third, and fourth steps creaked.

With his hand off my mouth, I drew in as much air as I could and yelled, "Cade! He's—"

And that was as all I could get out. Dylan's deathlike grasp obstructed my air supply. The look in his eyes turned feral. It was anger unlike anything I'd ever seen. The incident in town suddenly felt like a day at the beach. In all my life, I'd never been as scared as I was in that moment.

Footsteps pounded the hardwood in the hall, and a second later, Cade's voice came, faint over the sound of my own erratic heartbeat, floated from across the room. "Dylan, stop!"

"I swear if you take one more step—either of you—I'll snap her neck."

"Just chill, man." That, from Noah. He must have gotten back from the base sometime after I'd passed out.

"Oh, I'm chill. Trust me. So chill, in fact, that I'm giving you a chance to break your losing streak. We're gonna change it up a bit."

"Change," Noah repeated. There was an air of caution in his voice. Like he was talking to someone standing on the edge of a building, preparing to jump. "Change how?"

"It means we're going to play a new game, boys. And this time, we're getting everyone involved." He turned back to me, eyes traveling over my body with a lecherous grin. Easing up, he slowly unwrapped his fingers. The relief was instant, the pressure from his grip disappearing to leave only a dull ache and the need to cough. "I'll even let you play this time."

Crazy. They're all crazy.

"Sorry," I said between shallow gulps of air. I could barely hear him over the sound of my own pulse, stuttering along like an engine trying to turn over. My chest hurt—more from fear than the fact that I'd had some wacko camped out on it for five minutes—and the adrenaline pumped through my veins like jet fuel. Heart attack. I was on the verge of having a heart attack. Add all that to the soreness from our previous encounter, and my body was in full-on craptastic mode.

Show no fear.

"Not interested. Maybe you should just go play with yourself?"

Dylan snorted. He slid sideways, allowing me to sit up. "I like this one much better than the others." His gaze swiveled from me to the boys. "And before you contemplate something heroic, I want to remind you what happened two months ago."

Cade's furious expression faltered, morphing to stricken, but the cryptic taunt seemed to enrage Noah. Eyes narrowed, he clenched his jaw, visibly taking a deep breath as if to remain in control. "Why should we play your game at all?" he asked. "I mean, what's the point?"

"To keep history from repeating itself," Dylan replied, cocky.

Noah, in turn, shrugged. "Maybe it's time to break the cycle. Stop trying to undo your brand of crazy and just take you out. You feel me, right, man?"

I was almost thankful for the abstruse innuendos. They chewed at my fear, nibbling away and leaving irritation at being so obviously excluded from the loop. I felt like I was sitting on the outside of a soundproof glass room. These people inside were having this conversation—one that plainly included me—and I couldn't hear them.

"Good," Dylan said. "That's good—and I actually believe it. I did the crime, so I deserve to do the time, right? We all *know* that's what Cade thinks—which I find extremely hypocritical. You know, all things considered. But what about her?"

Noah stiffened. "What about her? She's nothing to me."

Ouch. I knew the guy didn't like me, but that was harsh. And stupid. I had a feeling Dad wouldn't be handing out commendations to the two guys who let his daughter die.

Dylan laughed. A twisted sound that screamed of lunacy. "She's *nothing* to you? Really? Does Cade feel that way as well?"

What *the hell* was going on here? They had some kind of history. That much I'd figured out on my own. In the beginning it seemed like this had something to do with Dad. As a general, he had his fair share of anti-fans, and they'd gotten the commander involved. There were the hushed whispers I'd overheard speaking of some plan Dad was in on. Now, though, I was starting to think Cade and Noah had dragged their own crazy baggage to my doorstep.

"Just tell us what you want," Cade snapped. Our eyes met, and he quickly looked away.

Dylan's expression turned stormy. "You can't give me what I want." His voice was low and his words cutting. But there was something else. A spark of sadness in his eyes so fleeting, I couldn't be sure it had even been real. "You can't give back what you stole from me."

"What you planned on doing was—"

"I don't care," Dylan bellowed. He was literally shaking with rage.

I jumped. Cade and Noah didn't seem surprised by the outburst, though. They stood by the door, watching and waiting like they'd done this a thousand times before.

"I owe you hell for what you did to me. You, and Anderson, and the Tribunal."

Anderson...

I was sure he didn't mean me. Before tonight, we'd never met. I would have remembered. There went the dirty laundry theory. This *did* somehow involve Dad. And the Tribunal? What the hell was he talking about? Obviously these people—whoever they were—had wronged him in some way—or at least, that was his perceived version of it. But what the hell did it all have to do with me?

Dylan's expression softened. Just a little. He laughed. "She reminds me of Ava. All spit and fire, ya know?"

"But she's not Ava," Cade said, taking a step toward the bed. "She's just some innocent girl."

"She is innocent," Dylan agreed. "But we both know she's not just *some* girl. And you'll have to live with the outcome of all this. You and her damn father."

It happened so fast. One second I was leaning

against the wall, watching this sociopath get off on the sound of his own voice, the next I was being shoved back down to the bed.

I struggled for all of about three seconds. His arm tightened, wedged beneath my neck to keep me in place, and I knew in my gut there was no escape. This was it. No art school. No quirky best friend. No sex... Dead at seventeen before actually getting a chance to live.

I braced for the blow, but it never came. Instead, there was some shuffling, and a moment later, something clicked around my right wrist. It was warm and thin with a smooth surface and snug fit. I strained my neck to get a look, but Dylan held tight. Whatever the thing was, the feeling of warmth was growing. Fast. There was a sharp sting. Like a thousand tiny needles all plunging into soft skin. My wrist went from pleasantly toasty to mounting inferno that threatened to turn me to cinders in a matter of seconds. Poison? A bomb of some kind?

The pressure keeping me in place eased, then disappeared, and I was able to sit up again as the burning started to subside. Dylan removed his hand and stood watching me with a sinister grin. I couldn't help wondering why Cade and Noah were just standing there, staring at me like I'd grown a set of horns and a spiffy new tail instead of restraining him. Well, they weren't looking at me exactly.

They were gawking at my new bracelet.

Dylan folded his arms and leaned back against the wall, casual as could be. "I'm staying three days. Back off and let me do what I came here to do. Help me find me Ava. If you do, I'll give you the key to that thing before I leave."

Noah snorted. "Sure. You want us to stand by while you butcher people and help you kidnap some innocent girl? We'll get right on that."

"Give me the key, and we'll help you find Ava," Cade countered. He pushed past Noah and came several steps into the room.

Dylan grinned and tapped the side of his head twice. "You keep forgetting that I know you, Cade. I know how your mind works. Right about now you're thinking, *I can do this. Make a deal to buy myself some time to take him down.*" He shook his head slowly, grin fading. "The Tribunal has to pay for what they did to me. It's nonnegotiable."

"And the general?" Cade took a single step forward.

Dylan's grin grew wider. "The general's part in all this is also nonnegotiable. He has to pay. You find me Ava and I'll keep it between him and me." He inclined his head toward my wrist. "Better get moving. We all know what will happen if I leave and she's still wearing that thing."

My stomach turned over and I swallowed back a mouthful of bile. *OhMyGod.* It *was* a bomb. Something set to detonate on a timer. *A timer.* Just like Mom, each remaining second of my life had been assigned a number...

"Take it off," Cade yelled. He lunged forward and dragged me off the bed and across the room, shoving me behind him. I wobbled, and if it hadn't been for Noah, I probably would have landed on my ass.

I was too dazed to object. The thing Dylan slapped on my wrist was still warm, but had cooled significantly. The pain was gone, but I felt like I'd just run a marathon.

Out of breath and exhausted. It looked like a simple black leather band on the top, but when I turned my palm up, the underside was strange. A small digital screen, seven blue numbers long. I'd never seen anything like it.

"Why are you doing this?" I couldn't control myself any longer. The words spilled out, cracked and small, the fear unmistakable. Dad would be horrified. Good soldiers hid their emotions. They stood tall in the face of adversity and overcame whatever the world threw their way. But I wasn't a soldier. Nothing in my life until that point had ever made it more apparent. I was ready to crack. "What the hell is this thing?"

Dylan smiled. It was a condescending grin, and some of my fear turned to rage. All I wanted in that moment was to beat the look away with my bare fists. "You should ask your boys here about the Infinity Division. They'll fill you in—since apparently Daddy didn't."

Infinity? That was Mom and Dad's thing. Their *word*. What the hell did this guy know about it?

"What's to stop us from taking you down here and now?" Noah said.

Dylan shrugged again. "I'm giving you an opportunity to save her. You wanna blow it? Go ahead. You *might* have no problem living with her blood on your hands, but what about your buddy? Do you think Cade could do it? Do you think he'd *let* you do it?"

Noah leaned in, lips twisted into an ugly snarl. "We both know this is bullshit, Dylan. Part of the game. You've got no intention of giving us that key."

Dylan winked. "Maybe you're right—maybe not. You really willing to take that chance?"

"What if she's not here?" Cade asked. The poison in his voice was enough to make me flinch.

Dylan clucked his tongue. "Then things are looking pretty grim for the Andersons."

Cade hesitated. "She could be gone already."

They stared at one another for a moment, the silence heavy. Something dark hung in the air. History was the wrong word to slap on these guys. They were connected. In some weird way, a part of each other that seemed to push and pull and fuel their existence. The very definition of a toxic relationship.

"Better hope not, because I'm getting tired of looking. Hell, I may just move on and look someplace else." Dylan nodded once and started toward the door. Before leaving, he paused. "Oh, and Cade? Don't involve the base. I see anyone from Fort Hannity on my ass and she's as good as dead."

Without another word, he disappeared. None of us tried to stop him.

Chapter Seven

*C*ade spun around and immediately began trying to pry the band from my wrist like a demon possessed. His skin paled and his eyes sparked with fear—concern twisted and churned in my stomach. He scraped at my skin and yanked and cursed. None of it helped. The band stayed firmly in place, locked around my wrist like it was meant to be there.

Noah came up behind him and placed a hand on his shoulder. "Stop, man. You're going to make it worse. If you break it, there's a chance it'll fry her."

Cade shook him off and continued trying, and I finally found my voice. This girl had no desire to be *fried*. Ripping my arm away, I took a step back. Secret time was over. For real. "I'm done. This has been an insane trip and all, but I'm over it. One—or better yet, both—of you better start talking."

Noah wasn't interested in my speech. "Move it." He grabbed my arm and started dragging me toward the door. "We're taking you back to the base."

"Like hell," I snapped. A blow from me to a guy like Noah would probably be a lot like a tickle to an elephant. He was cut and then some. Possibly even more so than Cade. Since I knew damn well I couldn't get his attention with my fists, I decided to use my fingers. Gripping a section of skin on his forearm between my thumb and pointer, I twisted hard.

He cursed and let go, glaring with what looked to me like the expression of a man planning a murder spree. "You ever do that again—"

"Same goes for you," I snarled, and whirled on Cade.

He seemed to be the most reasonable. Not to say reasonable. Just the *most* reasonable. I opened my mouth to continue, but I glanced down at my wrist, and a tremor ran through me. Dad would tell me to use my fear as fuel. Let it propel me toward my ultimate goal. Living. Staying alive. That was the goal here. Not to end up dead as a result of someone else's fight.

Dad's voice echoed inside my head. *Don't lose sight of the goal, Kori.*

Deep breath. Okay. I could do this. "I don't give two monkey shits about whatever promises you might have made to my dad about keeping me safe. You can keep your war games and classified meetings and secret plans. I don't care about whatever it is you have brewing with this Dylan freak. But that wack job just came into my house—into *my bedroom*—and threatened to kill people. People like my *dad*. He snapped this thing on me." I held up my hand and gave it a wiggle. "Whatever it is, I get the impression that it's *not* the latest in wrist wear fashion. No more secrets. Whatever is going on involves me now, and I want answers. Is this thing a bomb?"

Please. Not a bomb. Don't be a bomb…

"It's not a bomb," Cade responded, and I let out a relieved breath.

Oh, thank God…

He stood a little straighter. The color had returned to his face, and he didn't look so much like a corpse now. But his expression bothered me. A cross between fear and sad acceptance. Almost like he knew I was a goner, but didn't have the heart to admit it out loud.

I tamped down my growing fears and pushed ahead. "And this Infinity Division? What is it and how's it connected to my dad?"

Cade took a deep breath. "Infinity is a secret government project headed by your father."

Okay. Now we were getting somewhere. Granted he was giving me as little as possible, but I could work with it. Start with the basics. "And this Tribunal Dylan was talking about? I get the feeling he's not looking to bake them cookies."

"Revenge," Cade answered. That was it. One word. No elaboration.

But I was nothing if not determined. The daughter of General Karl Anderson wasn't so easily deterred— mainly because, as Dad put it, I could be a pain in the ass when I wanted to. I took pride in that. "What does Infinity do? Are we talking tactical ops? Or covert rescue? Enemy infiltration?"

"That's classified," Noah snapped.

"What they do isn't as important as getting that cuff off," Cade interjected. He shot Noah an angry glare, then refocused on me. "I need you to trust me. Can you do that?"

"What is this thing exactly?" I looked down at the cuff on my wrist. There was nothing imposing about it. But judging by the way Cade had gone into Hulk mode trying to get it off, it was far from innocuous. We'd established it wasn't a bomb, yet Noah said it could *fry* me. Not really a win in my book.

And he wanted me to trust him? I tried not to laugh. Dad told me once that trust was a precious thing. It needed to be cultivated and earned. I agreed. These two hadn't cultivated anything other than fiction in the short time I'd known them, so trust wasn't really on the table.

Yet there was something in Cade's eyes that sent chills racing up and down my spine. Good chills—the guy was hot as hell and that kiss was still fresh in my mind—but bad chills as well. Whatever Dad was into—whatever the Infinity Division was—was on the verge of exploding. And this thing on my wrist? I got the feeling it was the detonator, and I was going to end up being ground zero...

He hesitated. I was about to push, but he sighed and said, "It's government issue. From the Infinity project. It's part of a larger device that, if activated, will start a timer."

My pulse kicked into overdrive and a wave of cold rolled over me. That word again. *Timer.* Timers were never a good thing. From the moment Mom learned her cancer was inoperable, there'd been a timer hanging over her head, ticking the seconds away. Every moment I spent with my dad was counted. Measured against his job and responsibilities to our country. Life, in general, was one big timer. Every breath we took was equal to a minute, counting down to our final hour.

No. Timers were never a good thing. At the end, you always lost something important. Something you couldn't get back. "Timer for what?"

"Infinity deals with highly advanced sciences. The work it does is decades ahead of where the world believes us to be." He inclined his head toward my wrist. "When Dylan activates his cuff and the timer on yours reaches zero, that cuff will do something I don't believe you'll survive."

I swallowed. He was being annoyingly vague and, judging by the look in his eyes, this was bad with a capital *B*. Obviously I hadn't expected him to say something good, like I'd be getting my very own pony and a year's supply of peach yogurt, but *ouch*.

Strategy. We needed one. A plan of attack. That's how wars were won. That, and knowing your enemy. "So Dylan is what, a rogue Infinity agent? Is that the beef he's got with my dad?"

"That would best classify him," was Cade's answer. Short, simple, and empty. There was more to it, obviously, but digging for specifics could come later. As long as the basics were laid out to start, I could move forward.

"Okay." I deserved a big cookie for pretending to keep it together. Really, what I wanted was to find a nice dark closet and scream into a pillow at the top of my lungs until my voice was gone and I'd cried myself dry. "What about these Infinity people? They made it, right? Can't they just give us the key?"

"It's not that simple," Noah said. "We should definitely try, but don't get your hopes up."

Wasn't he just the picture of positivity? I wanted to argue. If they made the thing, then why the hell couldn't they take it off? But we didn't have time right now. "Three days. Dylan gave us three days to find this Ava girl—"

"That's providing he keeps his word," Noah interjected with a sharp glance in Cade's direction. "He can technically leave any time he wants." He turned to Cade. "So why three days? Since when does he work on a specific timetable?"

Cade frowned. "I'm not sure, but it worries me."

"Maybe he's—"

Jesus. Was this something that needed to be hashed out now? Weren't there more important things to focus on? I whistled, and they both froze. "If these Infinity people can't get it off, then is finding Ava possible? I mean, do you know who this girl is?"

They exchanged another look. One that made me uneasy.

Cade was the one who answered. "We know who she is. But finding her might prove difficult, if not impossible."

"And why is that?"

"If it were that simple, Dylan would have found her by now. He's been here two days already. If he hasn't, it means she's not where she should be, or…" He looked from me to Noah, cringing.

"Or that she's gone," Noah finished. He reached across to my desk and snatched the open bag of potato chips. Popping one into his mouth, he shrugged and added, "She could be dead."

Dead. Like I was going to be. "Wonderful."

"First things first," Cade declared. "We should contact the general. Let him know that Kori is wearing a cuff."

"That might be tough to do." Normal parents left contact numbers when they went away on business trips, but Dad's job wasn't exactly playing register jockey at the local Stop and Shop. He checked in with me when he could, but getting a hold of him wasn't usually possible. "He went to Washington. I have no idea—"

More crunching from Noah. "He's not in Washington."

"Jesus, Noah!" Cade snapped.

"What?" He stuffed a small handful of chips into his mouth, crunching loudly. "It's the truth. Personally, I think this is a waste of time. We should be focusing on the important stuff."

The important stuff? Sonofa—

"Not in Washington?" That was it. I yanked the bag from his hands, balled it up, and tossed it across the room, scattering crumpled bits of potato chips across my floor. He cursed nonstop, pranced around in worn civilian clothing, and made himself at home in his superior's house? Everything about the guy screamed disrespect. "And what the hell kind of solider are you, anyway?"

He stalked across the room and retrieved the bag, making a show of tearing the foil open and dumping the remaining contents into his open mouth. "An unwilling one," he mumbled, mouth full.

"*Unwilling?* What the hell kind of answer is that?"

He swallowed and hitched a thumb toward Cade. "I go where he does. End of story."

"Oh. I'm sorry," I said in mock apology. After everything I'd been through, the last thing I needed was more of this guy's attitude. "I didn't realize another person could *make* you join the army."

Noah came at me, stopping inches from my face. I hadn't realized until now how tall he was. Over six feet. "I never joined the damned army—"

Cade, previously the more stable of the two, smashed his fist into the wall by my door. The plaster bowed, small bits and pieces spraying out in all directions. "Anderson!"

"What?" Noah and I roared at the same time.

Horror.

It was all over Cade's face. Slowly, I turned to Noah. The same was mirrored in his expression, but there was something else. Something angry. Something oddly *familiar*. Blue eyes narrowed to thin slits and lips pressed in a thin line, he reminded me a little of Dad when he lost his cool—which wasn't often. I'd seen it happen only twice.

"I want the truth," I said as quietly as I could. "The entire truth. None of this classified garbage. None of this *need to know* crap. The whole damn story."

"You don't have the clear—"

I held up my hand and stuck it in his face. "Do not finish that sentence. You never joined the army, remember?" I turned to Cade. "Talk. Now."

"We don't have time for this," Cade snapped. "We need to find out if anyone on that base can unlock the cuff. If not, we need to focus and find Ava."

"Fine." I stepped through the door, out into the hallway. "But this is my life, boys. I don't know you, so I have no intention of trusting you with it. I'm going with you."

Noah's face contorted, a mask of annoyance over my declaration, but Cade seemed pleased. He nodded and gestured to the door, snickering under his breath. "Let's all go have a chat with the commander, then."

*I*t took forever to get through the late morning gate check. It brought a rush of bittersweet memories. At Dad's last post, Fort Andrews, Mom and I had gone binge shopping. Shoes for her, art supplies for me. We'd come back sated, stuffed from a junk food lunch, and having to pee. There's nothing quite like being stuck in a line of ten cars while having your eyeballs float from one-too-many cherry colas.

Fort Hannity was huge. I'd never seen the entire thing. Hell, I'd never even seen the housing section. When we'd moved to Wells, I made a promise to myself not to get too involved with anyone. Dad never stayed in one place very long, and even though he'd promised this assignment was different, that we were here to stay, I didn't believe him.

Once through the security check, we were met by Sergeant Moore, a stocky man with no expression, wearing the regulation army greens. He'd escorted Cade and me to the commander's office, then left with Noah. No complaints from me. The entire ride over here, he glared at me through the rearview mirror like he wanted to eject me from the moving vehicle.

"That guy is the biggest asshole I've ever met. And that's saying *a lot*."

Cade snickered. We'd been in the commander's office for a few minutes now, and the silence was driving me nuts. "Noah? Most people say he's an acquired taste. But he'd give his life for me. We've been friends since we were born, practically."

"Well, then you're a damn saint." I took a deep breath. Time to ask. The question had been burning a hole in the roof of my mouth since his outburst back at the house. I wanted to know where my dad was if he wasn't in Washington—and how a lowly private and a fuzzy would be privilege to that intel, but more than that, Cade's outburst was driving me nuts. I needed to know. "You weren't talking to me. Back at my house when you said *Anderson*. You weren't talking to me."

This whole thing had passed surreal and entered impossible. Sure, Noah could have the same last name as me. There were plenty of Andersons out there. My second grade teacher was an Anderson of no relation. So was a guidance counselor in my last high school. He could also have the same intense blue eyes and sharp cheekbones as Dad, as well as the intense glare and commanding attitude. But what were the chances? Cousin? Was it possible that I had family I hadn't met? Why wouldn't anyone have told me?

"I was talking to Noah," he admitted. He sighed and dropped his head into his hands, threading his fingers through his hair. After a minute, he leaned back. In that moment he looked like he hadn't slept in days. Like someone who'd been on the run, trying to avoid his demons, for ages. "This whole thing is complicated, Kori. Like, more than you can possibly imagine."

I sat down across from him. "I'm a fairly intelligent girl. Try me."

"It's not really my place to—"

"Of course not." I folded my arms and bit down on my tongue to keep from saying something nasty. I wanted to rip this guy a new one—several new ones at this point—but I knew he was still my best shot at information. Even *my* temper wasn't bad enough to blow that.

I knew the score. There were things he wasn't allowed to tell me. Secrets and operational details that might possibly put people's lives at risk. I was a reasonable girl. I got that. But he had to give me something. Twice now. This Dylan jerk had come at me twice—three times if you counted that first weird encounter. That made me a part of whatever the hell was going on. Then there was the whole Dad's not in Washington bit. Like I was going to just let that go?

"What about you? This whole thing seems like it's pretty far up the food chain. What's a private first class doing in the thick of it?" I eyed him suspiciously. "Unless you're not really a private?"

"I am. Technically."

Beep. Beep. Danger alert!

"*Technically*?" Because that didn't raise a thousand more questions he probably had no intention of answering.

"I suppose it would depend on who you ask. Technically I've gone through basic training. Done my time in the trenches, so to speak. But fourteen months back there was an incident…"

"Let me guess. Involving Dylan?"

He nodded. "Yes. I was brought into the Infinity project—I volunteered, actually. That's how I was able to come to Fort Hannity. See, Noah and I—we shouldn't be here..." There was something about the way he lingered on that last phrase that made my stomach twist and the hairs stand up on the back of my neck.

"Be here? Like, alive? Are you trying to say the project saved your life or something?"

He thought about it for a minute, then sighed. "I guess you could say that, though not in the way you're thinking. Noah and I lost someone. Someone who was more important to us than anything else in the world. The work Infinity does made it possible to deal with our grief in a productive and potentially helpful way."

Things started falling into place. The disgusted scowls and angry glares from Noah. The attitude and venom. "This person you lost, I remind Noah of her, don't I? That's why he hates me so much." I still didn't like the guy, but I could almost understand his vitriol. Then I remembered the kiss. My skin heated, and I was sure my cheeks flushed. I cleared my throat and sat back in my seat. "I remind you of her, too. That's why you—"

"You don't remind us of her, Kori." He took a deep breath, and I was sure he'd let it go. Leave me hanging again, foaming at the mouth for an answer. But I was wrong. He turned and took my hands in his. They were warm, and I couldn't help noticing how my fingers fit perfectly into his palm. Like resting them there was the most natural thing in the world. Our eyes met and I wanted to look away. The intensity of his stare was like a blade cutting straight through me. But I couldn't. I was riveted. Enthralled by the pain and regret in his eyes. "You *are* her."

Chapter Eight

"I'm her," I repeated, and pulled my hands from his. "What exactly is that supposed to mean?"

He stood. "You, Noah, and I have been inseparable since we could pretty much walk. It was the three of us against the world. Your dad, the general, is like a father to me."

It's always the pretty ones, isn't it?

Apparently the army should have done a better job evaluating his mental health, because Cade Granger was certifiable. Like, bring the meds down in busloads and get thee to a rubber room kind of loony.

"I'd never seen either of you before you showed up on my doorstep for babysitting detail." I sighed. Maybe it wasn't insanity. Maybe this was his way of flirting. Kind of like telling a girl she was your destiny. The one you dreamed of every night. He either needed to revamp his romantic approach or was in need of professional help. You know, the kind they offer with white jackets and padded rooms? Possibly even strong narcotics and electroshock treatment.

He shook his head. I could tell he was frustrated. That made two of us. "I'm explaining this badly. Not you exactly, but a different version of you."

"A different *version* of me?" This kept getting better and better. Next he'd tell me he was from Mars, and that I, unaware of my super-secret one-of-a-kind heritage, was from Venus. Together, we could save the world.

"The device Cora built allows—"

His words were like thunder in my ears. Everything froze and my breath hitched, catching in my throat like month-old bread. I clamped a hand across his mouth and silently counted to ten. When I was finished, all I could feel was an allover tingle. An almost overpowering sense of surreal trepidation. "Cora? As in my *mother*?"

He took a deep breath and slowly peeled my hand away. As he knotted his fingers through mine, his expression changed. Not really a frown, but not a smile, either. If I had to guess, he wasn't happy about having to justify his fantasy world. With a slow, deliberate nod, he said, "The Infinity Division is the brainchild of Cora Anderson."

The flirting theory got axed, because I'd just officially decided the jury was in. He was nuts. "You're trying to say my mom worked for the government?"

He shifted from foot to foot. Apparently in his delusional scenario this was classified intel that he was hesitant to share.

"Please," I said, stalling for time. The commander would be out soon. I just had to keep Cade busy. Then, when I was surrounded by sane people with weapons, I would tell them all how he'd lost his ever-loving mind. "Tell me."

It was like a two-ton weight lifted from his expression. His posture loosened, and the tight set of his shoulders relaxed. Like he'd been waiting to spring his brand of crazy on me from moment one. "She and your dad spearheaded the whole operation. Cora is brilliant. One of the most amazing minds science has ever been graced with."

"So, my mom was some kind of super brain?" I said it with as much sincerity as I could muster. Why? Why were all the cute ones either taken, gay, or teetering on the edge of sanity? I was trying to keep my cool in light of his declarations, but I wasn't sure I would last until the commander returned. Every time he said my mother's name it was like a knife twisted in my gut. The way he kept referring to her in the present tense made my blood boil. He spoke as if she was a person he knew and spent time with as opposed to the mother who was stolen from me two years ago.

"The brightest," he confirmed. "That device I was talking about, the one she created, allows access to different dimensions. *Parallel Earths.* The Kori Anderson Noah and I knew was from our Earth."

I stood and took a small step toward the door. Parallel Earths? Yeah. That was my limit. "Oh. Okay," I said as neutrally as possible. "You're from a parallel Earth. That explains it all." My plan to humor him was starting to seem impossible. I opened my mouth to tell him to screw off, but thought better of it. Would he take offense to my sarcasm and attack? He was clearly unhinged, and there was no way I could take him in a fight.

No... He wasn't violent. I could tell by the sullen expression on his face that he really only wanted me to believe his delusions. "Kori, please. I know this is messed up, but you have to listen to me. Your brother and I, we—"

"My *brother*?" I half laughed, half cried, letting go of the charade completely. This was more than I could handle. My acting chops weren't good enough to sustain a ruse of this magnitude. "Noah? Is that who you're talking about? You think Noah is my brother? I think my parents would have remembered to mention something as important as a sibling."

"You don't have a brother, but our Kori did. Noah is—"

"Stop it!" I screamed. Screw it. If he was violent, let him come at me. Anything would be better than sitting here listening to this. "Just cut the crap."

"He's telling you the truth, Kori," Commander Simmons said, appearing in the doorway of his office. "Though he shouldn't be telling you anything at all." He stepped into the main room and his gaze fell to Cade, tinged with disappointment. I knew that look. Had been subject to it in its many forms throughout my time here. Cade, in turn, hung his head.

"I can prove it," he prodded gently. Like he was afraid I would crack or something. I didn't know what was more unnerving. The crap they were both spewing, or the fact that the commander's entire demeanor had changed. He was softer. More gentle. Not at all what I was used to.

Where was the hulking bear of a man with the ornery attitude? Easy. He was still in his office at Fort Hannity. It was me who was displaced. Maybe Dylan had killed me up in my room. He'd killed me and this was my own personal version of hell. I reached around and pinched myself—hard—and it hurt like hell.

Okay. Scratch the dead theory. Dead people couldn't feel pain, right?

"How? Take me for a ride in your spaceship? Hand me a tiny little bottle with the words 'Drink Me' on the label?" If this were a normal situation, talking like that to a high-ranking officer—*any* officer—would land me in water hot enough to poach an egg. But this wasn't a normal situation. The world seemed to have turned itself inside out. The commander was telling me Cade was dead on? Surely somewhere in the world pigs were tap dancing and cows were doing ballet.

"I'm not an alien," Cade said, exasperated. He paused, giving Simmons a sideways glance. It was only when the commander nodded that he continued. "And we don't want you to drink anything."

Disappointing, because maybe a drink would help the believability of their story... I could certainly use one for my nerves right about now...

"I believe I can clear all this up for you, Kori." Simmons stepped aside, giving me a wide berth, and gestured to the hallway. "If you'll follow me..."

"Follow you where?" The last thing I wanted to do right then was follow any of them anywhere. "Because I gotta be honest...right now I don't think I'd follow you into a church full of little old ladies giving away free baked goods and puppies." Could I realistically make a break for it? Clear the building, and then the gate before they took me down? Doubtful.

His lip twitched with the smallest hint of a grin. It was so fast that I wasn't even sure it'd been there at all. He gestured toward the door. "Down the rabbit hole, of course."

Simmons led us into the hallway and through another door. In fact, he led us down a lot of hallways. Through a lot of doors. Everyone we passed offered a stiff-armed salute, and I briefly thought about calling for help—this was something like a mass hallucination, right?

The air. There's something in the air. Biological weapons or something funky in the food source...

But thanks to indecision, my chance came and went. The farther we got, the fewer people I saw, until there was no one but the three of us, standing in front of an office door with the words AUTHORIZED PERSONNEL ONLY on it.

Simmons punched an eight-digit code into the dimly backlit pad beside the door, and with a soft whooshing sound, it breezed opened. He stepped aside and gestured for me to go in. I hesitated, not really sure I wanted to know more at this point, but he gave me a small nudge.

Don't do it. This is how most horror movies start...

"It's okay, Kori. I promise."

I didn't have the heart—or maybe it was the guts—

to tell him that I didn't really buy that. Anyone who believed they could travel between dimensions had a screw or two loose. But I sucked in a breath and did what Dad would have expected of me. I squared my shoulders, held my head high, and walked into the room.

Except, it wasn't a room. It was an elevator.

Instead of big buttons with the numbers one through nine, there was a single red square. A scene from a Bugs Bunny cartoon—Mom's favorite—flashed through my head. Never, ever push the red button. Bugs Bunny knew that.

Daffy Duck on the other hand...

Cade stepped in beside me, followed by Simmons. He pushed the button and the doors closed with a soft click. A second later, the bottom dropped out from my belly as the car lurched downward with a massive jerk.

The seconds turned into minutes. *Tick tock. Tick tock.* But the elevator didn't stop. We just kept going down. Like, subterranean mole people kind of far. I wasn't claustrophobic by any means but, as the minutes ticked by, I started getting antsy. When the doors did finally open, it was all I could do not to rush for the door and fall to my knees to kiss solid ground.

As I crossed the threshold, I half expected to step out into the center of the Earth. That would have made this all okay. Proved that these people were nuts— forgetting of course that the elevator existed in the first place.

Simmons stepped off behind me, and in a very official tone, said, "Welcome to the Infinity Division, Kori."

"No," was all I could muster. I closed my eyes and

shook my head. For a minute, I stayed that way. If I didn't open my eyes, didn't see the cavernous room spread out before me, didn't acknowledge the unlikelihood that the commander was insane, I wouldn't have to accept the inevitable. It was real. All of it. Every crazy, insanity-tainted word that had come from Cade's remarkably skilled lips.

I opened my eyes. To my left were a group of men and women, all in mid-length white coats. They were bent over what looked like a large circuit board. I shifted my gaze to the right. A large machine—it looked like a refrigerator to me, but I was fairly certain it wasn't—sparked and crackled. Two men stood in front of it. One punching buttons into a silver keypad on the front, and the other jotting something down into the notebook in his hands. They glanced up at us, momentary surprise in their expression, then went back to work as though we weren't there.

Simmons rested his large hand on my shoulder. The weight of it, or maybe it was the reality of what I was seeing, nearly crushed me. "If you will follow me, I'll have you briefed."

All I could do was nod. Speech was impossible at that point. Hell, putting one foot in front of the other was a trick. My body seemed to have forgotten how to function. The nerves sending impulses from my brain to each limb had gone on strike. Even my lungs weren't working right. Every few steps I'd hold my breath, only letting it out when the corners of my vision began to swim and the pressure in my chest became too much to bear.

"You must be Kori," an older woman said, coming up

to us. She held out her hand and, numb, I took it. "It's wonderful to finally meet you. My name is Elaina. Cora spoke of you all the time."

And there it was again. The inclusion of Mom's name in this rapidly growing conspiracy—which, despite the obvious unfolding facts, I was still having a hard time buying. Mom was my best friend. My only friend, really. We knew everything about each other. I knew about her secret Don Knotts obsession, and she knew about my irrational fear of frogs. I found it hard to believe that she'd accidentally forgotten to mention something as big as a specialized uber degree in weird science. "You knew my mom?"

Elaina smiled. It was warm and genuine and almost made me forget about the insanity I was knee-deep in. "Very well." She put her arm around my shoulder and gently guided me forward, farther from the elevator. Farther from reality. "I realize this must be very jarring, but I'm going to answer your questions to the best of my ability."

Cade came up beside me, and I glanced back the way we'd come. The commander had abandoned me. Spreading my arms wide, I said, "My mom did this? This is all because of her?"

Elaina nodded. Her face beamed with pride. "Everything you see here stems from Cora's work. Though she wasn't here to see the fruition of years of accomplishment, everything we are, and can do— everything we will eventually be able to do—is because of her notes and research. The world, though it may not know it yet, owes her so much."

"So it's true then?" I couldn't believe I was actually

going to say this out loud. "She invented a device that makes it possible for people to cross…*dimensions*?"

"Very sci-fi, isn't it?" Elaina laughed. "But, yes. That's the gist of things." She gestured to Cade. "Private Granger is from a different multiverse. Another timeline, if you will."

"A different timeline," I said, rolling the word—and the idea—around.

Her smile widened. "Parallel timelines. Alternate realities. Quantum universe. Interpenetrating dimension—"

My head was starting to spin. "Why?"

She tilted her head to the side, light brown hair spilling sideways. "Why, what?"

"I mean, aside from the obvious sci-fi awesomeness, why travel to other *dimensions*?"

There. You said it. How hard was that?

"Think of the applications this technology has," she said, starry-eyed. Like she was talking about fairies or unicorns. Yeah. I'd hit a geek nerve big time. "The possibilities are, quite literally, endless. As far as we can tell, there are an infinite number of alternates out there. Unlimited resources, different advances in medical and technological sciences. This is the biggest breakthrough in history." She grinned. "And, of course, the obvious."

"Obvious?" There was nothing about any of this that screamed obvious to me.

She winked. "To prove we can."

Cade tugged up the leg of his jeans. On his ankle, over the top of his sock, was a cuff that looked exactly like the one Dylan had snapped on me. "And this is what makes it all possible."

I lifted my wrist. The black leather strap looked so

benign. Maybe a little new agey if you flipped it over, but capable of transporting you to a parallel universe? I just had a hard time buying into that.

But, what if? If what they're saying is true, then maybe she's out there somewhere. Alive and well. Thriving...

I wasn't ready to jump on the insane-train just yet, but the wheels started turning in my head. The possibilities this opened up... "So you're saying this thing will let me visit another dimension?"

Elaina frowned. "Not let. *Force.* The cuffs are made in sets of six. Five drones linked to a master. This particular one, like Cade's and Noah's, is linked to the master on Dylan's wrist. When he skips—moves from one dimension to the next—the others will as well, only on a short delay."

"Okay," I said carefully. There was a "but" in there someplace. A big ugly one. "So couldn't I go and just come back?"

Cade sighed. "I know what you're thinking, Kori. And theoretically, yes. While there's no way to control where we go, the main cuff does have a way to return you here."

Elaina's frown deepened. "The molecules in our bodies are always in flux. Always vibrating. I've been talking to Noah at length—the whole thing is absolutely fascinating!" Her eyes took on that same starry gleam, and she tilted her head back, smile spreading from ear to ear. "The cuffs work by changing the...frequency, if you will, of how a person's molecules vibrate. Each parallel world has its own signature. Think of it as not necessarily traveling to another version of Earth, but more phasing. Like taking a step from one room into another. There's a button on the main cuff that will return all users to their original vibrational state, therefore phasing them back to their rightful places."

"But your body needs preparation before the first trip," Cade said cautiously. He looked from me to Elaina.

She nodded. "There are measures that must be taken or the consequences are…unfavorable."

"Unfavorable?" And there it was. The kink in the line. "How *unfavorable* are we talking here?"

"There are three possibilities," Cade said, taking over. He glanced from Elaina to me, nervous. "If *no* preparation is taken, you'd never survive the skip. When the cuff activates, it would just confuse your body and scatter your molecules all over the place. Full prep takes, at minimum, seven days. Seven days we don't have. The third possibility is called quick-prep. It has a slightly better prognosis."

I swallowed the growing lump in my throat. "*Slightly better?*" The news just kept getting brighter and brighter. In my experience, slightly better didn't usually amount to hopeful.

"The quick-prep method will let you survive the skip without full prep, but it could destabilize the molecules on a more permanent basis. There's a chance you could be caught in a kind of limbo."

"Limbo?" Something told me he wasn't talking about dancing with sticks…

"There's a fair chance that you wouldn't be returned home if the fail-safe button was pushed. You might simply be grounded where you stood. Stuck in whatever reality you were currently in." Elaina hesitated for a moment. "Or, a more likely theory is that you would return home, but continue to phase randomly—and uncontrollably."

I balked. "Randomly? For how long?"

She looked down, refusing to meet my gaze which, really, told me all I needed to know. "As I said, it's a permanent alteration."

Cade pushed past her and lifted my chin so that we were eye to eye. "We used the quick-prep before following Dylan. It hasn't happened to Noah or me. The truth is, there's no way to know for sure. The fail-safe button has never been used. There's no proof anything negative will happen."

"Yes." Elaina nodded. "From what I've come to understand, we know only that it changes your molecular makeup. There's a chance it could have no serious effect whatsoever."

A sick feeling bubbled in my gut. "How long do I have?"

"If Dylan stays true to his word, then a few days," Cade whispered. "But Dylan hasn't always proven to be a man of his word, so the truth is, there's no telling."

"Okay," I said, trying to let it all soak in. No freaking out. Soldiers didn't do that. "So, what you're telling me is, if we don't get this thing off, I'm going to be dragged along when you guys leave, which will kill me?" That wasn't an option I was willing to accept, and I was pretty sure Dad wouldn't be thrilled with it, either. I might drive him crazy on a somewhat daily basis, but total vaporization seemed extreme. "Well, just to be safe, since ya know I kind of like surviving, quick-prep me. There's obviously not enough time for the whole shebang, but I'd rather continue breathing somewhere else than stop altogether. Dad can figure out how to get me back once this is all over, right?"

Elaina shuffled from foot to foot, suddenly very nervous. She put both hands into her pockets, then pulled them out only to return them again.

"What? What are you not telling me?" They were looking at me as though I might explode. A ticking time bomb counting down the seconds to detonation.

Cade tensed, watching the woman with barely contained fear. He opened his mouth several times, but it took a moment for actual words to come out. "Elaina?"

She grabbed my hand and squeezed. Taking a deep breath, she said, "Kori, the semi-prep method doesn't exist on our Earth. We haven't even gotten the machine to function properly..."

Chapter Nine

It took me several tries to swallow down the growing lump in my throat. Air seemed to have become an issue, and an allover chill replaced the subtle warmth in the air. "Doesn't exist?" I repeated, numb. What was that supposed to mean? That I was a goner? When Dylan *skipped*, I was going to be dragged off into oblivion?

Cade's lips twisted into an angry grimace. "I was told the project was on schedule here," he snapped. "If you haven't gotten the cuffs to work, then that means you've never even made a trial run…" He let his head fall back and cursed. "That explains all the questions."

Maybe you'll just cease to be. Kind of implode or dissolve. Maybe it won't hurt much…

Elaina's face morphed into a mask of regret. And guilt. Apparently someone hadn't been completely honest with the guys. She threw up her hands and took a step toward me. "They didn't lie to you, Cade. The project is on schedule—our schedule. We didn't plan

to make our first runs for at least another two years."
She turned to me. "But we'll find a way to fix this.
We've been working with the boys for a few days now,
tweaking our tech based on theirs. As I said, we're still a
few years off as far as the actual cuffs are concerned, but
it looks promising. Noah is working with our medical
team as we speak."

"Noah?" I snorted. "Well, then let me prepare my
will."

Cade moved closer. "No. It's not like that with Noah.
You'd never know it, but he's Cora's son to the core.
Smarter than anyone I've ever met. He was pre-med
before this all went down. I know it seems like—"

"He hates me?" I yelled. It came out a mix between a
squawk and crying.

"He doesn't." Cade sounded sure, but I didn't buy it.
The guy had done nothing but snarl and snap at me from
the second he showed up on my doorstep—at least now
I understood why.

"We'll find a way around this," Elaina said, pushing
between us. I was hardly listening. I was having too
hard a time wrapping my head around all this new
information. Mom and Dad heading up a secret,
interdimensional travel agency. Noah Anderson. Brother,
med student—genius…? "In the meantime, I need you
to stay close to the boys. They're familiar with Dylan
and can keep you safe."

I blinked, then tilted my head and leaned closer.
No way. I had to have heard that wrong. "You want
me to stay with a couple of barely trained, unarmed
time travelers while there's a killer out there looking to
cut me down? Instead of, I dunno, staying on the nice

fortified *military base*?" She was insane. Or, maybe I was? Did I really want to stay here and leave my life in the hands of two strangers? Dylan said he'd give us the key if we found that Ava Harris girl.

"Technically, they aren't time travelers, they jump dimen..." Her voice trailed off as she realized that that wasn't the part of the conversation I cared about. "Staying on base won't help. This isn't a normal situation, Kori."

"You don't say!" I kind of snapped. I knew my tone was disrespectful, and Dad would be furious, because he raised me better, but I couldn't rein it in. "Alternate universe killers aren't something we deal with on a day-to-day basis? Color me surprised." I sucked in a breath, forcing myself to calm down and take control of the situation. That's what good soldiers did. "My dad. Call him."

Elaina looked even more uncomfortable. "That won't be possible."

"Not possible?" My mouth fell open. "Oh. I remember. He's in Washington—only *not* in Washington, right? You're telling me you can't contact him—or you won't?"

She shifted from foot to foot, looking over her shoulder like there might be someone standing there to help. "It's a bit of both, actually."

"A bit of both?" The words came out kind of squeaky and shrill. I was on the verge of losing it, and now I was being told they wouldn't—*couldn't*—contact my dad? This could be my last chance to see him. To say good-bye! "Why does that sound like you've *lost* my dad?"

"I understand your fear, but—"

"Do you know where he is or not?"

Eliana sighed. "We don't. We've tried contacting him—just once. He hasn't responded."

I was so ready to start swinging. "And you didn't think to try again?"

"It was decided," she said, nervous. "That it would be best for him to stay in the wind. From what Cade and Noah have told us about Dylan, if General Anderson reports in, he could be in grave danger."

I remembered the threats Dylan made, along with something about a Tribunal. "What's his problem? Why does Dylan hate my dad? Is he connected to Ava Harris?"

Eliana perked up. "Ava Harris? Who's that?"

Ahh. So the plot thickened. Elaina hadn't been entirely up front about their Infinity progress, but apparently the boys hadn't been totally forthcoming, either.

"Wish we knew. Dylan mentioned her," Cade said. Had to give the boy props. He was a convincing liar. That both worried and intrigued me.

Elaina let out a disappointed sigh and turned to Cade. He gave a slight nod and inclined his head toward the elevator. "Maybe we could talk?" He spread his other arm wide. "Away from all this?"

I hesitated a moment, then nodded. He wasn't crazy like I'd originally thought, and he was easy on the eyes, but that didn't mean I wanted to spend quality alone time with him. But, I needed information, and it seemed like he was the only one who had it. If the Infinity people here hadn't even gotten their machine to work, then Cade, from a place where they obviously were farther along, was my best bet of surviving this thing in one piece and finding my dad. "Okay," I said. "But only if you answer my questions." I leaned a little closer, giving him my best death glare. "All of them."

He didn't look thrilled about the idea but nodded. I hadn't said anything about Ava Harris—he owed me. "Just remember something, Kori. Sometimes questions are better left unanswered."

*C*ade took me back to the house—an arguable idea if you asked me. Dylan had already proven he could slip in and out unnoticed. Was this really the safest bet? But there was no fighting it. As per Simmons, he was in charge, and good soldiers never challenged the chain of command.

Reason number 268 why I would have made a horrible soldier...

"This makes no sense," I said, flopping back onto the couch. "No offense or anything, but you said it yourself. You're just a private. Barely out of basic. What makes you qualified to deal with this? You're taking point on something that, in my opinion, is the biggest thing in history."

Cade took the chair across from me. He looked tired. Not just in a sleep-deprived way, but also emotionally. Like he'd reached his limit. He held up his right hand. "Dylan killed her. My Kori... After I found—after what Dylan did, I knew he'd go right to the lab. Noah was with me, we called the general—he didn't know about Kori yet—and told him Dylan was planning an unauthorized skip."

There was a darkness in his voice that sent goose bumps skittering across my skin. His tone was grave, so I decided to let the questions keep for now.

"When we arrived I was in shock, still covered in her blood. Noah was so close to losing it... When the general got there, when he realized what Dylan had done..."

"He'd already gotten away."

Cade nodded. "No. He was still there. We fought, but he gave me the slip. Dylan took the test set, but in his rush to leave, two of the cuffs must have fallen out of the box."

"So the general sent you?" It still didn't jive. "I mean, Noah was a civilian, right?"

"He was," Cade confirmed. "And trust me, it took some convincing. We weren't the general's first—second, or third—choice. But, we were there and time was an issue. Plus, we were uniquely motivated and knew Dylan better than anyone else." He slumped against the wall. "I think in the end, the general knew that no one, not even his most loyal subordinate, would do as much to catch his daughter's killer than her brother and the guy who loved her..."

The guy who loved her...

The other me was a lucky girl. She'd had someone who loved her enough to chase a crazy person across multiple dimensions to avenge her death. I guess in a way it all made sense. I couldn't imagine what it had to be like for my dad—*her* dad. Sending them had to be an emotional response. Cade covered in my blood and telling him I was gone…

"Even the most decorated soldier wouldn't have stood a chance against Dylan. Not because he was better trained, but because they would never understand him. Noah and I, we got it. We knew the thing that was driving him."

"And that brings us to question number one. What would that be? The thing that's driving Dylan, I mean."

"Revenge…and Ava Harris."

The obvious question was, revenge against who? Obviously Infinity had done something Dylan deemed vile, but I wanted to know about Ava. The look in his eyes when he'd asked about her, fury along with something deeper, still burned me. "Who is she?" I remembered his cover-up with Elaina. "And why are you keeping her a secret from the commander?"

"Ava was the one. The perfect match for Dylan in every way. She challenged him, pushed him…made him want to be a better person. He loved her more than anything else on this—or any other—Earth."

"*Was* the one." He'd asked me where she was because he'd come here looking for her. One of her, at least. "She died, didn't she? Where you're from, she's dead."

"She is," Cade confirmed sadly. "And if we tell the army about her, they'll only get in our way. I've seen it happen before."

"When I first met him the other night, he seemed so sure I could tell him where she was. But why would he think I knew where to find her? I mean, that's why he's here, right? To find my Earth's version of Ava?"

"In part, yeah. But there's so much more to it." He shifted in his seat, getting comfortable. "Dylan and I enlisted in the army right out of high school. It was good for us. Gave us both something to focus on. We had a shitty childhood. Both had some anger issues—the general practically raised us. After Ava died, well, the general could see Dylan declining. Heading down a self-destructive path. Hell, we all could. You, him, Noah, and I were all so tight until... There was this project they were working on. Something they were having a hard time finding volunteers for. The general approached Dylan."

"Assuming this was for Infinity?"

Cade nodded. "We didn't know what the project was, and he refused to tell us anything. I had a bad feeling, though. I thought it was weird that they'd take such a low ranking volunteer for something so high level. We tried to talk him out of it, but he was angry and wouldn't listen. We'd had a falling out after Ava died."

"But he went through with it anyway I'm guessing? He volunteered?"

"Yep. I did some digging—you'd be surprised what kind of information you can get with the right bait, and found out about the Infinity Division. The reason they needed volunteers was, at that point, the trials they were conducting were unsuccessful. People were dying. I went there to stop him but I was too—"

I held out my hands to stop him, feeling sick to my stomach. "Wait. You're telling me this project was killing people, and the general—*my dad*—wanted Dylan to take it for a spin? Someone you're saying he cared about?" What kind of a monster willingly put someone he loves in the line of fire like that?

Cade frowned. "It's not like that. Not really. Our

version of the general is actually a much softer version than yours." He leaned forward, resting his elbows atop his knees. "I think it was basically a *shit or get off the pot* kind of thing. Dylan was in a dark place. It was either do something good with his life, or die on his own. He was drinking. Not taking care of himself. We all watched while he started to just waste away. No one could stand it anymore."

I wasn't convinced at his spin on the whole humanitarian angle, but didn't argue. "So assuming Dylan did it? It must have worked, right? I mean, he's not dead."

"Oh, it worked. The project was finally a success— and Dylan seemed to pop back. He was alive again. He stopped drinking. He even started talking to me again…"

"Okay…" Then realization hit, and I felt stupid for not seeing it before. It was the same thought I had had about my mother. "He thought he could use Infinity to find Ava."

"I don't think he understood how it all worked in the beginning. I think he thought he could find *his* Ava. Save her."

"But it doesn't work that way."

He was watching me, his gaze intense. It seemed like forever before he replied. "No. It doesn't work that way. The Infinity project isn't time travel. You can't go back and undo something. Gone is gone. Dead is dead." He let his gaze drop to the floor. "After the first trial, he went to the general and asked when he could skip again. It didn't go well."

"The general said no…"

Cade gave a dark laugh. "He told Dylan that while his services were appreciated, he was no longer needed.

He was not a part of the Infinity project—and never would be."

"That's horrible!" While I found it hard to sympathize with someone like Dylan, I couldn't imagine how used he must have felt. To be so close to the thing you wanted more than anything, then have it ripped away.

"Dylan had a taste of hope, and he wasn't about to let it go. If Infinity wouldn't let him skip again, then he'd sneak in and do anyway. It didn't take long to realize what he was planning to do." He shook his head and squeezed both eyes closed for a moment. When he opened them again, there was a spark of fierceness there. Conviction. "But it wasn't right. Against all the rules and principles. Everything that Infinity stood for... He wanted to take an innocent, unaware version of Ava and steal her away. I couldn't let him—"

"You turned him in." He didn't need to say it out loud, because he wore the guilt like a second skin. I had no idea why I hadn't seen it before. Like a black cloud, it shadowed his every move. Tainted every word.

I knew, because I had one of my own. An immeasurable weight that pressed down on me, unrelenting, every moment of every day. One I'd never spoken about with anyone.

"He was so convinced he could save her. Bring another version of the girl he loved back home and live happily ever after like nothing had happened. But he was wrong. It just doesn't work like that. So, yeah. I stopped him." He took a breath, eyes settling on something over my shoulder. "He blames the general for keeping him from Ava, and me for turning him in."

"And the Tribunal? What is that?"

"On my world, they're what you would consider judge and jury. Each state has one, as well as all the branches of government and military. With technology that allows people to travel to alternate timelines, there are rules in place to ensure the technology isn't abused and used for personal gain. Unbreakable and harshly punished."

I swallowed. "When you say harshly punished…"

He lifted his head and met my gaze dead-on. "Dylan was sentenced to die."

"Oh my God! That's not *too* barbaric. Christ. You couldn't just lock him away?"

Cade shrugged. "That's one of the big differences between our worlds. On mine, military crimes, as well as murder and domestic abuse, are punishable by death. It may seem harsh, but our crime rate is significantly lower."

It was a lot to process, but still didn't answer the initial question. "That still doesn't explain why he thought I would know where Ava was."

"She's your cousin."

"She's my—"

He held up his hand. "On our Earth, she's your cousin. Actually, on most of them, she is."

"But not this one."

He shrugged again. "Most of the time, Ava's mother divorces her father and ends up crossing paths with Cora's brother. They usually marry before Ava turns two."

I tucked my feet up and burrowed into the cushion. There was a chill in the air that had nothing to do with the low temps outside. "So he planned to use the Infinity technology to find another version of his Ava, but you said you turned him in. That he was caught. How did he make it here then?"

His demeanor changed. It went from sad but justified, to pained and, most of all, guilty. "He escaped before the sentence could be carried out."

"Escaped? How the hell do you escape the U.S. military? Especially in a hard-ass world like yours?"

He opened his mouth, but it was Noah, who'd just walked in the front door, who answered. "Cade let him go."

Chapter Ten

I stared at Noah, then turned to Cade. He wasn't looking at me. His gaze was fixed on Noah, the expression etched in an even mixture of guilt and pain.

Noah closed the door behind him and took several steps into the room. He threw his hands into the air and pinned his friend with a sad smile. "No judgment, man. I get it."

"You get it?" I shrieked, and whirled on Cade. "Well, I don't. You were the one who turned him in. You had to know what they'd do to him. You had a change of heart?"

"Yes, I did," he replied in a hushed tone. He bent his head for a moment, and when he raised it and his gaze met mine, there was fury like I'd never seen before. "But I regret it every waking moment. It's something that will haunt me until the day I die, and I would give anything to turn back time and let him die."

"Why, though? Why would you let him out to begin with?"

"Because I didn't think I could watch my brother die."

"Your—" The rest of it lodged in my throat. I opened my mouth, then closed it, speechless. His brother? That maniac was Cade's *brother*? How the hell did two people end up so different?

"Whatever blood once connected us means nothing now." Cade stood, eyes fixed on Noah. "He signed his death warrant when he started killing people."

I could see it in his eyes. Every word was the truth. For the most part. I had a feeling it wasn't the killing people in general that turned Cade against his brother as much as a particular person. "You were in love with her." The words stole my breath, and for some reason, made my chest ache. "Your Kori. You were in love with her and that's why Dylan killed her. To get back at you for turning him in."

A violent storm of emotion raged across his face. Agony and anger and regret. Guilt mixed with that painfully obvious self-loathing I understood better than I would have liked. If he'd never let Dylan out, none of this would have happened. His Kori would have never been killed, and he and Noah wouldn't be stuck, getting dragged from dimension to dimension with no end in sight.

But there was more to the sadness in his expression. When he raised his head and our eyes met, I found it hard to breathe. "Yes. And, no."

"I don't understand. No, he wasn't trying to get back at you?"

Cade shifted uneasily. He glanced back at Noah, who regarded him with what I could only classify as sympathy. "He was getting back at me, but not for turning him in. Well, that was part of it, but…"

Obviously something else went on between them. Something that had traumatized Cade as much as Ava's death had twisted Dylan. "But…?" I nudged.

"Ava. I was the one who killed her."

"You—"

"Bullshit." Noah slammed his hand against the arm of the couch, then stalked across the room toward Cade. He pulled him up and grabbed him by the front of his shirt, giving a harsh shake. "I'm so sick of hearing this shit." He shoved Cade backward and whirled on me. "He didn't kill her. It was an accident. We were all drinking, acting like assholes. Cade was the only sober one. The only one being responsible."

"Yet I still crashed the car," he interjected.

"When the only sober person in a car full of drunks loses control on icy roads, that's called an accident, man. Not murder."

"He promised to kill you," he said quietly, turning to me. "On our world and every other one he set foot on. Dylan swore that he would wipe you from existence."

"Well," I said with a wave in his general direction. "He's slacking, because I'm still here, and I've got no intention of taking the long dirt nap."

"This isn't a joke," Noah snapped. He nudged Cade out of the way and planted himself in front of me. "Personally, you're just some chick who happens to be wearing my sister's face, but to him—" He jabbed a finger in Cade's direction. "It would kill him to watch you die all over again, and I won't let him go through that."

"Aww," I said, crossing my arm. "Careful or I might think you care."

His lips twisted into a scowl. "Don't delude yourself. I don't give a shit about you, or anyone else on this damn rock. I'm here for one reason."

"And that is?"

"To make sure my boy makes it home in one piece."

And with that, he pushed past me and made his way into the kitchen. A few moments later, I heard the hinges of the fridge squeal, followed by loud, obnoxious crunching. "Jesus. Does he ever stop eating? How the hell is he not, like, five hundred pounds?"

"He's right about one thing. This isn't a game. Dylan might be letting us think we have a fighting chance. That putting that cuff on you is his way of giving you some kind of advantage over the others. But it's bullshit. He's got no intention of giving us that key."

The air was suddenly much thinner. Colder, too. The certainty in his voice made the bottom drop out from my stomach. The kind of feeling that came with the sudden, violent slide from the top of a twenty-story rollercoaster.

"Ava's death wrecked him. It tore apart his soul. There's nothing left in there. None of the person he used to be. All that's left is pain and anger. He's nothing but a time bomb looking for a place to detonate."

"Sounds like a fun guy." I refused to let him see how freaked I was. Couldn't. Dad once said the key to survival in times of war was equal parts persistence— aka stubbornness—strength, and good old-fashioned bullshit. Never let the enemy see you sweat. Cade wasn't necessarily my enemy, but it was the same basic principle. "So what do we do? Try to find Ava? Try to find Dylan? I'm sure the commander could track her down fast if we just—"

Cade shook his head. "You heard what Dylan said. No army interference."

"Okay." That didn't answer my question. "Then where do we start?"

His eyes grew wide. Like a bug, I couldn't help thinking. "*We're* not going to start anything. This is the first time I've seen you alive in almost a year. I intend to keep it that way."

That's when I lost it. I didn't know if it was the way he was looking at me—a strange mix of longing and determination mixed with guilt—or the tone of his voice. Dominating and just a bit accusatory. "This is the first time you've seen me, period." I stalked toward him, stopping an inch or so from his face. "I'm not *her*. I'm not your Kori."

"I know that!" He flinched at my suddenly harsh tone.

"Do you?" I fired back. "Because the way you look at me, I wonder if you're not exactly like Dylan." As soon as the words spilled out, I regretted them.

I'd hit a nerve. His face contorted, a mask of fury and pain. He balled his fists tight and stepped closer, effectively backing me away. "What the hell is that supposed to mean?"

But I wasn't a pushover. I'd never been one to back down. My mom always saw it as a weakness. Something that would get me into trouble. Dad fostered it. Fed my instinct to fight and challenge.

It didn't really work out the way he'd planned though, did it? When Dad encouraged you to stand tall, he probably didn't mean get into any and all trouble you can find...

I got right back in Cade's face. Shoved him as hard

as I could. "Do you think I'm blind? That I don't see the way you stare at me? Are you going to tell me it never crossed your mind? That when you did find me, an *alive me*, that it would be just like getting *her* back?"

We'd surpassed inside voices and had moved on to screaming. The neighbors on the right side would ignore it. They'd always been a bit weird. But my left side neighbor, Mrs. Davis, would be close to calling the cops. I didn't care, though. This needed to be said. It was something we needed to drag into the open, because I didn't want it coming out to bite me in the ass further down the road.

Noah came stumbling through the doorway, a piece of carrot hanging from his lips. "What the hell is going on out here?"

Ignoring his question, Cade's face reddened. He shoved me back. Not hard enough to hurt, but with enough force to send me stumbling backward. To let me know he wouldn't be bullied. "I'm never getting her back," he bellowed. "Trust me, I know that. And I know you're not her. You're the furthest thing from her. But if you think I'm going to let you die when I can finally prevent it, you're fucking delusional."

Noah threw up his arms and stepped between us. "Hey man, let's—"

Cade shoved him out of the way. He opened his mouth, but I wasn't interested.

"That's right. I'm *not* her," I repeated, louder and with more bite. "I'm not in love with you, and you're not in love with *me*. At this point I'm not even sure I'm going to be able to tolerate you long enough to figure this all out! It's not your damn job to watch out for me or to save me. I can save my own damn self."

"You're wrong," he seethed. The lower tone was actually more intimidating than his yelling. His eyes narrowed to thin slits as every inch of him tensed, a tightly wound string just seconds from snapping. "It is my job."

"Spare me," I countered before he could launch into some righteous speech about this all being his fault and how he wanted to make things right. I didn't give a damn. "You screwed up." I softened my tone but held my ground. "I get that you feel guilty. I understand that you feel like you need to fix it. I don't know crap about what kind of girl your Kori was, or how the dynamic between you two played out, but me? I'm not a damsel in distress. I don't need saving. I don't want it. And I don't want you."

Some of the anger left him, and his shoulders sagged. "You don't understand. Dylan—"

"Is a bad guy. Yeah. I get it." I gestured around the room, trying hard not to let my temper get the better of me. "But this is *my* world, Cade, not yours. These are my people to protect, and it's *me* who's going to lose my family—hell, my life—if we fail. If you need to be involved so damn badly, then help me figure out how to get this thing off. Help me stop Dylan from hurting more people."

Noah huffed. He looked from me to Cade and nodded slightly. "This isn't all about her," he said softly. His lips slipped into a frown. There was a spark of sadness in his eyes, but also something stronger. Something I recognized. That trademark Anderson determination. It was the same look I'd seen on Dad's face as he gave me his *life must go on* speech after losing Mom. "We left home to stop Dylan from doing more damage. She's right. We need to stop him from wiping out more innocent people. There's no Tribunal here. That means there are three clueless people out there on his radar. Three people who are currently unaccounted for. They don't deserve to die."

Cade refused to look at him. Instead, he kept his gaze locked on mine. A shiver shot up my spine. "And if it puts her right in the crossfire, then that's okay, because she's not our Kori, right?"

Noah held up his hands and shook his head. Just once. "I didn't say that, man. You know I loved my sister. We were close... But she wasn't like Dad. Wasn't like you or me. She wasn't a fighter. This one is annoying as shit, but I really think she can hold her own." He eyed me, tip to toe, then gave a slight grin. "She can hack it. I think she's too stubborn to go down easy."

Cade finally turned, glowering. For the longest time he didn't speak. Just stared. Like he was contemplating Noah's assessment. Trying to decide whether to lock me in the basement for safekeeping or let me help resolve this thing.

"This is a bad idea," he said finally. To Noah, he added, "I know better, but as usual, you've talked me into going along with something I know is going to end in disaster."

Noah grinned like a kid who'd just been given an entire candy store. "When have I ever done anything like that?"

Cade stared at him.

"Okay, okay. Maybe once or twice... But we *can* do

this. I think this is the shot we've been waiting for. A way to put this thing to bed once and for all." He punched Cade in the arm. "We can go home, man. *Home*."

Cade shook his head. "This is a bad idea," he repeated.

I smiled. It was forced. A tool used to hide the fear I really felt. But right then, it was all I had. Falling apart wasn't an option. Neither was running. This was something that needed to be faced head on. Laces tight and guns at the ready. I would kick ass or die trying. "Most of the fun stuff usually is."

Chapter Eleven

While Noah took the commander's jeep to check out some of Ava's more typical haunts, Cade and I "borrowed" Dad's SUV and set out to track down this world's version of his Tribunal. Three people named Odette Ferguson, Miles Hann, and Penny Bloom.

It was just after noon and we were sitting in traffic, still several miles from our first stop. Penny Bloom's. Cade had been quiet, and although I enjoyed the silence, I had so many questions. Questions I might not get another chance to ask.

"I—she—" I swallowed. There was a part of me that didn't want to know, and another that couldn't wait. "My mom—what's she like? Is she—"

"Alive?" he finished for me.

"Yeah."

His lips split with a smile. It made me instantly jealous for reasons I couldn't quite reach. "Very much so."

The bigger question on the tip of my tongue—the biggest one, really—was *what is she like*? Was she like my mom? Did she have a thing for tacky blue lawn flamingos and junk food? Did she love cheesy horror movies and chocolate-covered popcorn?

"Cora has always been a huge part of my life," he continued. "My parents were...less than what a kid could hope for. She and the general were the best kind of surrogates "

"Tell me something about her," I said, closing my eyes. I pictured Mom's face, the summer breeze fluttering her hair. I could still picture her smile so clearly, but lately I'd found myself wondering if I was starting to forget the sound of her laugh. I remembered she had the slightest accent—but only when saying certain words or when she'd get upset. She'd sort of rolled her *R*s. "Anything."

I opened my eyes to see Cade smiling. "She liked rats."

"Rats?" I giggled. "That's...weird."

"Not when you think about it, really. Cora loves animals—especially the ones she feels are misunderstood."

"Ahh," I said. They had that in common. My mom had loved animals. We would have had an entire zoo's worth if moving from place to place hadn't been our way of life. To supplement her critter craze, though, Mom and I made monthly trips to the zoo. Whenever we moved someplace new, it was the first thing we scoped out. Well, technically the second. The first thing we did was take note of all the local junk food joints for when Dad went out of town. "Bet she loves pigs, too."

He laughed. "Crazy about them."

I shifted sideways in my seat, feeling lighter than I had in a long time. Suddenly I was ravenous for more despite the ache in my chest. Even the most unassuming detail would fascinate me. It didn't matter that we weren't talking about *my* mom. This was still Cora Anderson. It was still, in some small way, a part of her. "Tell me something else."

He was quiet for a moment. "Ya know, she said something to me once. I didn't understand it at the time, but it makes so much sense now."

"Oh?"

"She said she was proud of you. Said that if there were an infinite number of you out there, she would love each and every one more than her next breath."

I didn't respond. Couldn't, really. My chest constricted, bringing the ache back with a vengeance, and suddenly breathing was that much harder. There was a lump in my throat, making it impossible to swallow. Was knowing she was out there, still alive and well, but unreachable to me, enough? I was starting to think it wasn't. I was starting to sympathize with Dylan despite his methods. The idea of getting a lost loved one back was tantalizing. The very definition of temptation.

"So you guys are close?" The words were cracked and frail, and in that moment, I was terribly afraid of losing it. Of breaking down and dissolving the carefully constructed walls that had held all the pain at bay.

He nodded. "We are. She's one of the kindest souls I've ever met. You're just like her." He paused, then frowned. "Well, my Kori was, anyway."

I tried not to take it the wrong way, but it was impossible. The wave of pain that had crept in was swept away by a sudden spike of anger. "What's that supposed to mean?"

He sighed. "I didn't mean it like that. Just that they were both softer. They saw the good in people no matter what." His expression darkened a little. "Even when the darkness is right there in front of them, they're always expecting change. Always thinking they can incite it."

"And what about us?" I felt the heat rush to my cheeks—and this time it had nothing to do with the way he was looking at me. "If you were so close with my— her—family, how did she feel about you being with her daughter?"

Cade shrugged, oblivious to my indignation. "In my world, it was an inevitability. The four of us had been friends since, like, kindergarten. We were always just part of the family. We got older and things progressed. I guess they all expected it. We complemented each other."

"That's sad," I said, folding my arms.

He pulled the car alongside the curb, in front of a pale yellow Cape. When he shifted to face me, his expression darkened. "How is it sad?"

I shrugged, slightly vindicated by his irritation. I should have just left this subject alone, but for some reason, I couldn't. It was like the universe was taunting me. Teasing me toward confrontation. One day, he might get to go home. His Kori might be gone, but his Cora wouldn't be. It was stupid, but I was jealous that he'd get to see *my* mother again and I wouldn't. Twisting his words in a way that might hurt him made me feel slightly better—which made me feel horrible. "Well, it doesn't sound like much of a relationship. I mean, I'm no expert, but *complementing* someone?" I snickered.

"Certainly doesn't sound like something epic. Love isn't supposed to be predictable, Cade." I'd never been in love, but my parents were soulmates and I saw how they treated each other. There was nothing boring about their relationship, even after all those years together. I still remember all the surprises they would plan for each other, each trying to outdo the last gesture. Their relationship was what I wanted mine to be one day. I wouldn't settle for anything less.

He twisted the key with a jerk and yanked it from the ignition. "You don't know shit about me. About her." He fisted the keys until his knuckles went white. "You don't know anything about our relationship—and something tells me you wouldn't know *epic* if it came along and smacked you on the ass."

"Oh." His irritation hit the spot. "So then I'm wrong?"

"I loved her," he said through clenched teeth. "More than anything else in this world."

I believed him. I mean, why else would he have jumped across realities to hunt down her killer? But love was a funny thing. There were different kinds. Different levels. The way he described the relationship with his Kori didn't sound like true love to me. Pointing that out to him, though, would have been pointless. He was clearly in denial, and I wasn't that angry.

I gave up and inclined my head toward the house. "This it?"

"Penny Bloom's." He nodded to the gray SUV in the driveway. "Think that's hers?"

I slid around and pushed open the car door. "Only one way to find out for sure."

There were no signs of activity, and the place was

dark. Cade got out of the car and made his way up the walk. I followed, staying behind a few paces. Acid bubbled in my stomach, that uncomfortable rumbling that went hand in hand with worry.

One foot in front of the other, we climbed the three steps onto Penny's porch. The methodic wooden tapping as Cade rapped on the door was like a gong in my ears. "Mrs. Bloom?"

No answer.

He knocked again.

More silence.

With a huff, he pounded his fist against the door, harder this time. When he met with the same response, he tried the doorknob. To our surprise, it turned without resistance.

"Huh," I said, pushing the door open a little wider. "That should have been obvious."

He rolled his eyes. "Breaking and entering isn't obvious."

I winked. "It's not breaking and entering when the door is open."

"I cannot believe how much like Noah you sound."

That was enough to shut me up instantly.

Cade stepped around me and crossed the threshold. The house was dark, and there was a stillness to the air that made the hair on my arm spike to attention. I knew without going farther that we were alone here. Still, we searched. Through the living room and into the kitchen, there were no signs of a struggle. Nothing was broken or seemed out of place. Dishes were stacked on the counter in neat piles next to the sink, while the table in the far corner of the room was decorated with dainty placemats and a vase with fresh-cut flowers.

I sighed and started for the stairs. "Is it possible she went out of town?"

"Anything is possible," Cade said, coming up behind me. "She's not the same as my world's Penny. Considering the door was unlocked though, that's probably unlikely."

At the top of the stairs, I hooked a right, while Cade went left. There was a bedroom on either side, both empty. "Now what?" I asked, leaning against the wall beside a large oak dresser. "Where do we go from here? She could be anywhere. Maybe Dylan isn't going to go after her."

He shook his head. "Not a chance. They sentenced Dylan to die, and I know my brother. He'll never let it go. Getting what he feels is justified revenge is just as important to him as finding Ava."

"So, then...?"

"I hate to just walk away, but my gut is telling me to move on to the next name. Dylan isn't going to waste time. We can double back and check here again."

Walking away almost felt like giving up on Penny, but in my gut I knew he was right. She wasn't here, and waiting around wasn't a good call. What if, while we hung around here waiting just in case she returned, one of the other two people were hurt? Killed? A good soldier knew how to make the hard calls. But, on the other hand, you never left a man behind.

"What about someplace else? Is there another place we could check?" I was grasping at straws, but I had to try. "Someplace your Penny might go?"

He frowned. Almost like he felt sorry for me. "We

already know she's not like my Penny Bloom. We don't know where she works, what her hobbies are. We don't even know if she has any family on this world."

"Where she works," I exclaimed. Why hadn't I thought about that? I dashed across the room to her dresser and began pulling open drawers. "Just look around. Maybe there's something that can tell us where she works. A pay stub—anything."

Cade didn't look hopeful, but he nodded and disappeared into the other room. I went to work rifling through her personal items and pulling papers from her desk. After I'd torn through everything in the room, I moved on to the next.

I pulled open the next drawer. We'd both moved into the last room. "So was this what you always wanted to do?" I asked, making conversation to distract myself from the fact that I was in the last room and had yet to find any information leading me to Penny.

"Travel from one dimension to the other, you mean?"

I rolled my eyes and sifted through a pile of neatly stacked papers. "Yes. Because that's every child's aspiration... I meant the army. Did you always want to enlist?"

Cade moved to the closet. The door opened with a squeal and he bent down to pull out a stack of boxes from the back. "Actually, I always wanted to go into veterinary medicine." He snorted. "Noah was going to cure sick people and I was going to help animals."

I stopped shuffling through papers to turn toward him. "Seriously?"

He smiled. "Sure. We had it all planned out. The Man and Beast Clinic."

I laughed, trying to picture them working side by side. I could almost see Cade as a vet, but Noah as a doctor? I still couldn't picture it. "Man and Beast Clinic?"

He shrugged and turned back to the boxes. "We were twelve. It was Noah's idea."

Of course it was...

I remembered what he said about his world's version of my mom. "Bet Cora loved it."

Cade laughed and grabbed another box. "She promised she'd be our best customer."

A lump formed in my throat. It was so stupid for me to be jealous, yet I was.

He was quiet for a moment, and when he spoke again, his tone was softer. "When I was nine, Cora found an injured bird. She brought him home and called me over." He snickered. "One of the few times I wasn't *at* her house already. Even then, she pushed me. Challenged me. She asked me what I thought we should do to get the bird back its his feet."

"It sounds like you love her very much."

He was quiet for a few moments. "I do."

The lump got bigger, but I tamped it down. This conversation needed to go in a different direction. "So what did you end up doing? For the bird, I mean."

"Well, it was my idea to give it two Advil, Nyquil, and a full body cast. Cora gently suggested a vet."

It was hard not to picture a younger version of Cade, with his serious expression and matter-of-fact attitude prescribing Nyquil to an injured bird. "Sounds like a smart lady."

"She is. I miss her." He turned to me, and I saw it. The

exact moment he realized what he'd said. "Shit. Kori, I'm sorry. I didn't mean—"

I held up my hand and shook my head, but the lump in my throat threatened to choke me, so I simply smiled and turned away from him to resume my inspection.

We searched the rest of the room in silence. It took about twenty minutes to get through the whole thing, and when we came up empty-handed, at least Cade looked sorry. "We're out of time, Kori. We have to move on."

I sighed and slumped back against the refrigerator. I'd gone through the living room and guest bedroom while Cade took on the dining room and bath. We'd tackled the kitchen together. "I just thought maybe..." My voice cracked and I couldn't finish my sentence.

Suddenly he was in front of me. "Hey." He grabbed my hands and squeezed tight. Just once. "I get it. I didn't wanna give up on her either. We'll come back, I swear."

"If we leave, that's it. We won't find her alive. Coming back later isn't going to cut it, and I know you know that, so don't bullshit me, please."

He brought his hands to my face, tipping my chin upward so that we were eye to eye. Expression going from soft to fierce, he said, "I have to believe that we will. And I need you to believe it, too."

What I believed was that he believed it. In that moment, standing there and looking into his eyes, I finally understood how he'd been able to do what he'd been doing. Jumping from place to place. Failing to save the girl he loved over and over. He *believed*. Not because he was innocently optimistic, but because he had no other choice. A walking, talking, version of *if at first you don't succeed…* Soldier determination never appealed to me. The *can do* attitude and slightly cocky air that the drill sergeants instilled in them from day one of boot camp had always put me off. But right then, I found his attitude about the whole thing the most attractive thing I could think of.

Before I could think twice, I leaned in and kissed his cheek.

"I'm sorry," I whispered, letting my head fall back against the fridge. I turned so that we weren't face-to-face.

"No. I'm sorry. I know what you must think, and it's wrong. I—" His eyes locked on something to my left. "No. No way is it that simple."

"Simple?" I twisted so I could see what he was looking at. I couldn't see the front, but it looked like a pamphlet of some kind, stuck to the fridge by a panda bear magnet.

He grabbed the paper and stepped back, holding it out for me to see. It was covered in lush trees and showed a happy couple walking up a wooded path. "Fallow Park," he announced, giving it a slight shake. "It's a trail map. We found our link! She hikes just like my Penny."

It was already two in the afternoon by the time we pulled into the parking lot. Almost halfway through our first day and we'd gotten nowhere. I was keeping my fingers and toes crossed that this little side trip changed all that.

On the way over, Cade called Noah and asked him to meet us here. With the three of us searching the park, maybe we'd get lucky—that was, if Penny Bloom was even there. Noah took the two first trails, and Cade and I had just finished walking the last two. We'd come up empty-handed.

I stuffed my hands into my pockets and fought a shiver. It started to drizzle the minute we got out of the jeep, and we'd been hiking down the main trail for a while now. My hoodie was nearly soaked through, and my socks, thanks to the generous hole in the front corner of my Keds, were a soggy mess.

"Back on our Earth, they close this park so that Penny can run."

"Are you serious? They close the entire park down? Just for one person?"

He nodded. "Tribunals are important to our legal system and society. Almost royalty in a sense. As you can probably imagine, just like with any other thing, there are those who don't agree with their judgments or the amount of power they hold. It's not uncommon for attempts to be made on their lives, so their security detail is high priority."

"That's crazy." I stepped over a large branch in our path. When I put my foot down, it slipped in a patch of wet leaves. The world tilted to the right, but Cade was fast. He grabbed me before I went down, lifting me up and setting me back down on the other side.

"Careful," he said, stepping away.

"Yeah," I countered, feeling heat rush to my cheeks. His gaze lingered a little too long, but to be honest, mine did, too. He wasn't what most girls would call conventionally hot. He was good-looking, sure, but it was more than that. The way he held himself and the strength in his eyes. Studying him, I noticed his right eyebrow sat slightly higher than the left, and his nose was a smidge crooked. Like Dylan's. I wondered if they did it to each other. It was those little imperfections, in addition to the scar, that made him attractive. Made him worthy of a good, long look. If you bypassed the controlling attitude, I could almost see why the other me fell for him. "I'm a klutz," I added, finally.

"And I'm a flying monkey," Noah said with a snort. He came up behind us and snapped his fingers several times, pointing to the end of the trail. "I didn't find anything on the other two paths. This is the last one. Could we please keep moving? I'm turning into a frozen prune."

"Not sure it's worth it." Cade stuffed his hands into his pockets and sighed. "We haven't found much difference in geography from Earth to Earth. This part of Fallow Park leads to the cliffs. The trail basically ends here."

Noah nodded. "It was worth a shot. I say we officially call it and try tracking down Miles and Odette."

They turned and started back, and I reluctantly followed. I took about four steps before the faint sound of something stopped me cold. "Is that—?"

We all froze, listening. It was faint, but I was sure it sounded like a woman. A woman calling for help.

"Penny..." Cade took off with Noah right on his heels. I followed. Through the thick trees, I stumbled after them, far less graceful, and broke through into a large clearing. But there was no one in sight.

"Where is she?" Noah scanned the area left to right and stomped his foot. "I don't see a damn thing."

"Someone! Help me!" the voice cried again, this time louder.

It took a moment, but when I realized where the sound was coming from, I almost threw up. "The cliff," I whispered, horrified. "It's coming from over the *edge* of the cliff."

We rushed forward and peered over the edge. Sure enough, there she was. Dangling precariously over the ravine below, from the middle of an unstable-looking tree trunk that jutted out from between two large boulders.

"Jesus," I breathed. She was secured by only her left wrist, angry red marks marring her skin. Her left shoe was gone, probably lost to the water far below, and mud streaked her blue and pink jogging suit.

Cade pushed me aside and settled on the edge, swinging his feet over. Just as he was about to drop down to the trunk, Noah grabbed his arm and yanked back furiously. "Are you insane? That thing won't hold you. You try to go out there and get her and you'll both fall."

He was right. The tree was thick, but it wasn't rooted in the rock well. Every few moments little bits of dirt and debris pulled loose from the base. It was holding Penny, barely, but it wouldn't hold Cade too. The chances of them surviving the fall was slim. It had to be at least thirty feet to the water below, the path obscured by multiple jagged rocks.

"Shit," he cursed.

"Please," Penny cried. Her grip on the rope slipped,

and her right hand pulled free. The movement jerked the tree trunk and shook several larger rocks loose from the surrounding area. I watched them fall, bouncing off the cliff until they splashed into the water below. My stomach tightened. "Please help me!"

"Ideas?" Cade said to Noah.

They stepped to the side, whispering, and I sank to the ground next to the edge. "It's going to be all right," I called as soothingly as possible. She struggled to look up, toward the sound of my voice, and the tree trunk shifted a bit. "Just stay as still as possible."

She wrenched her neck in my direction and a sob escaped her lips. "I was on the path. This guy came out of nowhere..."

"We're going to get you up." She nodded and I stood. There wasn't much time. Panic was a normal human reaction. Poor Penny wouldn't be able to keep it together much longer from the looks of it, and I couldn't blame her. Even the most badass soldier would have an issue with this situation. We needed to get her up. Now.

Cade and Noah were too big. They'd get her—and themselves—killed. And if that happened, I was a goner. There was no hope of me getting that key from Dylan without their help. Like it or not, I'd been wrong earlier. My life *was* in their hands.

The decision sucked, but it was the only one. Heart thumping, I said, "I'll do it." I wedged myself between them. "I'll climb onto the trunk and get her."

They stopped talking and stared at me.

"What's the other choice?" I pointed to the edge of the cliff. "That thing is unstable as it is. If either of you steps onto that trunk, it's pancake city. But if I go..."

"No way," Cade said, while at the same time, Noah shrugged and said, "Okay."

I should probably be offended by Noah's lack of regard for my life...

"If we don't do something now, she's going to fall," I pushed. My gaze went to Cade's. "I won't stand here and let that happen. Not when there's something I can do to help her."

"What can you do? You'll never be able to pull her up," he argued. He cast an angry scowl at his friend, who seemed oblivious.

"I'm stronger than I look," I countered, even though he was right. I'd never be able to lift her onto the trunk by myself, and even if I could, I doubted it would be able to take all the movement. The jostling required for me to possibly wrestle her up would knock the trunk loose, and we'd fall for sure. But I had a plan. One that might be able to work around my lack of upper body strength. "And just so we're clear, I wasn't *asking* for your permission. I was telling you so you'd help me."

Cade stared, wide-eyed, and Noah pushed him aside. "What's your idea?"

Deep breath. No pressure... "I realize this isn't ideal, but the alternative isn't an option." Dad always said I could take control of a situation like a true military brat. Time to prove him right. Turning my back to them, I counted to ten and crouched down. "Penny, I'm here with Cade and Noah, two soldiers from the Fort Hannity Military Base." Technically it was the truth. "We're gonna get you up."

She made a small whimpering noise, but nodded, and I stood. I pulled off my hoodie and handed it to

Cade. "There's a rock jutting out about five feet down. It looks just big enough for two small people. If you can lower me down, I can throw her the hoodie."

Noah wasn't impressed. "To keep her warm? What good will that do?"

I bent down and dug into the back pocket of my jeans. As a general's daughter, I'd learned to always be prepared. That meant having enough cash in case of emergencies—and a nice sharp pocketknife. I held it up. "He has her tied with one hand free." I took the sleeve of my hoodie and forced the ring at the end of the knife through the threads. "I toss it to her with the knife attached, and she uses it to cut herself loose and swing to me. You guys pull us up."

"You make it sound so simple," Cade remarked. He nodded over the edge. "I don't like it, but as you said, no other choice."

"Zactly." I peered over the side of the cliff again. God. It was a long way down. But, at least there was water. If I fell...I'd be screwed. I'd never learned how to swim—not that it mattered much. There was only a 50 percent chance I'd hit the water. Some of those rocks came out pretty far. Just far enough to smash my head like an old Halloween pumpkin on the way down...

I took the hoodie from Cade and tied it around my waist.

Noah pulled off his jacket and handed half to me. Then, wrapping the other half around his wrists and gripping tight, he leaned back. "Just like rock climbing," he said with a wink. He even smiled. Sort of.

I positioned myself at the edge and gave the jacket a

good tug to make sure he had a firm grip. Seemed solid. "Too bad I've never been climbing."

For an instant, there was a spark of sadness in his eyes. But he blinked and it was gone, replaced by the cold, volatile stare I was becoming disturbingly accustomed to. "Let's get this over with."

Getting down to the makeshift ledge was easier than I expected. There were more than enough crevices to use as footholds, and Noah's jacket provided sufficient leverage. When I felt the solid surface beneath me, I kept a tight hold on the jacket and pushed down with one foot to test it. Carefully, I eased more weight until I was standing on my own. Solid. Good. Now all I could hope for was that it stayed that way.

"Okay, Penny, here's what we're gonna do." I shifted so that my back was flat against the cliff and untied the hoodie from around my waist, drawing her attention to the knife.

Whatever you do, don't look down...

"I'm going to toss this to you and you're going to catch it with your free hand. Use the blade to cut yourself free, but make sure you hang on tight or you're going to fall." No sense in sugarcoating things. She had to know the score. "As soon as you have a good grip, carefully swing your legs so that you sway toward me. I'm going to grab you, and our friends up there will pull us up. Got it?"

She didn't respond.

"Penny?"

Her lip trembled and her head moved slowly from side to side. Still no response.

The last thing we needed was for her to go into

shock. It was time for some tough love. "Suck it up," I snapped. The sound of my voice echoed off the rocks, then faded into the distance. "You need to soldier up or you're going to fall. Going to *die*. Got it?"

For a second I thought maybe I'd made things worse, but after a moment, she nodded. Worked every time.

"Okay." I grabbed one of the sleeves of my hoodie tight and leaned forward as far as I dared. "We can do this." It wasn't clear who I was trying to convince. Her, me, or Cade and Noah up top. They both lingered at the edge, watching silently. This whole thing was a good, solid plan in theory. The problem with theories, though, is that they didn't always pan out.

One swing. Two swings. Three… It took five tries for her to grab the sleeve of the hoodie, and when she did, there was a moment my heart nearly stopped. The ring on the edge of the knife slipped through the threads and I was sure it would fall to the water below. But it didn't. With shaking fingers, she managed to fumble the blade free and went to work sawing through the rope.

I held my breath. Each second that ticked by felt like an hour. In order to hang on to the rope while cutting it, she had to rock the blade back and forth across a small piece below her wrist. The movement made the trunk shake, and my heart hammered double-time the entire way.

After several of the longest minutes of my life, the rope snapped and Penny gasped in surprise. "Now! Carefully swing toward me."

She began gently moving her feet back and forth. I made several attempts to grab her as she swayed near, but it was no good. I was too far away.

"I need to get closer," I yelled to the top.

A moment later, Noah appeared over the edge. He was on his stomach, leaning over the side. The end of his jacket dropped down. "I've got it. Try now."

I wrapped the sleeve around my hand twice and leaned forward, praying that he had a firm grip. My toes curled over the edge. Sweat broke out on the back of my neck and my pulse hammered. Extending my hand, I wiggled my fingers and said, "Again. Swing toward me again."

Above my head, small pieces of rubble and bits of dirt shook from the base of the tree. The more she moved, the looser the roots became. The gravity of the situation hit me right then. If the tree trunk pulled loose, there was a good chance it was taking me down with it. The rock I was on was small. There'd be no way for me to avoid it as it fell.

"I can't reach," Penny cried.

"Yes you can," I insisted, even though I wasn't sure anymore. Every second that ticked by poked more holes in my plan. She had to swing carefully, and it just wasn't giving her enough momentum. "Listen to me. When I say go, you're going to kick toward me as hard as you can."

"But you said—"

"Do it!" I screamed. "Now!"

She kicked back and swung both feet hard in my direction. That time I was able to grab her calves. I didn't think. Didn't hesitate. I pulled as hard as I could.

"Hurry!" Noah yelled. "My jacket is ripping."

The trunk of the tree groaned and buckled.

"You're almost there, Kori," Cade called from above.

He was right. Just…a…little bit…more. With one final tug, I pulled her onto the rock. She let go of the rope just in time. The trunk of the tree came free of the rock. I held my breath and pulled her forward, smashing myself against the side of the cliff, hoping that the roots didn't drag us down too. It sailed overhead, the bulk of it missing us by what felt like inches.

"You guys okay?" Noah appeared over the edge again, followed by Cade. He shimmied as far down as he could and extended both hands.

"Go ahead," I said to Penny. She was shaking uncontrollably and looked like she was going to pass out at any moment. That, or puke. Neither option was good. "They'll pull you up."

With Noah's help, they lifted her to safety, then dragged me back up. I'd never been so happy to have grass beneath me. For the longest moment I just lay there, face against the wet grass and heart thumping. Once I caught my breath, I sat up.

"A young man did this," she said, pulling the tips of her sleeves up over her fingers with a shiver. "He just jumped me and…" She closed her eyes for a moment, shaking her head. "I must have passed out. When I woke up, he was tying me to that tree. He wasn't making any sense. He told me I would die there." Wrapping both arms around herself, a violent tremor went through her. "He left me there to die."

I'd never been the touchy-feely type, but I threw my arms around her shoulders and squeezed. "You're safe now."

"Noah will take you to the Fort Hannity Military Base," Cade said. "You'll be safe there."

Noah nodded and led her away without question.

As they faded from view, Cade took my hand and gestured to the woods. His lips tilted upward, a smile so bright it could have blotted out the sun itself. "See if we can go two for two?"

Chapter Twelve

We'd caught a lucky break with Penny Bloom. Not only had we found her, but as it turned out, she was the first they'd managed to save since leaving home. Like the other incarnations of me, Cade and Noah were always just a hair too late. Dylan always got there first. Cade was different. Lighter and more alive. He didn't stand as stiff or scowl as much. Saving Penny Bloom had seemingly breathed new life into him.

I wanted to take Penny's rescue as a sign that maybe this time would be different. That Dylan's crazy revenge cycle would be broken. Unfortunately, if our current progress on Miles was any indication, our lucky streak had been short-lived.

When we didn't find Miles at his home and came up empty-handed on any clue as to where he might be, we headed back to my place. Cade's mood fell with each passing moment. Noah still hadn't gotten back, and I was sure we'd get a call from the commander long before he did. I tried to console myself into thinking he'd be grateful we'd gone out and saved a life. Truthfully, though, he was bound to be pissed. I'd disobeyed the direct order to stay under lock and key.

I rummaged through the fridge, looking for something to munch on while Cade sat at the kitchen table and stewed. He hadn't said much since we'd gotten back, but I could tell he wanted to. He was happy to have found Penny, but there was an underlying frustration eating away at him. Maybe it was the small victory. They'd succeeded in doing something they never had before—saving Penny. The pressure to keep up the trend seemed to be wearing on him.

I settled on a pint of fudge brownie ice cream, grabbed two spoons, and plopped into the chair across from him. "Talk to me."

He scowled at the table. "About?"

I deposited one of the spoons in front of him, then slid the ice cream between us. "Anything. Tell me what it's been like. You bounce from world to world, but technically you don't really *go* anywhere. That has to be a head trip... Does it hurt? When you...skip?"

He eyed the box of ice cream for a moment before jabbing it violently with his spoon. Putting the spoon into his mouth, he shook his head slowly. "You get a little dizzy. Feel slightly displaced for a minute or two. No pain though. The whole process is very seamless."

Seamless?

Yeah. That was exactly the word I would use to describe inter-reality travel...

"Have you ever bumped into yourself?" I scooped up another spoon. "Like, another version of you?"

He frowned and scrunched up his nose just a bit. Like he'd just tasted something foul. "I have. Right out of the gate, in fact. It's the reason we look ourselves up first thing."

"And nothing bad happened?"

He cocked his head to the side. With his right brow lifted just slightly above the left, his face took on a sort of whimsical tone. "Bad?"

"Like, you know, paradox inducing?"

He snorted. "You could skip a million times, and in each place, sit down to dinner with yourself, and nothing bad would happen. The world continues to spin."

"Huh." I took another spoon of the ice cream. "That's disappointing."

His right brow lifted higher and I kind of hated the way, despite the situation we were in, it made me notice him more. Cade was turning out to be more than just a soldier. Normally that's all I saw these guys as. But Cade…Cade was more than that. "It's disappointing that we haven't torn a hole in the fabric of time and space?"

I smiled. "Kind of takes some of the mystery out of it, ya know?"

His lips twitched. "You're very strange…"

"Careful, soldier boy. On this Earth strange is actually a compliment."

He set his spoon down and leaned forward just a hair. "Isn't that a coincidence? Mine too."

Heat rushed to my cheeks. "Yeah? Well—" The phone started ringing. I leaned to my right and snagged the cordless from the counter without bothering to look at the caller ID. "Hello?"

"I assume my baby brother is right there with you?"

Dylan's smooth voice floated from the other end of the line. "Put me on speaker, will ya, princess?"

I glanced at Cade, who watched me with a curious glare, then pushed the speaker button and set the phone down on the tabletop between us.

"I'm going to go out on a limb," — Dylan let out an obnoxious hoot — "and assume you went looking for the Tribunal." He snickered. "My guess is that you didn't find them."

This meant he didn't know we'd rescued Penny Bloom. On the other hand, it also probably meant we weren't going to find the other two by simply tracking down their addresses.

Cade's fists balled tight, and he clenched his jaw. For a minute, I really believed he'd stand and flip the table. I'd never seen such anger in someone's eyes before. Such poison. "Where are they?"

"It wouldn't be much of a game if I told you, brother."

"This isn't a game." I couldn't help it. My plan was to keep quiet and let Cade handle it. He knew Dylan better than anyone, after all, but his particular brand of crazy was something I couldn't stomach. "Whatever it was that happened to you, or to *Ava*, has nothing to do with anyone here. It has nothing to do with me."

A few moments of silence ticked by. I actually thought he might have hung up until there was a sharp inhalation of breath. "You don't know shit about what happened," he said in a venomous voice. "And it has everything to do with you. It doesn't matter what world you come from, you're still Kori. And watching you die kills a little bit more of him each time it happens. I won't stop until he's as dead as I am on the inside. As dead as he made me."

I should have left it there. You don't poke a rabid dog. But, like always, my temper got the better of me. "As dead as he made you? From what I hear, he saved your ass. They were going to kill you, and he let you go. You repay him by going on a killing spree? If you ask me, that Ava chick dodged a bullet. You're two slices short of a sandwich."

He laughed. Well, no. It couldn't be considered a laugh. There was too much pain in the sound. Too much poison. It was a strangled cry halfway between a howl and a scream. The sound I'd expect a dying animal to make as it struggled to hold tight to this life. "Saved me? Is that what the fucker told you? You poor deluded bitch. I guess it doesn't matter what reality we're in, you always fall for his crap. You never see the fact that he's just like me. Dark and hypocritical."

I turned to Cade, who refused to look at me. "What—"

"Time is ticking, kiddies. Forget about the Tribunal and find Ava," Dylan snapped. There was a click, and the line went dead.

"What is he talking about?" Really, it was stupid. I shouldn't care for so many reasons, the first of which, two innocent people's lives were on the line. Picking apart the ravings of a madness-tainted loony shouldn't be the first thing on the agenda.

And, second, Cade was nothing to me. Why did I care what he might or might not have done? He was a part of someone else's life. She might look like me. Might sound, and on some level, act like me, but she wasn't me.

Still, for some reason it mattered.

A lot.

"It doesn't—"

"It does." I stood and stalked across the room, jerking the table. The pint of ice cream toppled sideways, oozing melted goop across the plastic tablecloth. "It matters. I want to know. What did he mean? What did you do?"

At first his gaze was heavy and volatile. There was a spark of madness in his eyes that reminded me of the twinge in Dylan's voice. They were brothers, after all. Why not? But it didn't last. "He's right. I didn't save him. I mean, I did, but I backpedaled. I stole the keys and let him out of his cell the night before they were scheduled to carry out his execution. The guilt was too much. I was the one who turned him in. I betrayed my own brother…" Cade shook his head, and some of the tension drained from his body. He slumped in the chair and let his head fall back. "I figured he'd learned his lesson. That he'd accept Ava was gone and move on with his life. Get out of town and start over. That he would forgive me for turning him in…"

"But he didn't." I pulled my chair closer and sat across from him.

He shook his head, lips pulling downward. "I should have known better. Ava was his life. She grounded him. Kept him in check. He told me he refused to let her go, but not before he made me suffer."

"By killing her," I said softly.

"I never imagined he would take it that far. They were friends. We all grew up together. If I'd thought for even a second that he'd hurt her, I would have killed him myself. Right then and there." He took a shallow breath. "The next day I got a text from her telling me to hurry over. That she had some exciting news to share."

My stomach heaved. I couldn't imagine what it must have been like for him.

"I found her bleeding out. He'd cuffed her to the pipes in the basement and slit her wrists."

"Jesus…" It was hard to picture. Myself, cuffed to a pipe and bleeding out in a cold basement. I shuddered.

"Noah called an ambulance, but they were too late. She was already too far gone when we got there."

"I'm sorry, Cade." The pain in his voice was like a razor to my heart. It wasn't me who loved him, this complicated stranger with a beautiful face, but in that moment, all I wanted was to wrap my arms around him. To take away some small fraction of his pain.

"He keeps killing you to get back at me. At your father. I keep trying to stop him, insisting to myself that the driving force behind my actions are to right a wrong I made by freeing him, but he's right. I'm a hypocrite."

Not what I'd been expecting. "How so?"

"Because I'm just like him, Kori. I followed him out of vengeance, sure, but it was also because I knew you were still out there. I wanted to see you again."

This was where things got tough. Admittedly, I felt an attraction to Cade. He was strong and brave. Easy on the eyes to say the least. But I didn't know him. Not really. And he didn't know me. The problem was, did he understand that?

"You know that you can't see me *again*, right? Until the other day, you'd never seen me before. It doesn't matter if our DNA is an exact match, or that we like and say the same things. I know this must be a huge mindfuck for you, and I can't imagine how hard it must be to look at me and not see the girl who loved you, but

I'm not her."

"I won't lie. When we first met, I looked at you and saw her. My Kori. But after spending some time with you, I realize the only things you have in common with her is physical appearance. The sound of your voice… your talent for art. Aside from that, you couldn't be more different." For some reason, that sent a twinge of pain through my heart—which was stupid. That's what I wanted, right? For him to realize that I *wasn't* the girl he loved.

"It had to have been hard for you, for Noah… But for your own sanity, you have to let her go. Trust me when I tell you, holding on will poison you."

He watched me for a moment before breaking into a sad smile. "Your mom?"

"My mom," I confirmed, my throat thick.

He nodded. "I'm sorry. If she was anything at all like our Cora, this world lost an amazing mind and a bright soul."

His words were meant to comfort, I was sure, but they had the opposite effect. In that moment it became clear. Why he and Dylan were doing this. Fate had stolen someone important from them. Moving on with their lives, knowing that person was still out there, at least in some form, must be agony. How could you continue on blindly with your life having that information? Knowing that with the right amount of planning, and some luck, there was a chance you could see her again. Be with her. I almost understood why Dylan broke the rules and went to search for Ava. Obviously, it didn't excuse his methods or the trail of carnage he'd left in his wake, but the sentiment was forgivable…relatable, even.

I would do it. If given a chance, I would find her…

And couldn't I? I subtly glanced down at the cuff on my wrist. Say our Infinity Division could muster up a quick prep method for the travel. Would it be so bad if Dylan didn't give us the key? Would it be that horrible? Having a chance to see Mom again?

"Dylan has killed these people before, right? This Tribunal?"

Cade nodded. "His MO hasn't changed until now. Normally he goes after them, then works on tracking down Ava. He either doesn't find her, or finds her and, for whatever reason, fails to take her with him. He usually takes his time. He's a twisted bastard. You saw what he did to Penny Bloom; he likes to make them suffer. He wants to punish them for what they did to him. He can skip whenever he wants…whenever he feels vindicated."

"So what's changed? He's having you guys track down Ava while he takes his revenge on the Tribunal. It's almost like he's rushing. Like he's…"

"On a timeline." Cade finished. He smacked his hand against his head and groaned. "I still say it makes no sense. Unless… What if there's something wrong with the main cuff? Something that limits the time he—therefore, by extension, we—spend in one place?"

I threw up my hands. "Don't ask me. Until a day ago, I thought the world was round."

His lip twitched with the barest hint of a grin. "Or the cuff could simply be failing. From what I gathered, they weren't meant to be used like this. Continuous with no maintenance. Plus, the set Dylan stole was the first working trial. Who knows how long something like that was meant to last?"

A few hours ago I'd been desperate to get this thing off my wrist. Now, the possibility that it was broken, that certain *scenarios* might be impossible, chilled me to the core. "Well, what would that mean exactly? What would it change?"

He shook his head. "I'm not sure."

I pushed the weird mix of elation and fear aside. Whatever might or might not be wrong with the cuff, and what it could mean for my future—my life, even— wasn't the most pressing issue at the moment. "We know he took the other two people—"

"Miles and Odette."

"Miles and Odette," I repeated. "If he's gotten to them already, how can we track them?"

His expression turned stormy. "I don't know that we can. We got lucky with Penny Bloom. What are the chances—"

"Think," I urged. "There has to be something. Anything."

He squeezed his eyes closed hard for a moment before shaking his head violently. "We don't know anything about this world's Tribunal."

"Fine. You don't know this world's version of your Tribunal—but you do know your brother." I grabbed his hand and tugged him off the chair. "You've been through this before. Think hard. Where would he bring them? How would he do it?"

For a minute I was sure he'd argue that I was wasting time, but instead, he tilted his head slightly to the left, then let it fall back. After a moment, he said, "I don't know much about our Odette Ferguson, but Miles Hann had several run-ins on the base with Dylan after Ava died. He was always getting into something. Always finding trouble. Hann never liked him." He dropped his gaze to mine. "I think I have an idea."

$\mathcal{W}$e left Noah a note and set out for downtown. Cannon Park Cemetery, to be exact. There was no traffic—which made sense. Six p.m. on a Sunday evening in late October didn't find many people out and about—allowing us to make it in near-record time.

"You still haven't told me why we came here," I said, unfastening my seat belt and pushing open the passenger's side door. There was a chill in the air that had nothing to do with the October breeze, and we were losing the light. On one hand, I wanted to find Miles Hann as much as Cade did. On the other, I was worried we'd find him—and it would be too late. "Is this a typical hangout for your Miles?"

Cade ignored me and scanned the area. When he found what he was apparently looking for, he darted forward without saying a word. I had no choice but to follow. Down the main path and around to the mausoleum section. When he came to the gaudy granite enclosures, he slowed, stopping to inspect each one. "We're looking for the Hann family plot." He moved to the next stone enclosure. "Dylan's standard threat to Miles was that he would bury him one day. As far as I know, he hasn't had the chance yet."

"What makes you think he'd bury him in his family's

mausoleum, though?"

Cade stopped for a second and frowned. "It's Dylan. The guy never misses an opportunity to go for the dramatic."

He started forward again and I followed, glancing around. Kids were known to come down here and party on the weekends because, what's more entertaining than living it up in a place of eternal rest, right? When we'd moved here, I tried once. Came down and tried to pretend I fit in. After about twenty minutes, though, it became obvious I didn't belong, having no interest in ingesting obscene amounts of cheap beer and jumping from headstone to headstone. My time was preferably spent vandalizing walls and buildings. You know...just your normal, everyday teen.

Pointing to the far end of the first row, he said, "Start on that end. I'll go this way. See if anything turns up."

"Gotcha." I kept my head high and started walking. There was no need to tell Cade that places like this now turned the blood in my veins to cold molasses. That simply driving past a cemetery nearly induced an unparalleled sense of panic.

We separated and began to search. I counted down from one hundred as I went, to keep myself focused. I walked along the path that led to the gardens, then circled back and paced the grass closer to the woods, scanning the names on each stone building. I did this three times, insanely hoping that I might have missed something. It seemed hopeless. There was nothing to see except the shadows of old ghosts and dying grass.

Cade caught up with me on my last pass. "It was a long shot. At least we tried." He tilted his head to the side, studying me. "You okay? You look like you're going to throw up."

I nodded. Or, maybe I shook my head. I couldn't be sure because my world was on the verge of spinning into oblivion. "I—yeah. I have a thing about cemeteries."

He frowned. "My Kori hated them, too." Hitching his thumb over his shoulder, he said, "Let's head back. See if Noah had any luck."

I nodded and let him lead me around to the main path. We were almost back to the front gate when I noticed something in the distance. It looked like another mausoleum, set apart from the others. As much as I hated spending another minute there, someone's life was on the line. We were here. It would be irresponsible not to check. "Did you look at that one?"

He looked from me to the small building, then took off at a dead run. I followed, my heart kicking into overdrive.

Cade skidded to a stop a few feet ahead of me, in front of the small chipped stone construct. The door was slightly ajar, and dried muddy footprints marred the otherwise immaculate entryway.

The name at the top said Hann.

Chapter Thirteen

*C*ade dove for the door and hurled himself through the entry. I was right on his heels, breath held and pulse pounding. On each of the three walls were two large marble doors. The two at the back had names carved into them, as did one to our right. The one on the left side, however, was different. Like the others, there was a name on the door—except this one was written in large, bold black magic marker.

Here lies Miles Hann. A bastard in every world...

"He buried him," I said. In fact, I think I must have said it several times. Over and over, like a prayer, as Cade worked to get the tomb door open. Even though Cade had told me about Dylan's threat, I could still hardly believe it. Who did something like this? The same person who would tie Penny Bloom to an uprooted tree hanging over a cliff, that's who. The same person who strapped a time bomb to my wrist just to get me to play his sick little game.

It took a few minutes, but he got the door open, and lying where the casket would have normally been, was a man.

"Oh my God!" I positioned myself next to Cade and we each grabbed one of Miles's arms. When we managed to get him onto the ground, he wasn't moving. The air grew artic. His skin was unnaturally pale and cold to the touch without as much as a flicker of movement. "Cade…"

"Watch out," he said, shouldering me aside, then dropping his head to Miles's chest. I saw his shoulders tense about a half second before he bolted upright, slamming both hands down and beginning to pump. "No." He huffed as he continued compressions. One. Two. Three. "Breathe."

I touched a finger to the back of Miles's hand. It was cold. Far too cold for there to be a chance at resuscitation. "Cade." I placed a hand on his shoulder and tried to gently pull him back.

It was pointless. Cade was determined—despite the already obvious outcome—to save Miles. He violently shook me off and cursed, slamming both fists down on the man's chest. Noah was the loud, opinionated one, but it was becoming more and more obvious that Cade had a tightly controlled, volatile streak. Like his brother, there was darkness there. Maybe a different kind of darkness, but still. It simply needed the right thing to coax it out.

"No!" Cade pinched his nose and blew into Miles's mouth. A second later, he pressed an ear to the man's chest. "No," he repeated. "Not another one."

He began compressions again, pumping Miles's

chest several times before leaning in to breathe into his mouth. But it was too late. It'd probably been too late for a while now.

"Cade," I whispered, moving to sit in front of him. His eyes glazed over, and he kept his attention on Miles, still compressing his chest as though any moment the man would open his eyes and take that lifesaving breath of air.

But it wasn't going to happen.

"Come on, Miles." He ignored me and kept going, pounding on the man's chest. Or, maybe he just didn't hear my voice. It was obvious that he was lost in his own world. The pain etched on his face, the fear—the fury— made my chest hurt. I may have only met Cade Granger, but his dedication to saving these people, to putting an end to his brother's madness, was palatable. He knew he'd lost Miles. I could see it in his eyes. Yet still he tried. Seemingly possessed by the uncontrollable need to change something that couldn't be changed. To fix something he needed desperately to control but could not.

"It's too late," I tried again. "He's gone. This isn't—"

"No!" he roared, and began pumping harder. Beneath the sound of his breath, I heard something crack.

"Cade!" His head whipped around, his gaze pinning me with a borderline feral look. I stood my ground— well, kneeled it, actually—and met his stare with one of my own. "You can't save him. He's already gone. Snap out of it, soldier! Focus on Odette."

For a minute I wasn't sure he'd listen. There was so much fight in his eyes, and he was wound tighter than a guitar string. Even though this was pointless, I respected him for it. For having the courage, the drive, to fight against what seemed to be inevitable. Cade was a rare breed of people. I knew because I'd met so many. Having moved around the world, I'd been subjected to every kind of person out there. He wasn't perfect by any stretch of the definition, but he was real, and he was *good*.

After a moment, he let out a breath and slumped back against the marble wall. Dropping his head into his hands, he sighed. "His blood is on my hands."

"This is on Dylan," I said, rising onto my knees. I leaned forward and grabbed the sides of his face, forcing him to look at me. "Not you. You didn't bring him here. You didn't have a hand in ending his life."

"Didn't I?" He lifted his gaze to mine, and I swallowed back the growing lump in my throat. His eyes swirled with a storm of rage and pain. "Everything Dylan does, every life he ends and every spirit he breaks, is possible only because I set him free." He let his gaze fall back to Miles.

I, on the other hand, did my best not to look. Like Cade, I felt guilty, but it was more than that. If I looked at Miles, lying there as pale as paper and totally still, ice cold and stiff, I might lose it. I would have to admit that we'd failed. That an innocent man paid the price with his life. That there was a good chance we'd fail again... That *I* would pay the ultimate price.

First Miles, then me...

It was the first harsh dose of reality, bringing my own mortality into question. Cade stood, taking a single step away from Miles's body. Without looking at me, he said, "We need to move."

Numb, I nodded and climbed to my feet. I was about to ask where he thought we should start when my cell started ringing. "Hello?"

"Got a lead on Ava's family," Noah said on the other end. "Also inadvertently found Odette."

"That's great!" I covered the speaker and turned to Cade. "Noah found Odette."

He let out a breath. "Thank God."

"—me finish for fucks sake."

I rolled my eyes. "Finish."

"Don't get too excited about Odette. She's already dead." He paused for a moment and something crackled, followed by a chewing sound. "Locals got a call a few hours ago about a body floating down the Manard River. They just identified her. It's all over the news."

I didn't say anything, but as it turned out, I hadn't needed to. The look on my face gave it away. "It's too late, isn't it?" Cade growled. He tightened his fists and kicked at the mausoleum wall with jarring force. The sound of it, a muted thud that echoed through the small space, sent my stomach roiling.

Handing him the cell, I stepped through the doorway to wait outside in order to give him some privacy. I didn't know why I did it. Maybe it was the look in his eyes. That faint but unmistakable tint of defeat mixed with that tiny spark of madness always present in his brother's eyes. I didn't know Cade well enough to intrude on something like that.

After a few moments, Cade stepped from the mausoleum entryway with his shoulders squared and his head held high. A true soldier. In that moment, despite not being *his* Kori, I was proud of him. If I'd been in his place, losing a war of my own waging, time after time with what seemed to be no end in sight, would I have had the strength to keep going? Would I be able to face the enemy?

"Noah said Fort Hannity knows about the discovery of Odette Ferguson's body. Seeing as we'd given the commander her name, as well as Miles, and having sent Penny Bloom to the base for safekeeping, it's a sure bet he knows what we're doing."

"And where we're not." The commander's instructions had been clear. We were to remain at the house under all circumstances.

"This just got ten times more complicated." He folded his arms and leaned against the smooth marble pillar beside the doorway. "For starters, the commander will get involved. There's a chance Dylan will think we went to them for help. He—"

Still in Cade's hand, my cell started ringing again. When he glanced down at it, he frowned. Handing it to me, he said, "This won't be good…"

The caller ID said Brysen Simmons. "Oh, shit…" I took a deep breath, then lifted the cell to my ear. "Hello?"

I had to pull the phone away from my ear because the first few moments of the call were a jumble of incoherent screams and grumbles. Every time I opened my mouth to provide an explanation—albeit a poor one—the commander would begin again. All I could do was stand there and let him finish.

By the time I hung up, even Cade, still standing a few feet away, was cringing. "That sounded rough."

"He's not happy," I confirmed. "Says I disobeyed a

direct order from a superior. That you and Noah are bad news and I'm to return home immediately."

"He's right, Kori." He pushed off the building and took a step toward me. "We don't mean you or anyone else here any harm, but the shitstorm we brought with us *is* trouble. You should listen to your superior and head home."

It was my turn to fold my arms. I screwed myself up and stood tall, fixing my most challenging glare on him. "Technically he's not *my* superior."

"No." Cade shook his head slowly. There was a spark of defiance in his eyes. "I suppose he's not."

"I make my own choices," I continued. "Anyone who knows me is well aware that I'm perfectly capable of getting myself into trouble without outside help."

Again, he shook his head. "I don't doubt that."

"You're right, though." I sensed that for once he wasn't going to protest my involvement. I wasn't sure if he was finally learning to respect me or if he'd just given up on keeping me safe, and I didn't really care. What mattered was that I was a part of the team, and there was nothing Cade was going to do to stop that. "With the commander, and the entire base involved, this just got infinitely more difficult." I sighed. "Your Tribunal is accounted for. It looks like there's just one thing left to do."

"Find Ava," he said with a sigh.

"Right."

"This is your call, Kori. You can head back home or come with me. Like you said earlier, this is your life on the line. You have every right to fight for it yourself."

He held out his hand, and without hesitating, I took

it. Goose bumps jumped to attention all over my skin. I believed in that *meant to be* crap as much as I believed in Santa Claus or the Easter Bunny. Still, I couldn't shake the feeling of warmth, of an odd sense of comfort, as our hands rested against each other.

"They're going to be looking for you. Maybe they think it's for your own good, but this won't just blow over. You have to understand the weight of your choice if you come with us. You have to understand that every decision has a price. One that might last well after this whole thing is over."

That's assuming we all survive that long...

I shrugged. "I've never been one to back away from a fight."

His lips slipped into a grin. "I don't doubt that, either."

Chapter Fourteen

I hadn't known him, but nonetheless, I felt guilty leaving Miles all alone. Stupid, since he was beyond my help. Except for Penny Bloom, Cade and Noah's Tribunal were dead, but there was still a chance to save myself—and that couldn't be ignored.

I'd let the commander know where to find Miles, then inferred that I would head back home without actually saying it out loud. Technically that made me less of a liar—at least in my opinion. Somehow I doubted the general would see it that way, but as long as I was alive to take my punishment, I could deal with it. The thought of losing my freedom didn't seem like such a travesty anymore now that my life was on the line. We'd called Noah, and Cade arranged for us to meet him at someplace called the Doon.

There was a hulking rock formation on the left side of the car, the top of which jutted out above our heads like an awning. That, coupled with the trees and absence of light, made the scene look eerie. Like something out of a dark fairy tale.

Yep. The last thing the girl sees before some monster swallows her whole...

Still, creepy or not, it was beautiful in its own way, and I found myself itching to get my hands on pencils. Several shades of green and brown, accented by dark gray. On paper, I could make it something it wasn't. Inviting and pure. On paper, I could turn it into something magical. That was the beauty of art. The thing my dad never understood. He fought against the world, making it safer for the people by using force. Tactical strikes and well-thought-out defense plans. I used something different. Something that, while not as direct as his methods, was still sorely needed. Art was my way of giving people hope. Supplying them with the knowledge that beauty still existed. That it was worth fighting for.

"So, why here?" The silence in the car wasn't uncomfortable, really, but I think that's why it bothered me. I'd always been somewhat of a lone wolf, and when we began bouncing from base to base almost once a year, I resigned myself to the life of a loner. It was something that didn't bother me anymore. Except now, sitting here with Cade, I almost felt like I'd been missing out. Maybe it was because I didn't have Mom anymore. My best friend and partner in crime. Or maybe it was something else...

"We come here because buildings aren't static," Cade said, pushing open the driver's side door and sliding out. I followed his lead. "They change from world to world. But the landscape generally doesn't."

I followed, closing the door and moving around the front of the car to stand beside him. "What about the people? What are you like? In other places, I mean."

"Pretty much the same. I mean, I'm not always enlisted, but my general personality seems to be consistent." He rapped his knuckles against the roof of the car lightly and looked away. "There are always some differences, but most people have certain constants."

"Constants?"

"Things that stay the same. Personality traits, hobbies, mannerisms…" He hesitated. "Relationships."

"Relationships," I repeated, wary. I wasn't the Kori he knew, but that didn't change the fact that every so often I'd catch him staring, almost longingly. If I had to guess, he didn't even realize he was doing it. And, although I almost didn't want an answer, I was morbidly curious. "Like yours and mine?"

"Yes…and no." He sighed. "The same circles of people tend to exist on each world, give or take a few. Certain people just seem to gravitate toward each other. The relationships differ sometimes, but they're usually there in some capacity."

"I think I would have remembered meeting you." I mentally kicked myself for the way I said it. Kind of like a chick version of *How you doin'?* "You know, because you're so damn irritating."

Oh, yeah, Anderson. Nice save…

"Like I said, the first thing Noah and I do when we arrive after a skip is look ourselves up. As far as I can tell, this time Cade and Dylan Granger were never born. It seems like my parents never got together."

"And Noah?"

He frowned, and almost hesitantly said, "Records show Noah Anderson died at birth."

I opened my mouth, then closed it. I tried to swallow, but there was a lump lodged in my throat. "Died at—he wasn't born. I think my parents would have told me if I'd had a brother."

Cade looked uncomfortable. He turned, focusing on the tree line with too much intensity.

"No," I said, shaking my head. "It just can't be true. Why wouldn't they tell me?"

When he met my gaze again, he was sad. "Because really, what would it have changed?"

"What would it have—are you nuts? That's something I deserved to know!"

"So, your parents should have told their small child that her brother died a year before she was born?"

"Maybe not when I was younger, but as I got older? Hell yes." My head filled with images of the life I could have had. A brother…a partner in crime…a real friend. I pushed the thought from my mind, halfheartedly reminding myself that I wouldn't have wanted a brother like Noah. Loud, stubborn, annoying. Insanely loyal…

He shrugged again. "Maybe they just ran out of time."

Ran out of time…

And there it was again. Time. Mankind's mortal enemy. Always working against us, skulking in the shadows, waiting to steal away minutes by the handful until only a precious few remained.

I didn't know how to respond, but thankfully, I didn't have to. Noah picked that moment to come jogging into view. "You both okay?" he huffed, stopping by a large rock to catch his breath.

"Yeah." Cade nodded. "What did you find out about Ava? Is she—?"

Cade was cut off by the sound of rolling tires and scattering debris. He took a step back, positioning himself in front of me as two large SUVs skidded to a stop in the dirt a few yards from where we stood. "Shit." Whirling on Noah, his lips twisted into an angry snarl. "Seriously? You let them follow you?"

Noah gave it right back. He jabbed a finger violently in my direction. "They wouldn't even be looking for us if you weren't so obsessed with my sister's fake."

Simmons extracted himself from the black SUV and stalked forward, never taking his eyes off me. The way his shadow loomed in the glow of the truck's headlights was just about as ominous as his expression. I swallowed, holding my ground, and stepped out from behind Cade.

"Sir, if you'll just—" Cade started.

"Do not finish that sentence, son." Pointing to me, he said, "Get in the back of the truck. Now. Before I restrain all of you."

I knew better than to talk back to an officer, but I couldn't help it. He was wrong and, by dragging us back to the base, would probably be condemning me to death. "If you would—"

"Now!"

I bit down hard on the inside of my lip and started for the car. The look of unadulterated fury in his eyes left no room for argument. Cade was right. This would hang over my head for a long time. The level of shit I'd gotten myself into was going to bury me. That was, if Dylan didn't manage it first. But staying wouldn't work, either. The general had backup. If I resisted, there was a chance he'd hurt Cade and Noah, thinking he was doing what was best for me.

I didn't look back at the boys as I pulled open the back door and lifted my right foot to slip inside. I didn't really think anything of it when I heard footsteps slapping against the ground, or Cade's voice telling the commander that this was a huge mistake. No, what got my attention was the rage-filled howl that Simmons let out, followed by the SUV shuddering violently back and forth.

As I turned, the driver cursed and struggled with his seat belt, but Noah was faster. He rammed his elbow up, catching the man right beneath the chin, following through with a brutal right hook. The driver's head snapped back, then fell forward, missing the horn by inches.

I stumbled from the back seat in time to see Cade overpower Simmons, snatching his gun and turning it on him as the driver of the second SUV got out of the truck.

Dad had known the commander nearly my entire life. He and his family had joined us for everything from holiday dinners to mini vacations. He was an army man through and through, and I knew the only way Cade got the better of him is because the old-timer had underestimated him.

Simmons backed up a step, moving protectively in front of me. The gesture almost made me feel bad about what I'd put him through the past few days. Almost. "Easy, son."

"This is not a sign of disrespect, sir. But you're not equipped to deal with Dylan. You won't be able to stop him." Cade nodded in my direction. "You won't be able to save *her*."

"I don't know how things work where you're from, but threatening a superior is a serious offense." Simmons kept his voice even, but the underlying fury behind the words was crystal clear.

"That's not what this is," Cade responded. He leaned to the left and, meeting my gaze, nodded slightly. "Again, your call, Kori. Stay or go."

What was I supposed to do here? Simmons was doing only what he believed to be in my best interest. But, a not-so-small voice in the back of my mind told me this *wasn't* in my best interest. He might think it was, but so far, from what I'd seen, Cade was right. They couldn't deal with Dylan. Not because they weren't equipped, but because they didn't know him. Cade and Noah had an inside line to his specific brand of insanity. They didn't understand his motivations. If there was any hope of getting this thing off my arm, then there was really only one choice to make.

I sucked in a breath and stepped out from behind the commander. "I'm sorry, sir."

Taking that first step was hard, but I did it. I put one foot in front of the other, and started forward. Didn't get very far, though. The commander cursed and grabbed my arm. "Where's your head at, kid? Do you really think your father would approve of you disobeying a direct order?"

I whirled on him. The buildup of anger and fear I'd been keeping stashed away since this whole thing began, exploded. "First off, I'm not one of your soldiers. You can't give me orders." His eyes narrowed and he opened his mouth, but I kept going. "But I think my dad would approve of me doing the right thing. And right now, the right thing is to make sure I don't end up dead."

"This is not the way to do that, Kori."

"It is," I insisted, taking another step away.

Simmons eyed me, then settled his gaze on Cade. He let go of me and held up his hands, seemingly relaxing a bit. "Then we'll work together."

Relaxed or not, I could see it in his eyes. It was all an act. He was lying. Saying whatever he thought I wanted to hear to get me to come back to the base with him. I didn't know what to say, so I didn't say anything. I simply shook my head and crossed the small clearing to Cade's side.

Noah came up behind us. When I glanced over my shoulder, I saw that, for the first time, he was looking at me with something other than disgust. There was sadness in his eyes, but also pride. "If your general is anything like ours, he'd be proud of his daughter for fighting for her life."

"He wouldn't want her in harm's way," the commander said, tight-lipped. Realizing that we weren't going to play along, he'd lost his neutral expression and had settled on furious. "He'd want her safe. He'd want her with his people."

"We *are* his people, sir." Cade pushed Noah aside and took a step toward Simmons. He aimed the gun at the commander's car and, after a moment of hesitation, fired off two rounds. One shot to each front tire.

I jumped, and Noah snickered. Cade lowered the gun then, after hesitating, removed the clip and set the weapon on the ground between them. "If we don't deal with Dylan, she isn't safe." He took a step back. "None of them are safe."

Simmons was furious. His shoulders rigid and jaw clenched tight, there was fire in his eyes. "And what's to say I don't stop you?"

Cade sighed, then dug in his pocket. He held up something shiny and thin. "Because of this."

Simmons cocked his head but said nothing.

"See, where we come from, technology is far more advanced than it is here. We're at least three decades ahead of you in some aspects." He wiggled the thing in his hand. "This will stun you for at least an hour. If you try to stop us from leaving, I'll have no choice other than to use it."

Simmons was normally the master of cool. Really, the guy was like ice. You never saw him sweat, never saw him lose his temper. Cade, though, was cracking him. The commander narrowed his eyes, clenched his jaw, and after a moment of hesitation, stepped aside.

"I'm sure you know that once you leave this clearing I'm going to call in reinforcements. They will hunt you down, and the punishment will be harsh." He leveled his gaze at me. "That goes for you, too, Kori."

"I'm not a soldier, sir. What I'm doing, simply disobeying my dad's orders and going off with two boys I barely know, is nothing more than simple teenage rebellion. That's hardly an act of treason."

He couldn't argue with that, so he focused on Cade again. Knowing the commander, he thought he could scare him into handing me over. Bully the boys into doing what he wanted. "The consequences of these actions are going to come back on you, Granger. There's no scenario where this ends well. For anyone involved."

Cade's shoulders shook with a laugh. He turned and held out his hand to me as Noah made his way around us and started for the path.

For some reason, this felt like a turning point. One of those moments you remember for the rest of your life—no matter how long that actually ends up being. The threshold of something...be it good or bad.

He tugged me into motion. "There won't be any consequences," he said over his shoulder. "We won't be here long enough."

Chapter Fifteen

"So I have to ask." I leaned back in my seat and scanned the room. We sat huddled in the back corner of a small dive called Metro's. The music in the club was loud and it smelled like cheap perfume, but it was safe—I hoped. We'd crossed over the town line, and this was probably the last place Simmons would think to look for us. "What was that thing back there? The weapon you threatened Simmons with?"

Cade's expression lightened a bit, and the corners of his lips tugged up—just a hair. He reached into his pocket and pulled out a small silver disk. "A watch battery that's been in my pocket for the last year and a half…"

I blinked several times, then picked up the small thing. It was true. The deadly weapon was nothing more than a watch battery. I let out an unattractive snort. "The Commander of Fort Hannity had been taken down by a *watch battery*. This really should have been documented on YouTube…"

"So…" Noah cleared his throat and slouched back in his seat. "I couldn't dig up much on the Harris family, but I did get an old address for Ava's father. Doesn't seem like they live there anymore, but it's a place to start."

It was eleven p.m. on a Sunday night, so the place wasn't as crowded as it could have been. Finding a table hadn't been hard, and getting in had been a breeze. An extra twenty to the freakishly tall bouncer at the door and we waltzed through without having to show ID. The boys had even ordered beers without being carded

Noah pushed his beer away from the edge of the table and tapped the tabletop hard. "With the Tribunal dead, Dylan might head to Ava himself. With a little digging, he could find the information just as easily as I did."

"And there goes our bargaining chip," Cade added with a scowl.

"Then we just need to get there first." I downed the rest of my coke and fixed them with my best hard-ass stare. "Because I have no intention of dying."

"The old address I have for Harris is about five hours from here, in Westchester," Noah said with a yawn. "My vote is that we hole up for the night, catch some z's, then get a fresh start in the morning."

"It's been a long day," Cade agreed. "I'm just gonna hit the bathroom and we'll go."

He slid from the booth and disappeared around the other side of the bar. Noah watched him go, then went out of his way to position himself so that he wasn't facing me. I got that he was probably hurting, but enough was enough. "Why the hell do you hate me so much?"

At the sound of my voice, his shoulders stiffened. For a minute I was sure he'd simply ignore me. But after a few moments, he turned slowly and pinned me with a stare that sent a shiver down my spine. "I don't hate you. I don't think anything of you at all, honestly. You're no one to me. A ghost. A shadow of someone else."

It wasn't so much his words, but the way he said them—with loathing and barely contained poison—that made my heart thump faster and caused a lump to form in the back of my throat. It shouldn't have bothered me at all, yet it did. "Then why are you helping me?" I managed.

"I'm not helping you. I don't care about you." He inclined his head toward the floor as Cade rounded the bar. "I care about him."

"I saw a motel down the road. We can probably scrape together enough cash for a room—" He looked from me to Noah, then tilted his head. "What? What'd I miss?"

Noah stood so fast that the chair wobbled over backward. The sound barely registered over the music. "Go ahead."

Cade narrowed his eyes. "You're not coming?"

"I'll catch up." There was a distinct chill in his voice, one I knew was meant for me. "I'm hungry. Going to grab something to eat." And without another word, he turned on his heel and stalked to the door.

"He's hungry. What a shocker."

As I followed Cade from the club, a nagging feeling nibbled at my gut. Stopping to crash for the night was the right call. We'd be useless if we were too tired to think straight. But I couldn't help feeling like it was a mistake. Like something bad would happen. I looked at the clock. We didn't have much time left.

I don't have much time left...

*W*hile Noah scurried off to sate his seemingly endless appetite, Cade and I took the bus down the road to the small dive motel. They were surprisingly full, the only room left being one of the larger suites with a balcony. Of course, we were short on cash. But Cade, being a charmer when he wanted to be, was able to flirt the night clerk into giving the room to us at the standard rate.

Cade texted Noah our room number, then settled on the bed closest to the door. "How you holding up?"

I flopped down on the bed across from him and began untying my sneakers. "Well, I can't say it's been boring..."

He snickered and tipped an imaginary hat. "I aim to please, ma'am."

Silence stretched out between us then, and even though it was annoyingly comfortable, I felt compelled to fill it. Maybe because time was running out. If by some miracle we succeeded and found Ava, if Dylan kept his word and unlocked the cuff, I'd be safe and staying here, and the boys would be moving on. And on the other side of that same coin, if we failed, they'd still be moving on and I'd be bidding farewell to the land of the living. Either way, our time together was coming to an end, and there were things I couldn't help wondering.

"You mentioned something about constants. About the same general circles of people."

He leaned back and kicked his feet onto the bed. "Yeah?"

"Is it—when you—" Crap. Why the hell was this so hard? "In the worlds where we both existed, were we..."

"Together?" he finished for me.

See? How hard was that?

"Yeah."

He didn't frown exactly, but neither did he smile. The sadness in his eyes hit me like a punch to the gut. "I'm not sure what you wanna hear, Kori."

"The truth."

"The truth is, yes. In all the places we've both been, we're together. Always. Without fail." He slid off the edge of the bed and stood.

I opened my mouth, then closed it. I couldn't say it's not what I expected him to tell me, but his words, spoken out loud, were like a two-ton weight wrapped around my neck. "Is that—do you see that often?"

He was still standing. "It's not like my sphere of knowledge goes out that far. We skip from place to place—technically the same place—and deal with the same people." I noticed the fingers on his right hand had begun to fidget. "I mean, sure, it's not like we're the only ones. Your parents are always together. And there's this girl, Ash, who's popped up in other realities, always tied to Noah."

"But not where you're from?"

His expression was sad. He glanced at the door,

almost like he was worried Noah might walk through, then sighed. "Not where we're from. If we ever get home, I know the first thing he'll do is look her up. She's kind of his white rabbit, you know? Each time he sees her it gets a little harder for him."

"Did he—is she here?"

Cade shrugged. "I don't think so. He doesn't say it outright, but I know that's why he's always going off on his own. He's looking."

"But why be so secretive?"

"Because he's Noah?" Cade let go of a short laugh. "I mean, he knows I know, but it's not something he has to verbally acknowledge, so that makes it okay. In case you haven't noticed the guy's a little rough."

"So it's what, like fate? You and me? Mom and Dad? Noah and Ash…?"

His gaze locked on mine and I found that my heart rate had inadvertently jacked into overdrive. He shrugged. That was all. Yet the action had me swallowing back a lump and consciously telling myself not to stand up and back away. "When this all started, I would have laughed at the idea of that. Now? Who knows? I've come to realize there's a lot about this—about the universe—that I just don't understand."

My body lost the war with logic, and I stood to meet him, taking a single step forward until we were nearly nose to nose. "I think I might understand how Noah feels."

"Oh?" His voice came out thick, and he, too, visibly swallowed.

"I'm betting he feels cheated. Kind of like I do." A powerful wave of sadness washed over me, but that wasn't all there was. It brought with it something else. Something empowering in a way I'd never felt before. "You come into my life from out of nowhere and stir things up. If that wasn't bad enough, I find out that you're apparently like this perfect match for me. That somewhere out there, multiple versions of me are happy...with multiple versions of you." I sucked in a breath and dared myself to move just a fraction of an inch closer to him. "Yet here, in my reality, the universe cheated me out of the chance to know you."

"It doesn't seem fair," he said, voice husky.

"It doesn't," I agreed. "And now you're standing here—" I let out a short laugh. "Basically against all odds and what most people would say, common sense. You're literally an impossible situation made possible. A miracle."

His expression didn't change. His gaze didn't flutter. There was hardly any air in the room, and all the warmth in the world seemed to be pooling in the pit of my stomach. It was like ten thousand pounds of pressure was building up inside me, and if I didn't do something to alleviate it I would explode and take the entire world with me.

"I know I'm not yours. You had your me—and I'm so sorry that you lost her." My voice wavered just a little. "But..."

The small bit of distance that existed between us was banished as Cade grabbed my arms and pulled me forward. A second later, his mouth covered mine. His arms wrapped tight, holding on as though I was the only real thing in the world. Like I was the last safe place amidst a raging storm. I'd never felt anything so intense. Purely cosmic and right with the world, while at the same time, wrong.

Very, very wrong.

This boy didn't belong to me. I had no right to feel the things I did. I shouldn't be taking comfort in the way it felt to be locked in his embrace or taste his electrically charged kisses. It was like I was betraying myself, that other Kori. She didn't deserve to have the man she'd loved stolen by her doppelganger. Yet despite what that little voice was whispering in my ear, I didn't pull away. I couldn't. I'd never believed in destined pairs. The idea that everyone on Earth had that one true love—that soul mate—walking around just waiting to be found, made my head spin. But standing there with Cade, this boy who existed, yet had never been born, made me question my previous way of thinking. It made me wonder...

With a gentle nudge, I was on the bed, on my back with Cade hovering just above me. A lock of hair fluttered across his forehead, dipping in front of his left eye and making the scar more visible. Our eyes met and his lip twitched, tugging up at the side with a wicked grin. He bent his head, and a second later, began planting a series of tiny, yet scorching, kisses along my neck.

This was something on an entirely new level for me. It was equal parts exciting and terrifying. Add to that the black cloud of danger and the possibility of my imminent demise swinging overhead like a freshly sharpened pendulum, and my future was looking much shorter than anticipated. The truth of it all gave me courage. Made me bolder.

This might be the only chance you get...

I slid my hands down Cade's torso and gripped the edges of his shirt. After a single moment of hesitation, I was pulling it over his head. The motion was awkward and graceless. The material caught at his arms, then snagged at his right ear. He had to help in order to free himself. But he didn't seem to care. If anything, it made him more enthusiastic.

He brought his lips back to mine and, with even more vigor than before, kissed me. It was like all the air in my body leached out with that kiss. From the tips of my toes to every single strand of hair on my head, I felt it. My insides quivered, and my skin hummed. Raw passion and unequaled desire. A need so intense that it nearly overshadowed the entire world. In that moment, I wanted it to. I wanted it to drown me.

And I *almost* let it.

There were so many reasons to keep going and just one to stop. Unfortunately, for me, it was a doozy. I braced both hands against his chest and pushed gently. He froze instantly.

"Cade," I whispered, my breath coming in short, uneven pulls. His eyes blazed with hunger and I had to focus hard on what I wanted to say to keep from pulling him back down. "I—"

With one fluid move, he was up and sitting beside me. "If I apologized it would be a lie, and I'm not a liar, Kori. That's one thing I've never been. We're here and alone, and I wanted to kiss you. So I did."

I heard the words, but his voice betrayed him. He might not be sorry in the traditional sense, but he *was* feeling guilty. I sat up and tucked my feet beneath me. "There's nothing to apologize for. In case you didn't know this, it takes two people to do what we were doing." I sucked in a breath. I could do this. Tell him the truth.

"And it's not like I didn't *want* you to kiss me."

His eyebrows lifted. "Then—"

I held up my hand. "Please. Lemme get this out."

He nodded.

"Under different circumstances, I can see this." I gestured between us. "I think we'd have a shot at being something amazing. But *I* didn't get a Cade." I reached out and pressed my index finger to his chest lightly. "I didn't get *this* Cade. A different Kori did—and she has your heart. She always will. I'm nothing but filler—and that's not something I want to be."

"Kori—"

"I wanted to know what it would have felt like. To have a *you*...just for a few minutes. And I shouldn't, because I don't have a *you*. I think I just need to take a step back because, if I make it out of this alive, things will go back to normal. It'll be ten times worse if I fool myself into believing this thing between us is more than it is."

"More than me trying to hold on to the girl I lost, you mean?"

I swallowed back the lump creeping up my throat. Did he have to put it so bluntly? "Yeah."

His eyes darkened. Not anger, but a sadness so profound, it seemed to drain the life right from his body. "I'm sorry that I—"

I slid off the bed and took a step away. "Please, don't. I meant it when I said you had nothing to apologize for." I forced a smile and wondered if he could tell it was 100 percent fake. "It was a fun way to pass some time. I should go get cleaned up. Get some sleep, ya know?"

"Yeah." He stood as well. "I think that's probably a good call."

Chapter Sixteen

I took one of the bedrooms while Cade took the other. Sometime after I'd gone to sleep, Noah must have wandered in, because when I woke up a few hours later and ventured into the sitting room, I saw him perched on the balcony.

I watched him for a minute, wondering what my Noah would have been like had he survived—not that I'd wrapped my head around him existing in the first place. Would I have followed him around as a child, idolizing and irritating him at the same time? Would we have bickered until Mom couldn't stand it anymore? Noah hated me, but I realized in that moment that I didn't feel the same. I found myself wanting to ask questions. To connect with him in some small way. And despite every cell in my body screaming at me to turn around, I made my way out to the balcony.

"Hey." I stepped out the door and tugged the sleeves of my hoodie down over my fingers. It wasn't freezing, but the breeze in the air was chilly enough to make me shiver. "Can't sleep?"

I expected a snide remark, or possibly a simple-but-to-the-point *go the hell away*, but instead all I received was silence.

"You can crash in the other room," I tried again. I felt like an idiot for being so nice after the way he'd talked to me at the diner, but for the first time in my life, I found myself wanting to gain someone's approval. I didn't *want* Noah to hate me. Obviously we weren't going to be BFFs, but hell. I would have taken a simple, civil conversation. "You know, if the couch was keeping you up. I won't be able to fall back asleep."

Still nothing.

And that was my limit. There was obviously no gray area with Noah. He would never see me as anything other than an imposter. "Whatever," I whispered under my breath.

I jerked open the door and lifted my foot to step inside when he spoke. "Something happened."

"Something…?"

He turned and pinned me with a glare. "With you and Cade. Something happened between you. I tend to wander off. He hates it. Will sit up and wait until I walk back through the door no matter how long it takes."

"So?"

"So, he wasn't waiting tonight. Only one explanation for that."

"Maybe he was tired?" I let the door close and took a step away, thankful for the darkness, because there was no way my face wasn't cherry red.

Noah stood and came forward. "You slept with him,

didn't you?"

A million fury-fueled responses sprang to the tip of my tongue, but I just couldn't push them past my lips. I was too shocked to be insulted. "No."

Eyes narrow, he folded his arms and leaned back against the railing. His expression was neutral, but the spark in his eyes screamed disbelief. I'd never wanted to punch anyone more than I did in that moment.

But the desire came and went, and I found myself feeling uncharacteristically vulnerable. "He kissed me." I had no idea why I said it. I didn't owe Noah an explanation, nor did I have any desire to give it. Yet I found myself preparing to vomit one regardless. "He *really* kissed me."

He was quiet for a moment before snorting. "I'll bet." The venom in his voice held the smallest hint of pain.

The shock dissipated, replaced by white-hot fury. While I was sympathetic that the guy had lost his sister, I wasn't going to stand around and let him insinuate something seedy had happened. "What the hell does that mean?"

He grinned. "Whoa there. Ease up. I'm not implying anything scandalous." The smile faded just a little. "I've seen you two together. Multiple versions. I get the attraction. The *I'll bet* was all on Cade."

Not what I'd expected. "Why?"

He pulled the chair around and gestured for me to sit. I did, and he slid to the floor. "If you hadn't noticed, he's an *all-in* kind of guy. Cade wanted my sister's heart, body, mind, and soul. The entire package. Kori wasn't as hardcore as him." He snorted. "In fact, she was kinda cold. She was my sister and all, but man, the way she shut him down sometimes... You wanna talk about repression? My boy could be a case study."

"So they never—"

He laughed. "Are you kidding? She'd barely kiss him."

A chill that had nothing to do with the cool breeze washed over me. I knew Cade's interest in me had more to do with what I looked like than who I really was, but hearing Noah say it like that, basically implying I'd been used to get something he hadn't been able to get from his Kori was like a bullet to the brain.

"I loved my sister. We were real tight. But she wasn't like me. Wasn't like Cade." He picked at the edge of his jacket. "Honestly, I never understood what they saw in each other. Don't get me wrong. I love the guy like a brother—I'd take a bullet for him ten times over—but he was never what I would have called Kori's type, ya know?"

"Why not?"

"Kori always fit inside the box. Good grades. Good attitude. Never got in trouble, always followed the rules. Cade and I were the troublemakers—well, me more so than him—but, you get me? I guess you could say she was kind of like our voice of reason, ya know? That little whisper of conscience that sits on your shoulder and steers you in the right direction when you make a mistake?"

"It doesn't sound like a very healthy relationship." I suddenly understood Cade's comment about how they complemented each other, but to me it seemed more likely that they held each other back. Mom and Dad had disagreed, sure, but when it came down to it they egged each other on. They were constantly pushing each other toward the next adventure, the next challenge. They made each other more vibrant, not less.

"It wasn't. But Cade didn't see it. He had it all planned out." Noah made a sound halfway between a laugh and a snort. "The guy plans everything. Drives me nuts. They were gonna get married, have the whole two-point-five-kids and picket fence... But he never stopped to ask her what she wanted. What she had planned." He glanced my way, then turned in the opposite direction. "It was never going to happen."

I thought about the light in Cade's eyes when he spoke about her, the unmistakable devotion. Could he really have been that blind? "What was never going to happen?"

He didn't answer right away. His expression contorted. An odd mix of amusement and regret. "Them. Not in the way he wanted. They weren't right for each other. I knew it. Kori knew it..."

Again, I was speechless.

It didn't matter, though. He kept going as though he'd forgotten I was even there. "She loved him, just not the same way he loved her. I never told him. Never will, either. I wanted to. Would have if things hadn't gone down the way they did." He looked at me, then turned away again. "Probably... Now though? What's the point?"

"Why didn't she tell him herself?" Obviously a part of me was hurt by Noah's revelation, but another part was angry—for Cade's sake. "Why string him along?"

"It wasn't like that." There was a twinge of anger in his voice. His expression hardened—then softened a moment later. "Not really."

I folded my arms. "Sounds like a real peach."

"My sister loved Cade. She did. It just wasn't the right kind of love. Everyone expected them to end up together, and she didn't want to hurt him or disappoint them."

"So she, what, would have just gone along and never said a word?"

He shrugged. "Yeah. Probably would have married him, too. But the connection he was looking for, the one he felt, would never have been returned."

For a moment I was speechless. Who the hell would marry someone they weren't *in love* with? It took a minute, but I found my voice. "Why tell me?" I grabbed his arm and turned him so that we were face-to-face. I couldn't put my finger on it exactly, but I was horrified by his admission. Angry. I just didn't know on whose behalf I was pissed. The other me for her obvious betrayal, or Cade, because Noah should have told him. I threw my hands into the air. "Why the hell would you tell me that? You can't stand me. Why confess? Why now?"

He shook his head and pulled free. "You're nothing like my sister but, and I hate to even admit this, you *are* like me. I know exactly what was going through your head when I explained about their lack of a physical relationship. You were thinking he used you."

"He did," I spat without thinking. The pain and betrayal in my voice made me cringe. And as Noah stood, watching me with a justified expression, I sighed. "This is all moot. I'm either dead, or you guys will leave. Not like I'm going to have to awkwardly run into him for years to come. Besides, it was just a kiss. There's nothing between us. We don't know each other."

"You're dumb as shit, aren't you?"

My blood ran cold. "Excuse me?"

Noah's lips twisted into a fierce scowl. "You haven't known him long, but there's no way you can't see it. What kind of guy he is. He'd never pull a dick move like that." He backed down a bit. "I won't tell you he's not still in love with my sister. The guy was blindly head over ass. But I know him. Better than I know myself in some ways. And if he was doing anything with you—FYI I *don't* want details—it was because of you, not her."

It was a nice thought, but when I called him on it, Cade had even started apologizing, because we both knew I was right. And, as much of an ass as he was, Noah was fiercely loyal. I didn't want to be the one to shatter the oddly perfect perception he had of his friend.

I was about to head back inside, but lights in the parking lot below us caught my attention. "Wow," I said, leaning over the edge. A row of cars eight long was pulling into the parking lot. "Either someone decided to throw a motel party, or gypsies just rolled into town."

Noah joined me at the railing. "Kinda late for a mass check-in."

As I watched, the cars parked side by side, and one by one, the engines died. Then, when at the far side of the lot, the driver of the first car emerged, I nearly fell over. A familiar hulking form stomped toward the building.

Noah cursed and I pushed off the railing. "They found us."

Chapter Seventeen

"Cade!" Noah bellowed, shoving past me and sprinting into the hotel room. He pounded on the small bedroom door, then dove for Cade's jacket. "Gotta bounce, man. Rise and shine."

A few moments later a still-sleepy Cade appeared in the doorway. "What the hell are you—"

Noah threw the jacket at him. "Simmons is here with half of Fort Hannity. Probably better if they don't find us."

He thrust both arms into the leather and began collecting the few supplies we'd gathered along the way. "How did he—" He froze, then slammed a fist down against the end table next to the couch. "Damnit!"

I grabbed his hand and tugged him toward the door. "How later. Escape, now."

I pulled open the door, but Noah came up behind me and slammed it closed. "Are you insane?"

I blinked, genuinely confused. "Um, if you don't

want them to find us, staying here is *bad*."

"So is walking right out the front door." Cade went to the window and peered down. "By now they've made it to the clerk's desk. They'll be getting our room number."

We'd paid cash and used a fake name, but all it would take is a description and they'd know who we were. Two guys and a girl? Not exactly inconspicuous. As it was, the desk clerk had eyed me with disdain when we checked in. "Okay. So then what are our options?"

The boys exchanged a look, then both turned to the window.

"You want to jump?" I exclaimed, backing away from them. "That's insane."

Noah rolled his eyes. "Of course it is." He crossed the room and threw open the window. "There's a ledge. We'll head to the next room."

"Oh," I said, throwing my hands into the air. "Is that all?"

Noah rolled his eyes. "Says the girl who dangled herself over the edge of a ravine less than twenty-four hours ago?"

Cade glared at him and took my arm. He steered me toward the window. "It'll be fine. The ledge is plenty big enough." I peered out the window. He was right. The ledge was pretty wide. That wasn't the issue. The problem was, it didn't look to be in pristine condition. It wasn't dilapidated or anything, but it wasn't brand-new. There were cracks in the cement.

"Time to go," Noah said, giving me a nice hard shove. "I'm behind you."

I slipped my right foot over the sill and snorted. "And *that's* supposed to make me feel better. You'll probably push me."

"Don't be an ass." The second my other foot hit the ledge, Noah climbed out behind me. "If I pushed you, they'd know we were up here."

"God," Cade huffed as he climbed out behind Noah. "Am I going to have to separate you?"

"She started it."

Noah nudged me gently. "Hurry. We can't stand here. Start moving toward the next window."

With a deep breath, I started inching my way to the right. I didn't have an issue with heights—we weren't even that high up—still I refused to look down. I kept my back to the lot below and moved sideways, facing the building. It was a great plan until my foot came down on a loose piece of the ledge.

It wasn't one of those moments where time seems to come to a jarring stop. There was no freeze-frame picture of horror mere seconds before I fell. It was instant and blurring. One second I was standing on the ledge, the next I was plummeting like a stone.

Stars exploded in my eyes, and a sharp pain prickled up one of my arms. At first I wasn't sure which one. Everything was spinning at warp speed. But, I was vaguely aware that the jarring stop and assumedly sickening crack of multiple bones that would have surely come with crashing to the ground below, were not present.

"For fuck's sake! Stop squirming," Noah bellowed from somewhere above me.

Heart racing, I lifted my head as my vision cleared. Noah's hands were wrapped around my left wrist as I dangled off the side of the crumbled ledge. His grip slipped an inch at first. Then another. "Don't let me fall," I cried.

He was teetering on the ledge, leaning back with all his weight, and it still didn't seem like it was enough. Cade leaned forward to grab the back of his shirt, but Noah shook him off. "Don't! Stay back."

The concrete on either side of us was cracked and crumbling. Cade straightened and shimmied a few steps back toward the window. "Be careful."

"I'll think about it," Noah said, adjusting his stance. What was there to stop him from simply letting go? If it was a choice between me dragging us both down, or simply me plummeting to the ground below, I knew which way it'd go. I wasn't his sister. His Kori. I was an imposter in his eyes. Someone wearing her face and polluting her memory.

"Hang on," he snapped. "I have to—" His grip shook. "Get a better foothold before I can pull you up."

While he struggled with his footing, a million thoughts raced through my mind. Everything from what I wanted my last memories on Earth to be, to the things I'd never done. Things I'd never said. Dreams I'd never followed.

With a mighty heave, he managed to get my shoulders above the ledge. I kicked out my feet until I was able to hook the right one over the edge of the concrete, but it wasn't enough. I couldn't get the leverage I needed to hoist myself up.

Noah's grip slipped a bit. "Cade…"

A second later, Cade grabbed me. I'd never been happier to have someone pawing my ass. "You okay?" he huffed once all three of us were securely propped against the building.

I rubbed my shoulder, now sore from Noah catching me. "Oh. Yeah. I'm peachy. Let's do it again sometime."

It wasn't funny, but for some reason we all burst out laughing. In fact, we kept laughing until we were out of breath and my sides were sore.

"We have to move," Cade said, climbing to his feet. Noah and I followed suit, and we carefully made our way around the corner of the building and to the next room.

Luckily the window to the room next door was unlocked and we'd been able to get inside. Hearing commotion in the hallway, we waited, then snuck down to the main lobby as soon as the coast was clear. Simmons and his men were still there, but we managed to slip unnoticed into the employee lounge and out the back door.

We'd been driving almost an hour now. Our new ride—a "borrowed" station wagon—had a full tank of gas and a wide array of SpongeBob SquarePants toys. I felt guilty for taking the car, but we'd had no choice. It was the only vehicle at the far end of the lot, away from Simmons and his men. I made a mental note to check the registration and send the family an anonymous apology, as well as an address where the car could be found once we were finished with it.

We made really good time, and just after sunset, found ourselves three blocks from the old address Noah dug up on Mr. Harris. Since it was just after seven in the morning and far too early to go banging on doors, Cade and I settled at a picnic table at the community park while Noah ran for breakfast.

It was Monday, and I was officially skipping school—which kind of sucked. We had someone coming in from the Drovan Program—an organization that took on art students as apprentices of sorts—to talk to the class. I'd been hoping to do some schmoozing. Possibly even some bootlicking. Drovan was notoriously hard to get into. I wanted every advantage I could get. But instead of showing off my portfolio, I was chasing a lunatic on a quest to commit inter-realm abduction and mass murder for the slim chance to see my eighteenth birthday.

Not exactly how I saw my senior year going…

"We've got this, Kori," Cade said. He was sitting across from me, carving out a pattern in the wood using the station wagon's key.

There was a pressure in my chest, a nugget of fear that had been growing bigger and bigger since that first moment with Dylan in the alley. If we didn't find Ava and get the key to remove this ticking time bomb on my wrist, it would explode and take all of me with it. It was taking all my willpower not to let that fear consume everything that I was. I knew if I let it in, I'd be nothing more than a fetal ball waiting for the end.

Suck it up, Anderson!

That's not what a good soldier would do. A good soldier would fight—so that's what I chose to do. "When this is all over, you guys should be able to head home, right?"

"Hypothetically," he responded. "My main concern is

getting that key. A lot could go wrong."

"But it could go right."

He shrugged and tilted his head up to the sunlight. It was shaping up to be a beautiful day. Not a cloud in the sky. "It could, but we've been close before. A month ago I had him cornered. It was just him and me, and he was injured. I should have been able to take him out."

"What happened?"

He paused, then sighed. "I hesitated. He'd been shot—"

"Shot?" I exclaimed.

"He tried breaking into Ava's house. Her dad was home and was simply defending his family." He set down the keys and brushed his hands over the design he'd carved into the wood. "We were in that alley. Just the two of us. I could have taken him out—I had the advantage. But he made me think the wound was worse than it was. He... The truth is, my brother is a weak spot for me. We'd always been so close. It was us against the world, ya know? Well, until Ava..."

"You were worried about him."

"I made a mistake. I hesitated." His expression darkened. "Don't worry. I'm past all that now. He has to pay for what he did."

How would I feel if I were in his position? If someone I trusted, someone I loved, took everything from me? Would there be lingering loyalty? Would I be able to look past their transgressions? I didn't think so. Cade was a rare soul. A truly good-hearted person. And even though he swore he'd kill Dylan for what he'd done, I wasn't sure I believed it.

I leaned over to get a better look at what he'd carved

into the table. It was an infinity symbol made up of Celtic knots. "So what's that?"

He looked down at the carving. "The Infinity Division shield. Since Cora was born in Ireland, you thought it was fitting."

I ran the tip of my finger over the marred wooden surface. "I thought?"

He smiled. "Well, my world's version of you."

"She designed it?" The scroll work was beautiful. Twisting lines that wrapped elegantly together with an almost embossed-looking center. I knew my mom would have loved it. She'd always gone out of her way to share her Irish roots with me. Histories and pictures and stories of growing up just outside of Dublin. I'd never met my grandparents, but Mom assured me they were real *spitfires*. We'd planned a trip there right after my graduation. If I made it out of this, I'd go for both of us.

"She would really like you," Cade said with a grin. "Our Cora. She's a lot like you. Resilient. Tough. Nothing ever holds her back."

I didn't say anything, letting my gaze fall to the cuff.

Noah returned not long after that, with a tray of coffee and two brown paper bags. Donuts, bagels, and five egg and cheese sandwiches. By the time nine o'clock rolled around, all that remained were a pile of crumbs and three empty cups.

"I can't believe we ate all of that." And by *we*, I meant Noah. Cade and I each had a coffee and bagel, while Noah inhaled the rest. It had to be a miracle of science, something in the water of their world, that he wasn't four hundred pounds.

He frowned and balled up one of the brown bags.

"Woulda gotten more if I hadn't run out of cash."

Cade frowned. "There's no more?"

"Not unless you've got a money tree growing out your ass." Noah shook his head. "We're hoofing it to Harris's place."

Chapter Eighteen

We took our time and ended up on the Harris doorstep just before ten a.m. There was a small white sedan in the driveway and several lights on inside. I took it as a good sign, and as Cade stepped up to knock on the door, crossed my fingers.

But after five minutes, my hope was beginning to wane. "Don't think anyone's home, man," Noah said, peering around to the side window.

"There are lights on," I said, not willing to give up yet. "Maybe they just didn't hear the door."

He rolled his eyes and pushed Cade aside before pounding hard on the door. The sound echoed through the porch.

"Yoo-hoo," a gravelly voice called.

We whirled to see an elderly man on the sidewalk in front of the house.

"If you kids're looking for the Richardsons, yer outta luck. They gone on vacation a few days back."

I came around the side and made my way down the steps. "Richardson? We were actually looking for the Harris family."

The old man hobbled up the walk. "Don't remember the name—" He tapped the side of his head. "The old noggin isn't what it used to be. But there was a military family here at one time. They left years ago." He was wracked by a series of body-quaking coughs. When he calmed, he added, "Took that sweet little baby of theirs and moved away."

Cade was suddenly beside me. "Any chance you know exactly where?"

"Can't say as I do. Sorry. Might want to ask in town, though. The Mr. was an army man. Might've kept in touch with some of the good ole boys."

Noah grumbled something—presumably rude—but I elbowed him and smiled. "That's a great idea. Thank you so much."

The man tossed us a shaky wave, then hobbled on his way. I turned to the boys. "Now what?"

Cade didn't look nearly as discouraged as I felt. "Might be worth a shot. We could ask around. Not much else to go on."

"We can split up. Dig and see if we can't come up with something," Noah said, zipping his jacket.

Cade nodded. "Good call, but we can't stay too long. We'll meet back in the park at two."

Noah nodded and took off down the walk. A moment later, he turned the corner and disappeared from view. I was about to ask Cade where we should start, but a shadow fell across the walkway, followed by a wicked laugh.

"Don't you two look cozy?" Dylan stepped around and came to stand in front of us. He inclined his head toward the house, grinning. "Looks like the deal's off."

Cade returned the grin. "Is it?" He nodded toward the house. "Go ahead. You won't find her inside."

Dylan stood there for a minute, watching his brother. Probably trying to decide if he was bluffing. I waited for him to storm up to the door, but he remained where he was. Voice like a razor, he asked, "Where is she?"

"Someplace safe." Cade grabbed my arm and held it up. "Fork over the key and we'll tell you where."

Prickles of ice trickled down my back at the sound of Dylan's laugh, and the look in his eyes? It sent wave after wave of goose bumps jumping up all across my skin. The look in his eyes was rage brought to life. "Really? You think I'm that easy? You should know better by now, little brother."

Cade held his ground. "You want Ava? Then give me the key."

Some of the anger leached from Dylan's expression. He was quiet for a moment. "I give you the key and you'll take me to Ava. No games?"

Cade relaxed a little. "You've got my word, Dylan. I swear. As soon as the cuff is off, I'll take you to Ava."

Another moment of hesitation and Dylan sighed. He dug into his back pocket, and a second later, held out his palm. In the center was a small silver disc. He lifted his head and met my gaze head on. "Here. Take it."

I almost didn't reach out. It seemed too easy. Lacking the dramatic flair Cade said he loved so much. It was cool, nestled between my thumb and pointer, and when I handed it to Cade, he wasted no time in flipping my wrist and moving to set the key in place.

"Oh," Dylan said, almost as if an afterthought. "Just one thing. Before you use that, you should have all the facts."

"The facts," I repeated, swallowing the sudden lump in my throat. A shudder rippled through me. Of course it wouldn't be as easy as using the key and being done with this whole mess, would it? I took the key from Cade before he could use it, then sighed. "What facts?"

He turned to Cade. There was a glint of satisfaction in his eyes. "There's a choice to make. You can save only one of them."

Cade tensed, and I couldn't contain myself. "One of them? Meaning what? Who is *them*?"

He kept his gaze on Cade, refusing to look me in the eye. "I think this is a more fitting end to the game. Don't get me wrong. I've loved our previous rounds, but I think changing things up this time around did me good. Considering you screwed me over with Penny Bloom—" He winked. "Yeah. I know about your daring cliffside rescue. But I'm in a good mood. I'm going to let one of them live. The ghost of the girl you loved—or the only father you've ever known."

Cade's jaw tightened, and at his sides, both fists clenched and quivered. While I didn't understand Dylan's cryptic message—well, except for my part in it—he was visibly rocked. Fear swelled in my chest. I didn't know what exactly he was referring to, but if it had Cade this scared then it couldn't be good. He squeezed his eyes closed and pressed his lips into a thin line, nostrils flaring slightly as he seemingly struggled to keep his breathing even. Every muscle in his body went rigid, from the twitching line along his neck, to the stiff, troublesome set of his broad shoulders.

In short, his response scared the crap out of me. "What?" I tried. "What does it mean?"

Cade opened his eyes but refused to look in my direction. In the end, it was Dylan who finally gave in. "I decided General Anderson would look spiffy wearing one of those cuffs. That's the choice my brother needs to make. You or him."

My entire universe started to spin. Each breath gutted me, handfuls of razor-sharp glass moving in and out of my lungs with no other purpose than to rip me apart. It wasn't true. Couldn't be. Dad wasn't here. He was safe. "Bullshit. You'd never capture him." Yet, as I said the words, doubt crept in, poisonous and sharp.

"I figured you might not believe me," Dylan said, breaking through my haze. Shifting, he leaned to the left, plunging a hand into his pocket. A few moments later, he held out a small silver pin.

I couldn't bring myself to take it from him, but I couldn't tear my gaze from it, either. The small, shiny infinity clip that Mom had given him three years ago on their anniversary. He took it everywhere with him, clipped to the inside of his jacket when he went out of town. "No… How?" I lifted my gaze to meet his. "How is that even possible?"

Dylan laughed. It was dark and full of arrogance, and infused me with more rage and hatred than I ever thought possible. "It wasn't hard." He inclined his head toward Cade. "These idiots ran right to him when we got here. Told him all about how I was a threat to his precious daughter. He left them to babysit and set out to find me. Old bastard did all the hard work for me."

The fury bubbled over, and I launched myself at him. Luckily—for me or Dylan, I wasn't sure—Cade had amazing reflexes. He caught me and yanked back hard, bringing me in close to him and holding tight.

Dylan wasn't impressed. "Now that we've gotten that out of the way, let me make a new suggestion—you give me Ava and I'll give you the general."

The world fell away. The birds chirping in the distance, the cars passing on the main road—it was all just gone.

Dylan looked like a little boy who'd just stolen the very last cookie. "Oh. I'm not playing fair, am I?"

Anger unlike anything I'd ever known boiled up inside me. "If you—"

"Oooh. And here come the meaningless threats. Spare me, princess. There's only one way this is going to go. *My way*." Dylan leaned in, smile fading. "This is nothing personal. I actually like you. But I love Ava and nothing, no one, is going to keep me from her." He tapped his wrist. "Better hurry, though. Time's almost up."

"Fine," Cade said with a growl. "We'll get Ava and meet you back in Wells. At the park by the mural."

"You have until just before midnight on Tuesday." He turned and started to walk away, then paused. "Oh, what the hell. I'm feeling funny today. Let's sweeten the pot."

Cade regarded his brother carefully. "I'm listening."

"Bring me Ava and I won't even make you choose between them. I'll give you the general *and* the last key. I get Ava, and everyone gets to live." He snickered and, without waiting for an answer, strode away with his head held high.

We watched him leave, and it took everything I had not to tackle him and start pounding.

Cade lifted his head to look me in the eye. "We still have time. We can find him."

There was confidence in his voice, but the glint of fear in his eyes told a different story. There was something wrong. A catch he didn't want to tell me about. "If that's the case, then why are you so freaked?" I was done being coddled. "Why the hell would we need another key? We already have one. What aren't you telling me?"

For a minute I was sure he'd keep going. Spitting out soothing platitudes in an attempt to keep me calm. On another girl it might have worked. Made her feel safe and secure. On me it only made things worse. I didn't like beating around the bush. Head on, full throttle. That was my motto. There was no point in dancing around a problem. It wasn't going to go away.

With a twist of his lips and the slightest furrow of his brows, he sighed. "From what I understand, each key can be used only once." He shook his head. "I dunno about other worlds, but ours are one-time use. Something about the electricity in the cuffs frying them—I don't know. If the general is really wearing a cuff, then unless Dylan keeps his word, we have one key for two people."

"Do you think he's lying?"

"About the general? No." He stuffed his hands into his jacket pockets. "About having another key? Hard to say."

Even if he did have one, I doubted he had any intention of letting us use it. But facts were facts. You needed to have them in order to make important decisions. To weigh the options and make the choices. "How do we know it's even true? He could be lying. He might not even have another cuff."

"We can't afford to take that chance." He took a step toward me but I backed away. I was afraid he'd try to steal the key and ninja the cuff from my wrist. "I know for sure he took two cuffs. When Noah and I skipped, we found only the two we're wearing. I wish I could say for sure about the keys, but everything happened so fast. There was no time to take inventory…"

"Well, if there's only one key, then we're pretty much back to square one." My voice rose. This was the moment I'd been holding out for. Getting our hands on the key. Now that we had it, things seemed to have gotten even worse than they'd been before. I hadn't thought that was even possible. "Because you can be damn sure I'm not unlocking this and letting my dad die."

"We're not back to square one," he said. "Not exactly. I might have an idea."

He draped his jacket over my shoulder as I tried hard not to shiver. "An idea?"

"Rabbit," Cade said, squaring his shoulders. He dialed Noah, and after a moment, said into the cell, "We have to see the Rabbit."

Chapter Nineteen

"So this guy is some kind of computer genius?" I fidgeted with the seat belt as Cade pushed the jeep past fifty. We'd met Noah in the park and were on our way to sneak back into Wells—not the smartest idea in my book, but the boys assured me it was necessary. All they'd told me about this Rabbit person was that he was a trusted friend where they came from and that he'd freelanced for the government for the last five years.

"That's putting it one way. Rabbit is like a technological savant." Noah twisted around in his seat so that we were face-to-face.

"How do you know we'll find him? I mean, you said Ava was my cousin, yet here we've never met. Cade and Dylan were never born, and you..." I couldn't finish the sentence. "What if Rabbit is here, but he's like a checkout guy in the Stop N Shop?"

Noah shrugged. If he knew where I was going with it, he didn't seem to care. Then again, if he regarded all his other incarnations the way he did mine, then why would he? "Rabbit is one of the few constants we've seen. He's always here. Always smart as hell. We've gone to him a few times for help."

That made me feel a little better. "And it worked? When you went to him for help?"

Noah twisted back around in his seat, and Cade sighed. "Not every time."

My hope started to fade. "How many? How many times has he successfully helped you?"

"None," was Noah's answer. He glanced across the car at Cade, who returned the look with an irritated glare.

"Ignore him," Cade said as he slowed the jeep. He made a left onto Stamford Drive, then another quick right onto Muller. "We've gone to Rabbit about our cuffs a few times. Wanted to see if he could slice us from the main while still allowing us to track it."

"And I take it he had no luck."

"Nada," Noah said with a snort. "Because it can't be done. And now you want him to, what, unlock that thing without killing her?"

"It can't hurt to try," Cade responded tightly. "Got a better idea?"

Noah didn't answer. He sank back in his seat and proceeded to look out the window for the rest of the ride, which lasted all of about ten minutes. By the time we pulled up to the small white Cape Cod at the end of a partially empty cul-de-sac, I was ready to scream.

"Remember," Cade said, closing the driver's side door. His gaze was fixed on Noah, an even mix of concern and irritation. "Let me do all the talking. Every time you go in, you freak him the hell out."

Noah threw up his hands and slowed, stepping behind me. "Go for it, man. It's not my fault the last one had just come off a three-day bender."

Cade rolled his eyes and stepped onto the stoop. He turned to me. "Same goes for you. Let me do the talking."

Without even thinking about it, I threw up my hands just as Noah had. "And what would I even say?"

He looked from me to Noah and groaned. "Dealing with one of him was bad enough, but two? I'm not sure how much of this I can take."

Before I could argue that Noah and I were *nothing* alike, Cade turned away and rapped on the door several times, then took a step back. A few moments later, it opened and a tall, broad-shouldered boy stood framed by the doorway.

He had eyes as dark as the night sky and skin the color of mocha. There was a thick silver bar in his left eyebrow, and when he turned his head to the right to study Cade, I noticed a small rabbit tattoo just beneath his ear.

"Phil, my name is—"

The guy snickered. "Pretty sure no one anywhere calls me Phil." He leaned against the doorframe and tapped the screen three times, then leaned close and squinted. "Also pretty sure you knew that already. Am I right?"

Both boys hesitated, but not me. I'd never been the *sit back and be quiet* type. "He's Cade." I hitched a thumb over my shoulder. "That one is Noah. I'm Kori."

"And I'm Rabbit. But, like I said, most people who

come around here looking for me know that already."

Since I'd already broken the no-talking rule, I decided to keep going. I nodded. "We do. We came to see if we could get your help with something."

He cocked his head to the side, a slight grin splitting his lips. Both arms folded across his chest, he gave me a small nod. "Illegal?"

"Not even a little bit," was my response, while at the same time, Noah said, "Depends on who you ask."

"Hmmm. My interest is piqued." Rabbit looked among us and waggled his eyebrows once before pushing open the door and waving us inside.

Without question, we filed inside one by one, Noah bringing up the rear. We followed our pierced host down a long hallway, then down a flight of narrow steps that emptied into a large blue bedroom.

Without invitation, Noah flopped down into the squishy-looking couch against the far wall and kicked up his feet. Good to know he was rude no matter whose house he waltzed into.

Rabbit eyed him but said nothing. Instead, he turned to me. "So what is it you need my help with?"

I looked to Cade. This was where he needed to take over. Technically he knew Rabbit. Or, a *version* of Rabbit. He'd know better how to approach this—and exactly what to ask. I still didn't understand how this guy could help us. Genius or not, if we didn't have the key, we didn't have the key. I was willing to bet all the paint in the world that this was one lock we couldn't pick.

Cade took my hand and held it up for Rabbit to see. "I need you to break into this."

Rabbit squinted at the cuff. "What is that thing?"

"It's something that needs to come off. But it's locked. We need you to unlock it if at all possible."

He straightened and regarded Cade like he had two heads. "Dude, I'm not sure what you heard about me, but I'm a computer man. Ask me to hack mommy and daddy's bank account, or fix your grades in school, and I'm golden. But picking a lock?" He leaned forward again and frowned. Nudging the cuff with his pointer finger, he shook his head. "A really weird one? I'm not your guy."

"Yeah," Noah said, hoisting himself off the couch. "You are. This isn't a normal lock. Its tech. Tech that you helped create."

"I helped create this?" Rabbit snorted then backed away, looking uncomfortable for the first time. His gaze bounced between Noah and Cade as he inched toward the door. "Not sure what you're on, but it's customary to share when you come into someone else's house."

"Please." I pulled my hand from Cade's and took a step toward him. "I'm desperate, and I really need your help. Could you at least try?"

I thought he'd turn and bolt up the stairs. He had that look in his eyes. I'd seen it before on the faces of people about to tell my dad something he didn't want to hear. A mix of fear and self-preservation. Fight or flight.

I lifted my wrist and gave it a subtle shake. "This thing? It's going to kill me if I don't get it off. Soon."

That got his attention. His expression morphed from fearful to intrigued. Not concern, but hell. I'd take it. He cocked his head to the side, regarding me skeptically for a moment before jabbing a finger in my direction. "How is *that* supposed to kill you?"

"This whole thing is complicated and believe me when I tell you that you don't want to know the whole story." Cade stepped up beside me. "What I can tell you is that piece of tech is government issued and ended up on her wrist by mistake." He pulled a tiny silver disc from his pocket. The key Dylan had given us. "This is the key. We need you to duplicate it."

"Duplicate it? If you have the key then why do you need me?" The skepticism in his voice was now mirrored on his face. If Cade wasn't careful, we'd lose him altogether.

I decided the truth—or as close to it as I could get without freaking him out—was the best bet. "This key will unlock it—but I can't use it. There's someone else wearing the cuff. Someone else whose life is in danger." I took a deep breath. "Someone I care about. The key can be used only once. If I use it to unlock mine, then he dies."

Rabbit narrowed his eyes. He took the key from Cade and turned it over in his palm several times before looking up at me with a quirked brow. "What kind of a key can only be used once?"

"This one," Cade answered for me. "Please. Just take a look at it. See if you can do anything."

Rabbit hesitated, then nodded slowly. "Okay—but no promises."

Chapter Twenty

Rabbit was an incredible host. He let us raid his fridge and gave us access to his video game collection—much to Noah's delight. With the sounds of electronic slaughter and game-world mayhem drifting out from the other room, I tucked my sock-clad feet under me and curled into my borrowed fleece hoodie.

"He's still working," Cade said, coming into the room. He sat down on the chair across from the couch, never taking his eyes off me.

You'd think I'd have gotten used to his weird scrutiny by now, but the truth was, I hadn't. It was different now, though. His gaze didn't make me uncomfortable like it did in the beginning. Now it kind of made me jealous. I'd never had anyone look at me like that. Like they were seeing the sun, the moon—the entire universe—all wrapped up in one person. But that was the thing. The major hitch. He wasn't looking at me. Not really. He was looking at her. At his Kori. The girl who shared my face and body. A girl long gone.

Because of all the moving around we did, I'd learned to create distance. Or, in most cases, just not get involved. The few friends I'd had, the few guys I'd messed around with, had been nothing more than a distraction. A way to kill time between moves. That was all I could afford—and it'd never bothered me. Mom was my best friend. My confidant and cheerleader. I'd never wanted—never needed—more than that. Not until now. Not until seeing the depth of devotion Cade had for this girl.

Not until realizing what I'd been missing.

I shook it off and pushed aside the lingering feeling of loss, of something I didn't quite understand, and forced a smile. "Well then, keeping my fingers and toes crossed. How much time do we have?"

"Not a lot. We need to figure out what we're going to do about Ava. Noah didn't have any luck in town hunting down an address for the Harris family." He leaned forward, resting his elbows on his knees. "But forget about all that for a minute. How you holding up?"

I couldn't help it. I laughed. Not an amused sound, but something dark. Riddled with the loss of hope. The stink of defeat that I hoped to God he couldn't see. "Hanging in." I stretched my legs out and arched my back to be rid of an annoying kink. "I'm sure we'll figure this out."

He didn't buy it, though. I could see it in his eyes. With the subtle twist of his upper lip and the slight narrowing of his left eye. "I know you think I see her when I look at you, but the more time we spend together, the more apparent it is to me that you two are nothing alike."

"So you've said—multiple times." A streak of anger, red hot and fierce, blitzed through me. "Sorry to disappoint. We can't all be perfect."

His mouth fell open, and he shook his head. "Not at all what I meant, Kori." He sighed and straightened a little, slouching sideways against the armrest. "If my Kori would have said to me what you just did, I would have believed her. Not because she was good at hiding things—she actually sucked. The girl was the worst liar I've ever met." He looked almost angry. "No. I would have believed her because she believed it."

He'd pretty much lost me. "Okay…"

For the longest moment, he said nothing. Just kept looking at me with an expression filled with a mixture of awe and resentment. "What I'm saying is, she was naive. Kori saw the world through stained glass windows. Rose-colored glasses. Whatever euphemism you use in your world. She didn't see things clearly. Everyone was good inside and all the bad shit worked itself out eventually. You just had to sit back and the universe would right its own wrongs."

"That doesn't happen," I said. "Ever."

"Exactly." He leaned back. "Kori's world was like a damn Disney movie." The hint of resentment in his voice grew more prominent. "Picture-perfect with everything neatly wrapped up just before the ninety-minute mark."

I didn't know how to take what he was saying—or how to respond—so I just sat there and listened.

"We all babied her." I could have sworn his breath hitched. "Put her up on a pedestal and closed her away in a house of glass. I keep thinking that maybe if the general was harder on her, if we all didn't coddle her so much, she would still be alive. If she'd just seen things more clearly, then maybe she would have been able to fight him off."

I couldn't imagine living my life the way he was describing. People falling at my feet and trying to shelter me from reality. Walking around in a haze of fluffy pink, misplaced hope. I would never admit it to a living soul, but a small part of me was jealous. She wasn't made to feel like a screw-up. She had Cade and Noah and, from the sound of it, never had to deal with the loneliness that comes with bouncing from base to base. She'd never had to endure the loss of her mother…

I swallowed and found my voice. It bothered me to see him so upset—especially knowing what I knew about her. "I don't believe that." Kicking out my feet, I set them on the floor and leaned forward. "Maybe things happened the way they needed to."

The change in him was instant and fierce. He stood, towering over me like a storm cloud, ready to unleash hell on Earth. "The way they needed to? What the hell is that supposed to mean?"

"It means," I said, taking a deep breath. My heart thundered against my ribs as I rose to meet his gaze. I remembered what Noah said to me on the balcony. How Cade and his sister loved each other, but were never the right fit. How even though she loved him, she hadn't *loved* him… "That maybe she was holding you back." The instant the words left my mouth I could tell they'd hit him hard.

The fury on his face had me continuing. I'd never had a way with words. Usually I tended to stick my foot so far down my throat, it could come out my ass in an attempt to get an eloquent point across, but tongue-tied or not, Cade needed to hear this. He needed to move on. Chasing Dylan across God knew how many versions of Earth, being tied to the cuff, wasn't the thing that was keeping him trapped.

He was doing it to himself.

I'd just met the guy and I could see it, clear as day. He wore his love for her like shackles, never allowing himself the freedom to move on. He may not be my Cade, or my responsibility, but it was time someone knocked some damn sense into him.

"Not exactly how I meant for it to come out, but pretty much the gist of it," I said, my tone softer now. "It's harsh, I know, but I'm not sorry, Cade." I waggled my finger between us. "Maybe we—any and all versions of us—don't fit. Maybe that's why I'm as strong as I am. As independent. Because I never had a Cade. And maybe, just maybe, the universe knew you would never grow to be the person you were supposed to be, the person the world *needs* you to be, with her in your life."

"That is a fucked-up theory, Kori." he snapped. His fingers knotted tight, arms shaking with anger. "And an incorrect one. I've seen it work out for us. Multiple times."

"In other realities? How do you know what you saw? You only get a glimpse, Cade. A few snapshots from someone else's life. That's not enough to assess a relationship. That's not enough time to see the issues. For all you know, we're dysfunctional as hell."

He leaned in with a truly volatile expression and said, "You don't know what the hell you're talking about."

"Sure I do," I responded. "You need to move on with

your life. Anyone with eyes can see that."

"Forget for a minute that Noah and I are stuck. Forced to go where Dylan goes. You're saying I should just let it go? Turn my back so he can continue to murder people?"

"No. I'm saying that you need to be doing this for the right reasons."

"Well maybe you should enlighten me. I mean, you obviously have a better handle on the situation than I do."

I let the dig go and focused on keeping my cool. He had every right to be annoyed with me, but I wasn't trying to bait him. I was trying to make him see what was right in front of his face. "You want to bring him to justice? Fine. You want to prevent him from hurting anyone else? Awesome. But chasing him from here to the end of whatever Earth you end up on, so far, has been about nothing more than revenge."

He didn't say a word.

"Tell me I'm wrong," I challenged. "Tell me that you're not looking to get your hands on him so that you can make him pay for taking her away from you." I moved a few inches closer. I was toeing the line, but someone had to say this out loud. "The truth is, you're wasting your life!"

The change in him was instant, raw and real. In that moment, it was like his entire body had been enveloped in a black cloud. Anger and pain and loss and things far darker than I could possibly comprehend spun round and round.

"Wasting my life?" he repeated. His voice was low, but held the distinct tone of fury. If I hadn't been so preoccupied with getting him to see my point of view, I probably would have been afraid. *Very afraid.* Because in that moment? He looked and sounded exactly like Dylan. "Maybe you're just jealous. Standing here all eaten up by the fact that you'll never have a bond like we did. You see what she meant to me, and you know that you'll live the rest of your life without that. No one will ever love—"

I slapped him. I'd never slapped anyone before—it hurt like hell—but if anyone deserved a good whack in the head, it was Cade Granger at that very moment.

He touched the tips of his fingers to his cheek as the slightest hint of a grin spread across his face. Not necessarily a happy one, but more satisfied. Like I'd justified something huge by reacting. "Hit a nerve, did I?"

I wasn't a spiteful person. Mom raised me better than that. And even though he was being so horrible to me—despite the fact that he was hurting, there really wasn't any excuse—I still didn't set out to shatter his world. "Wake up, asshole! She loved you, but she wasn't *in love* with you."

I felt it. The palatable shift that engulfed the room. Cade looked like he'd stopped breathing altogether and was watching me, mouth agape and face pale. He swallowed several times before saying, "What did you say?"

Open mouth, insert entire leg.

"Answer me!"

All I could picture was quaking dishes and broken glass at the sound of his voice. I jumped about a foot in the air, stealing a quick glance back at the door. The last thing we needed right now was an audience.

Probably should have thought about that before you poked the lion...

"I'm sorry," I said. And I was. The anger in his eyes was nothing compared to the anguish. It didn't touch the hurt I'd unintentionally inflicted. "She loved you. So much. But she knew you weren't right for each other. She didn't love you like you loved her. Noah told me—"

"No," he snapped. "Bullshit. I've seen us together. Everywhere. There isn't any way we weren't *right* for each other!"

"Cade..."

"And let's forget for a second that Noah wouldn't have kept that from me."

"He didn't want to hurt you. What good would the truth have done?" Something inside me broke. My heart, my soul, hurt for him. I grabbed the sides of his face and tilted his head down so that we were eye to eye. "It wouldn't have changed anything, Cade. If you'd found out the truth, would you have let Dylan go?"

"No," he answered softly. "I loved her."

His dedication to the service and to my dad. His almost blind devotion to Noah's sister. The ferocity with which he pursued Dylan. The way his lips lifted slightly higher on the left when he smiled. In that moment, standing so close to what my dad would surely dub a truly good man, I fell victim to that pull. I couldn't help myself.

Pulling his face down to mine, I brushed my lips to his. Tentative at first. A part of me was afraid he'd move away. Terrified, actually. I didn't doubt his sincerity. He'd loved her. The other Kori. His life, his heart, his kisses... They'd all been reserved for her. But in that moment, I was desperate to know what that was like. Because maybe he was right. Maybe I would never have anyone as devoted to me as he'd been to her. I wanted— no, *needed*—to understand why she hadn't loved him like he'd loved her. Because from where I stood, Cade was just about as amazing as they came. Smart, sexy— complicated. I couldn't imagine ever being bored with someone like him.

He wrapped his arms around my waist, deepening the kiss. One hand clutching a fistful of my borrowed hoodie, the other skimming its way up my back and beneath my long hair, settling at the base of my neck. The skin under his fingers ignited, sending waves of warmth rippling through me.

I need to stop this…

Dangerous. This was dangerous. An experiment gone too far. This wasn't for me. His passion and fire. It was for her. It's why I'd stopped back at the hotel. Still, I found myself drowning in it all. Slipping beneath a haze of sensation. A wash of feeling so overwhelming that I wondered if I'd ever find my way out.

The kiss grew more intense. Cade's fingers around my neck tightened, his nails coming so close to pressing into my skin. There was need in his actions. Desire—but something more. Emotions that, while not quite angry, were shrouded in darkness. The hand at my waist twisted harder, gathering more of the hoodie until it pulled taut. I responded, equally enthusiastic, slipping my tongue between his lips.

The action seemed to surprise him. He sucked in a breath, then let out a small sigh. The sound of it did amazing things to my stomach. That allover tingle that comes from standing right next to a toasty bonfire. That building excitement as you bound down the stairs on Christmas morning.

It was equal part foolish and reckless, but I wrapped my arms around him, hooking them behind his neck, and dragged us together the rest of the way. Our bodies pressed close, Cade rolled with it without missing a beat.

This is stupid.

That annoying little voice inside my head kept getting louder.

He's using you! And why wouldn't he? You basically just threw yourself at him—right after he was a dick to you...

I knew I should pull away. Put an end to this before... before what? I got hurt? I wasn't some love-struck girl who hoped Cade would see what an awesome couple we could potentially make. I didn't think he would be sticking around when—if—we got the cuffs off Dad and me. We weren't going to hook up and he'd suddenly realize that I—not her—was the girl of his dreams. That was fantasy. It didn't happen in the real world. This wasn't some romantic comedy where the unlikely matchup turns out to be true love. This was a sci-fi nightmare that couldn't end in happily ever after.

I didn't love him.

I do like him though...

And that was, once again, the reason I pulled away. Or, the reason I *would* have pulled away if a loud creaking on the steps hadn't alerted us to someone coming. We stumbled apart and, in my haste to put distance between us, I lost my footing. I ended up sprawled on the couch, breath held and face probably flushed with embarrassment as Cade struggled to get his own breathing under control.

"Okay, let's—" Rabbit stopped as soon as he crossed the threshold. Shit. Did we look guilty? Faces flushed and lips swollen? Was my shirt all rumpled?

Thankfully he didn't say anything. He recovered quickly and came to stand behind the couch. Holding up a small bronze disc, he said, "All righty then. Ready to give it a go?"

Chapter Twenty-One

I stood, hesitant to believe he'd actually duplicated the key. The small bronze thing pressed between his thumb and pointer could be almost as dangerous as that kiss Cade and I just shared. Hope could gut you in the end. When things took a sharp turn south and landed you smack in the middle of a dark inevitable. That's how it'd been with Mom. The doctors were so sure they could control the disease. They'd given us hope—only to crush it. It was my life that teetered on the line now. I didn't want to be crushed. I wasn't strong enough to withstand the aftermath.

Cade tugged at the edge of his shirt and stepped around me to where Rabbit was. He took the bronze disc and held it up to the light. "This will unlock the cuff?"

Rabbit shrugged. He did that a lot. "Might. Might not, though. That key was unlike anything I've ever played with. I'm not even close to understanding how it works."

I nodded to the imposter in Cade's hand. "Then how did you make that?"

"I faked it," Rabbit said, frowning. "I took it apart—" He must have seen the sheer terror on my face, because he threw up his hands. "Don't freak. The original is fine. I needed to see what made it tick in order to make a new one. Problem is, there are a lot of components that I just don't get."

My chest hurt. "So then it won't work. I mean, it can't, right?"

"There's a small chance it'll work, but I'd prepare yourself for failure. Maybe if I had more time—" His eyes sparked with interest.

"We're out of time," was Cade's sharp response. He grabbed my arm and pulled me closer, fingers hovering above the small circular indentation on my unwanted fashion accessory. "You ready?"

No...

"Yeah." There was a nervous flutter in my stomach. This was it. The moment of truth. If it worked, all we'd need to do is find Dad and use the original to unlock his cuff. Easy peasy. If it didn't work...

Don't think like that! Good soldiers don't give up...

I squeezed my eyes closed. "Do it."

Cade's hand was warm as he angled my wrist up. A second later, his other one slipped into mine, fingers threading together and squeezing tight. There was a faint snap—assumedly as Rabbit clicked the key into the small hole—and then nothing. Seconds passed. Then minutes. When I finally dared open my eyes, I found Cade and Rabbit staring at the cuff, both wearing frowns. It was all the answer I needed.

"Well, that—" All the air left my lungs in one single, brutal push. Intense pain unlike anything I'd ever experienced washed over my entire body, radiating at my wrist and fanning out to every other limb. "What's—" But it was no use. Words were a lost cause.

I crumpled to the floor between the boys as a scream tore from my throat. It ripped free, shattering the space around us, and a second later, Noah's panicked voice filled the air. Good. That was good. Something to focus on. Cade was on the ground in front of me, but I couldn't hear him. His lips were moving, but most of the sound seemed to have seeped from the room.

"What the hell did you do to her?" Noah yelled. I was vaguely aware of him shoving Cade out of the way. "Kori? Can you hear me?"

I opened my mouth to tell him that I could—that he was the only one I could hear—but another spike of pain sent me reeling.

"Told—work—key—" I couldn't make out who was talking, but they didn't sound thrilled.

"Listen to me." It was Noah again. For some reason his voice was like a beacon, reaching out and pulling me in. Grounding me. I clung to it, trying as hard as I could to stay focused. He grabbed the sides of my face tight. "You'll be okay. I won't let anything happen to you."

Another pain bloomed in my wrist, this one very different from the first. I opened my eyes, my vision adjusting to see Noah's hands around my wrist, slamming it against the corner of the table, then again against the floor. I didn't know how many times he did it, but when the pain finally ebbed, he looked almost as relieved as I felt.

My breath caught, my gaze falling to the cuff. To the empty divot where Rabbit's fake key had been moments ago. "What just happened?" I asked once I was sure I wouldn't puke. My entire hand was numb, and I was afraid to move my fingers in fear that he'd broken them. "Because that felt like the reaper was trying to separate me from my skin."

"Close," came Cade's voice. A moment later he appeared in front of me, watching Noah from the corner of his eye. "I can only guess it was the cuff's defense mechanism. The key wasn't right, so the cuff fought back."

"By trying to kill me?" I sucked in a blissfully pain-free breath and scowled at the cuff. "That's it. You're off my Christmas card list." Noah rocked back on his heels and let his gaze move beyond me to something on the other side of the room. Before I could think twice, I leaned forward and grabbed his hand, giving it a single, brutal squeeze. "Thank you."

Our eyes met, and for a second I could see it. All the love and pain and loss that encompassed his sister's memory. For just a single instant he saw her, not me, and it brought the most amazing smile to his lips. Beaming like the sun, his fingers tightened around mine. His lips parted...but instead of speaking, his mouth snapped closed like a steel door, jaw tight and eyes narrow. He pulled his hand from mine and stood, stalking from the room without another word.

Cade watched him go then stood and turned to Rabbit with a murderous expression. "You could have killed her."

Rabbit, in turn, gave it right back. "Which is exactly

what I told your boy in there." He jabbed a finger at my arm. "I don't know what the hell that thing is, much less what makes it tick. It was a gamble—and you're lucky the outcome wasn't worse."

I jumped up and rested a hand on each boy's chest, pushing back with as much force as I could. "Cool it, kids. I'm fine. No harm done." When nothing further was said and no fists flew, I took a deep breath. "So what's our next move? We can't get it off, so we should…?"

Cade was quiet for a moment. "Ava Harris." He didn't sound happy. Directing his attention to Rabbit, he asked, "You can't get that thing off her, but could you locate someone for us?"

Rabbit, having obviously learned his lesson the hard way, was more cautious this time around. "Why? Who is she?"

"We think she might be able to help get this thing off," I answered just as Cade opened his mouth. I didn't like the expression on his face, and friends at home or not, he looked ready to start something, and that wasn't the best way to get Rabbit to help us.

"If that's true, then why come to me first?"

Shit. Smart one, this guy. "Honestly we didn't want to involve her unless we had no other options."

Rabbit regarded me skeptically for a moment before sinking onto the couch. "This chick has a key?"

"Not exactly," I said, cautious. "But she might be the key to getting one." He still didn't look convinced, so I kept going, remembering what Cade told me about her. "She's my cousin."

Technically it was a lie. Sort of. Somewhere out there, there was a version—several from the way Cade made it sound—of Ava that *was* my cousin. So really, it was only half a lie. Unfortunately, Rabbit didn't buy it. "Your cousin? And you don't know where she is?"

"That cuff is the product of a secret government project that allows the wearer to travel to alternate Earths," Noah said, coming back into the room. He crossed to where Rabbit was and folded his arms, casual as could be. "Someone put that cuff on her as leverage, and if we don't get it off, it will drag her from this Earth to another—which will kill her. Ava Harris is the reason. We're hoping by finding her, we can force the guy with the key out of hiding and wrap this thing up once and for all."

Crickets.

That's all you could hear. Literally. There must have been a zillion of them hanging out right outside the windows.

I imagined my expression was pretty close to Cade's. He watched Noah with unsurpassed shock, mouth hanging open and eyes wide. "Jesus, Noah. Again?"

Again? That must have been what Cade meant when he told Noah to keep quiet earlier…

Noah didn't seem to care. He shrugged and said, "What? You and I both know our Rabbit would totally appreciate the honesty. They all do. Every time."

"*Your Rabbit*?" Rabbit frowned. "As in, another me on another Earth. Do I have that right?"

"Yep," Noah said with a sharp nod.

"Meaning—" He waggled a finger between Cade and Noah. "—you two are from another Earth?"

"Yep," Noah said again.

Rabbit's eyes widened, and he shook his head slowly.

"That is—"

Cade glared at Noah. "If you'll just give me a sec—"

"The coolest thing I've ever heard," Rabbit finished with a stomp of his foot.

"What?" Cade and I exclaimed in unison. "You believe him?" He was messing with us. Because, he had to be, right? Who the hell believed a story like that?

Rabbit stuffed both hands into his pants pockets and flashed a sly grin. "The government thinks it can keep an airtight lid on this stuff, but chatter always leaks out. Granted, most people don't lend any credence to it. I mean, only a hemp-obsessed punk genius would ever buy into a rumor like that, right?"

Noah slapped him hard on the back. "That's my man." He shot Cade an *I told you so* glare.

"So then you'll help us?" I didn't want to get my hopes up. Rabbit might have a record IQ, but he was just about as strange as they could get. Just because he bought what Noah was selling didn't mean he'd want to jump into the crazy end of the pool with us.

"Hell yeah." He dove for the computer chair a few feet away and pushed off hard. The chair glided across the linoleum, coming to a jarring halt as his feet braced against the far wall. Fingers poised over the keyboard, he said, "Hit me."

"Ava Harris," Noah replied, moving to stand behind him. "Born July fifteenth 1999. Possibly in California. Sacramento. Another possible location is Long Island, New York."

As Rabbit's fingers breezed across the keyboard, Cade and I made our way over to the other side of the room. It was impossible to follow his movements as he skated across the keys. Page after page popped on the screen as Rabbit's eyes seemingly devoured the information.

"Nothing. What else can you tell me?"

"It wouldn't be Harris," Cade said. He stomped his foot and growled. "She's not Kori's cousin on this Earth. Her mom never met and married Cora's brother. The last name wouldn't be Harris! How the hell could I be so stupid?"

"Do you know what her father's name was? Maybe her parents never divorced here."

Cade thought about it for a moment, then snapped his fingers. "Fairfield. Ava's father is John Fairfield. Where we're from, he was a drunk, abusive bastard, but he was also a marine. Can you check service—"

"Two steps ahead of you, bro." Rabbit snickered. A second later, he tapped the screen and announced, "Bingo!"

We all leaned forward to get a better look. It was an address in Pennsville, just outside of Wells.

For a marine named John Fairfield.

Chapter Twenty-Two

We thanked Rabbit for his help and were back on the road by four in the afternoon. It'd been hard to get away. After realizing we were moving on, he tried everything he could to get us to stay and answer questions. Everything from scientific queries that made my brain itch, to questions about the roles of house pets in their society.

The GPS in our newly borrowed Toyota said John Fairfield's address was about three hours from Rabbit's place. The last thing I wanted was to sit in a car with nothing else to do other than obsess about my impending demise for hours at a time, but tagging out wasn't an option.

I shifted to my left and stretched my leg. My right hip and arm had fallen asleep and were starting to needle. I would have given just about anything at that point to get out and stretch, but the sand in the hourglass was almost gone. The little luxuries would have to wait. Hell, bathroom breaks required fierce argument. Cade didn't want to stop for anything. "So say we do find Ava. Then what?"

"We call Dylan," Noah said. He was stretched out across the back seat, feet kicked up and resting on the window frame. He and Cade decided to take turns driving. I hadn't been given a turn because, apparently, the other me was a horrible driver and they weren't taking any chances.

I twisted in my seat. "Call Dylan? Are you crazy?" Like I'd let them just fork this poor girl over?

"Relax," Cade said from the driver's seat. "Dylan would never hurt Ava. Any version of her." He glared into the rearview mirror. "But so we're clear, we're not going to call and tell him where to find her. He might not hurt her, but that doesn't mean he won't try to take her with him."

"But how can he do that without killing her?"

Cade didn't answer, but Noah snorted. "He was afraid to get your hopes up."

I stared at Cade. "Hopes up? What does that mean? What aren't you telling me?"

He palmed the wheel, then tapped it several times. "We figured that was his plan all along. Find Ava and bring her home. Remember I told you that when we found him in the lab, right before he skipped, the place was trashed? A few of the cuffs were gone. We're pretty sure he has a dose of the quick prep with him…"

"Why wouldn't you tell me that?" I screamed, slamming my hand against the dashboard. "You let me sit here thinking I was going to die if we didn't recover the key." It wasn't the most ideal setup, but at least if there was a working dose of the quick prep floating around out there, I had a shot.

I could see Mom again...

"We still don't know for sure that he has it, Kori. For all I know, his plan is to find her and stay here."

I folded my arms and straightened in the seat. Turning toward the window, I said, "You still should have told me."

B y the time hour two rolled around, I could tell Cade was starting to fade. None of us had really had much sleep since this whole thing started. Well, none of us except Noah, who had been snoring in the back for the past forty minutes. I guessed because it wasn't his neck on the chopping block, drifting off to dreamland was easy. As tired as I was, there was no way I could shut my eyes knowing what was at stake. Knowing what might now be only hours away...

"Pull off. Let's get some coffee and switch drivers."

"I'm fine," Cade insisted—all while trying to cover up a yawn. He rolled his shoulders and flexed the fingers on his right hand while giving me a sideways glance. "We're almost there."

"And I'd love to spend those few hours alive. Please," I tried again. We'd hit some traffic due to a car accident and were still about an hour and half out. "I'm starving. I could use munchies, and I seriously need to stretch."

I didn't think he'd give in. The one thing I'd learned in the short time I'd known him was that he was even more stubborn than Dad. The first person I'd ever met who could give the general a run for his money, Cade didn't seem like the compromising type.

"We're almost out of time, and considering by now we probably have half the U.S. military scouring the streets for us, I'd really rather not stop."

"But if—"

"Don't argue," Noah mumbled sleepily. "You know he's even worse than Dad." There was a rustling sound, and a half snort, and a moment later, soft snoring filled the car.

I hadn't missed his "Dad" slip up, and even though I tried not to read too much into it, the truth was, it gave me a warm feeling in the pit of my stomach. "It won't do us any good if you fall asleep at the wheel."

He didn't answer. Not that I'd really expected him to. It was obvious from the hard set of his jaw and the rigidness of his shoulders that he wasn't going to give in. I folded my arms and settled into my seat, preparing for the longest two hours of my life.

*W*e arrived at John Fairfield's address just before seven thirty. We had just four and a half hours left before Dylan skipped. My heart thundered as I slid from the car and followed Cade and Noah up the walkway of the large colonial on the corner of Fifth and Gerber. I had no idea what was waiting for us behind those doors, or if it would be the answer we were hoping for, but something about this moment felt huge. Like knocking on that door would be a turning point.

"And what are we supposed to say to her?" Noah grabbed Cade's arms just as he stepped onto the porch. "What's the *plan*?"

Cade frowned. He glanced at me, then back to Noah, swatting away a moth that had drifted down from the light above the door. "There isn't one. I'm just kind of coasting here."

"Coasting?" Noah's eyes widened. "Man, this isn't a *coasting* situation. Say she's in there. Then what? Do we drag her out kicking and screaming and fork her over? Trick her into coming with us?"

"I told you I have no intention of handing her over to Dylan."

"That's all well and fucking awesome. But it doesn't answer my question—or solve the problem. Your plan was to use her to get the key. *How* exactly do you plan on doing that?"

Most of the time when Noah opened his mouth, I wanted to smack him. This time, he had a point. We were here, but now what? What was the point of tracking Ava down if we weren't going to call Dylan? Just walking up and introducing ourselves wasn't going to fix anything. And what were we supposed to tell her?

Hi! I'm Kori, your almost cousin, and these two guys are from an alternate reality where, apparently, we're both dead. If you'd kindly come with us, you could help stop a multiverse-hopping lunatic, who has a serious hard-on for you, from killing a lot of people.

Um, no.

I stepped between them. "He's right."

There was a loud creaking sound, followed by a

booming voice. "Can I help you?"

The three of us whirled toward the door. A tall, broad-shouldered man, somewhere in his forties if I had to guess, stood behind the screen. He regarded us with a friendly, but cautious smile.

"You're John Fairfield, right? Sandra's husband?"

His smile faded a little. "Yes. And it's after eight at night."

A spike of hope surged. He was still married to Ava's mother. That meant she had to be here. "We're here to see Ava. Is she home?"

The man's brow furrowed. He leaned against the doorframe and folded his arms. "Ava?"

"Your daughter?" I tried, desperately clinging to that small spark of hope as it fizzled into nothingness.

"I think you three have the wrong house. I've got a son, Avery, but no daughter." He straightened and, taking one last look at us, nodded and closed the door.

The sound it made as it closed was like an explosion in my head. That was it. Our last chance. Ava didn't exist here. There was nothing stopping Dylan from offing me as promised and moving on to the next world. To the next possible Ava.

I gripped the banister and sucked in a breath. Everything started to spin.

Cade said something. All I heard was white noise. A constant crackle of nothingness—something it seemed was destined to fill my future. He grabbed my arm, but I shook him off with a violent jerk and bolted down the steps. Whatever it was he had to say didn't interest me. I needed to let this sink in. To come to terms with the fact that I'd just essentially been handed a death sentence.

Dylan wouldn't take pity on me. He wouldn't unlock the cuff and spare my life. I wasn't Kori Anderson in this scenario. I was a convenient tool to carry out an unrelenting revenge.

Past the car and down the suburban sidewalk. The stars were out, the sky was clear and the night air crisp. It was the kind of night I normally hated. The chill in the air usually found me retreating to warmer accommodations. But tonight I didn't feel it. Not really. The only real thing was the faint thumping sound my sneakers made as they pounded against the sidewalk. Slow at first, then steadily increasing until the rhythm was consistent and fast.

It wasn't until I came to a small colonial bordered by a privacy fence that I stopped. Someone—more than likely the owners of the house—had painted various sayings from end to end. Different colors and styles. All sizes and shapes. Each one was unique except for the singular thing they all shared.

Wars are not won by evacuations—Winston Churchill...

There is no failure except in no longer trying—Elbert Hubbard...

Survival can be summed up in three words. Never Give Up—Bear Grylls...

They were all about hope.

There was a strange beauty in that fence. Something I could relate to in the deepest level of my being. For once it wasn't about the colors or various textures. It had nothing to do with the fancy fonts. It was about the art. Not the same as something I'd have done, but powerful nonetheless. Art brightened life. It brought meaning to things otherwise left forgotten. It gave hope…

I had no idea how long I stood there, taking great care to read each and every last one, but when I turned around, Noah was standing behind me. "This whole thing sucks. I know. And since I don't believe in lying to spare someone's feelings, I'll come right out and say this looks grim. Even if Dylan has a quick prep on him, getting it away from him will be impossible. The guy would die before letting it slip away."

I snorted and, without thinking, punched him lightly in the arm. "Great pep talk."

He rolled his eyes, then shrugged. "I've never been a pep-talk kinda guy. But, I'm also not a quitter—and neither are you."

"You don't know anything about me," I fired back. My words were defensive, and the fear tasted foul rolling off the tip of my tongue.

"Yeah." He folded his arms and fixed me with a familiar glare. It was straight out of Dad's best intimidation expressions. "I know you. I *am* you. You and I? Cade's right. We're alike." He flashed me a wicked grin. "The universe's way of making sure my awesomeness was alive and kicking in this world, no doubt."

"Wow," I said, trying hard to hold back a smile. I was starting to think I might miss this back and forth once he was gone. "I'm standing at death's door and you still manage to find a way to make it about you. Kudos."

He stepped back and gave a sweeping bow. When he straightened, his grin was gone, replaced by that trademark scowl I'd grown eerily accustomed to. "Seriously, Kori. If this goes badly, then at least you tried.

You didn't just lie down and wait to die. It ain't over until it's over."

"And I take it it *ain't* over yet?"

He held out his hand. "Not by a long shot."

Did I think we stood a chance? Not really. The odds were stacked high against us, and we had no ammo to work with. Sure, I had a key, but would I use it to unlock my cuff while my dad was still wearing one? There was no chance in hell. I imagined if Mom were here, she'd say something inspiring. Something colorful and grand in that charmingly long-winded way of hers. Dad, on the other hand, would simply look me in the eye and tell me to soldier up. Suck back the poison and push through it.

So, that's what I did. I took Noah's hand and we stepped into the night to finish what Dylan had started.

Chapter Twenty-Three

No one spoke as we made our way back to Wells again. I didn't see a way around this. We had about four more hours. That wasn't enough time—not that I knew how much *would* be enough. Dylan was smart. He was motivated by rage and had nothing left to lose. People like that were the most dangerous kind.

Maybe this whole thing had been doomed from the start. Maybe I was destined to end up like all the others. Dead to pay for Cade's mistake.

Dead to pay for your own…

I'd never been a pessimistic person, but I knew when I was out of options.

"What now?" It wasn't Cade who finally broke the silence in the car. It was Noah. "Because I know we're not just going to give up." He twisted in the passenger's seat and glared into the back. "There's no one in this car who swings that way."

"I don't know," was Cade's response. That was it. Just three simple, sharp words.

I glanced over at the console and noticed for the first time that he was speeding. With everything going on, with my life hanging in the balance, for some reason that scared me most of all. It was stupid. Such a small thing. But that single slip screamed volumes. His control, while slightly irritating, had been something of a comfort. Like, no matter how insane things got, there would always be that constant.

I hadn't realized it until that very moment, but I'd come to rely on it in my day-to-day life. Dad was always the picture of restraint. No matter what was going on around him, he kept his shit together. And while I was sure I hated him for it, for burying his emotions and letting that outer shell do all the talking, deep down I envied it. It was something I knew I'd never have. Mom always said I wore my emotions like a neon sign. If Cade was on the verge of breaking, then the world was coming apart at the seams—and I couldn't have that.

"Think," I forced myself to say. "There has to be another way. Something else we can do. Another tactic we can try."

"Short of giving Dylan what he wants and hoping he holds up his end, I've got nothing." Cade wrapped his fingers around the wheel until his knuckles turned white. "We've got nothing."

Noah twisted in the seat again. His gaze traveled up, then down, then up again. With a huff, he faced forward. "Then I say we give him what he wants."

Cade snorted. The car accelerated just a bit faster.

Obviously I was missing something. "What he wants

is Ava. We don't have her. We can't get her. Do you know a suitable substitute?"

"Yes," Noah said. He turned the rearview mirror in my direction, grinning. "You."

"Me? How exactly would that work? Pretty sure the only thing he wants from me is my inability to breathe."

The car slowed a little, and Cade's grip on the wheel loosened, and the car slowed just a bit. "You're suggesting a stand-in?"

"Exactly!" Noah clamped his hands then hitched a thumb over his shoulder in my direction. "Look at her. She's the right height. Right weight. Even the same build. With darker hair… Can't believe we missed it."

"He might not be able to tell the difference if she's far enough away," Cade finished for him. "It'll be dark. It might work."

"No way." I didn't know Ava. Had never met her. But I'd seen the picture Dylan waved in my face back in the alley. We looked nothing alike. She had a dainty, heart-shaped face and deep-set eyes. "It'll never work."

"It's our only hope, Kori," Cade said. There was determination in his voice. "We can make this work."

"She'd have to have her back facing him, of course," Noah said. "And she wouldn't be able to speak."

"Okay." If there was a chance to pull this off, we needed to be sure about all the angles. Before they ran with it, we needed to get some of the details straight. "Say you could pass me off as Ava. Then what? I dye my hair, sit with my back to him…and? Do you think he's going to just hand over my dad, and the other key, just because he sees me from across the way?"

Cade readjusted the rearview mirror and glanced

into it, frowning. "Obviously there are kinks to iron out."

That was an understatement. Still, it was our last chance.

I nodded. "Okay. So what do we do first?"

We drove another twenty minutes and found a cheap motel. Cade didn't want to go all the way back to Wells, because he thought it would look suspicious. We figured I could dye my hair quickly, then let it dry during the remaining drive. We settled in a town called Pleasant Hill. Noah had volunteered to run for hair dye and food. I didn't question where he'd gotten the money. Cade said I didn't want to know—and I believed him.

I was betting he wanted to give Cade a chance to say good-bye. Just in case. That, or he was just as skeeved out about this place as I was. It was the kind of establishment that rented rooms by the hour, and judging by the lecherous gleam in the front desk clerk's eye when he saw us, it was hard not to cringe.

Noah had been gone less than fifteen minutes now, and Cade busied himself by pulling off his boots and attempting to shine them with one of the pillowcases from his bed. It was ridiculous considering they were worn and tattered, but something about the sight of him sitting there, trying to buff away the scuffs and mud, reminded me of home.

Every once in a while he'd look up then quickly look away when our eyes met. It was obvious that he wanted to say something. It was also obvious that he wasn't going to say it without a good, hard push.

I sighed and tucked my legs up under me, scooting farther onto my bed. "What?"

He looked up from his boots. "Hmm?"

"You have something to say. I can tell. Out with it."

He set the boot down and laid the pillowcase over the top of his pillow. Smoothing out the edges, he sighed.

I kicked my feet out from under me and slid to the edge of the bed. There was something so compelling in his eyes. So vulnerable and needy. On the outside, Cade Granger was the perfect soldier. Obedient and loyal. Methodical and thorough. But in that moment I realized he was missing something. There was a hardness in Dad's eyes that I didn't see in Cade's.

That I didn't *want* to see.

"Tell me." It came out as a whisper. A desperate plea for something more. I didn't know what, and I didn't care. Right then I just wanted to feel a connection. Something real to keep me rooted.

Without saying a word, he slid to the edge, then off, taking a knee in front of me. It brought us eye to eye. "There's so much I wanted to say to her."

My chest constricted, the air moving in and out of my lungs burning like fire. "Then go ahead. Say it to me. Pretend…"

His expression pained, he shook his head slowly. "Then what about the things I want to say to you?"

I swallowed. "Me?"

He didn't answer. Instead, he brought his hand up and ran the tips of his fingers across my cheek. The sensation was electric. A million tiny sparks roared to life beneath my skin. I leaned in to his touch as that little voice inside my head chided me for taking comfort in something that was meant for someone else.

"I want to kiss you."

"You want to kiss *her*," I corrected, my voice barely a whisper.

He looked like I'd slapped him, and that killed me. I didn't know why this boy had gotten under my skin. His sadness weighed on my shoulders and hurt my heart as though it was my own.

"Maybe you're right." He let his hand slide down the back of my neck, warm fingers resting against the skin. Confusion swirled in his eyes. "I don't know."

"If you could say something—tell her anything—what would it be?"

His head dropped, and for a moment he was silent. When his gaze rose to meet mine again, there was acceptance there. A sense of finality. "I knew it wasn't right. I think that's why I got so angry with you back at Rabbit's place. Deep down, I knew we weren't perfect. But I loved her. I loved before I even knew what that meant. She was goodhearted and pure. So forgiving—everything that I'd never had in my own life. That's what drew me to her, I think. She had a light—"

He faltered, and I grabbed his other hand. "Keep going."

"She was brightness and life." He sucked in a breath. "So much life… My parents never showed me love. Dylan and I were on our own at a young age. Emotionally and physically. We had a roof over our heads, food and clothing, but were left to raise ourselves. Noah and Kori came along, and that all changed. They welcomed us into their home. Eventually, their family. She welcomed us… I never got a chance to thank her. To really explain what that meant for me."

"I'm sure she knew."

He nodded. "Yeah. Probably. She was sharp. Saw things long before I did."

"And I'm sure she loved you." The words were thick in my throat. "It might not have been the same kind of love you felt, but hearing you guys talk about her, she doesn't strike me as the kind of girl who fakes it, ya know?"

Again, he nodded. "It was her," he said, so low. So pained. "From the very beginning, it was always her. There'd never been anyone else. I'd never—"

"It's okay, Cade."

"It's not," he insisted. "I claim to have loved her— to still love her—yet I can't deny the subtle truths that have surfaced over the last few days."

"Truths?"

"I feel something for you." He squeezed his eyes closed for a moment. When he opened them, there was a spark of pure fire. "I don't know what it is but I can't ignore the fact that it's there. That it's real and it's *new*."

The guilt he'd placed on himself over her death— repeatedly—was enormous. It was bound to cause confusion. I could say with certainty on my end that there was something there. A spark I would have loved to explore. But I wasn't confident that he saw things clearly. That he saw *me* clearly. "I'm sure it feels that way, but—"

He stood. "And there it is." There was a twinge of anger in his tone. He grabbed my hands and pulled me off the bed. "Always questioning me. Always challenging. I need to know. I need to know for sure."

Before I could react, Cade wrapped his arms around my waist and pulled me close. His lips covered mine. Fierce and desperate, they moved with a need I felt in every inch of my body. I couldn't help myself. I responded, equally desperate.

I'd been frozen. Trapped in ice and buried beneath a thousand layers of my own pain. In that moment Cade was the blowtorch. A flame that had burned its way into my life and melted the shell away to expose my raw insides to the world. A part of me resisted. That little voice of reason inside my head fought against awakening. It fought against the fact that I was beginning to understand that life without connections was pointless. Being alive without living—without loving—wasn't really being alive at all.

I threaded my fingers through his hair and kissed him like he was the only thing keeping my heart from stopping. If the plan failed, then this would be my only chance to feel like this. One-sided or not, I felt connected to Cade. I wasn't ready for it to end.

A soft moan escaped his lips. The sound stoked the fire already burning in my belly and drove me to be bolder. Mimicking what he'd done at the other hotel, I braced my hands against his chest and pushed him back. He stumbled, taken off guard, and fell back onto the bed. Before I could blink, I was being dragged right along with him.

Lips, hands, and limbs. There were no discernable lines. I couldn't tell where I ended and Cade began. I wasn't some starry-eyed girl. We weren't in love. This wasn't going to be a fairy tale ending. But maybe it could have been. Under different circumstances, maybe we could have fallen in love. The basics were there. I felt it. There was fire and interest. Challenge and so much room for both of us to grow. I wanted someone who could make me feel again. That one person who could—and would—break through my walls. I needed a person I could be myself with— pushy and sometimes a little controlling—someone who could handle my ups and downs and stubborn nature. He was looking for someone to help him stay on the straight and narrow. Be the man he wanted to be. Someone who could make him smile again... I knew deep in my heart I could have been that for him. Would have wanted to.

Just not in this world...

It was me who finally pulled away. Again. I felt bad. This was the third time I'd done this to him. You'd think I would know better. I sat up and scooched a few feet away, to the other end of the bed.

Cade propped himself up on his elbows. His expression was serious. "And now I know."

I didn't ask. Really, it didn't matter. If by some miracle the plan worked, then he was leaving. I wasn't going with him. He wasn't going to stay behind. There was no future in this. Whatever it was he thought he *knew* was irrelevant.

"I can see it in your eyes, you know." He watched me but didn't come any closer. "You try to hide it, but it's there."

The defense alarm rang, and my walls went up. "Oh yeah?"

"You feel something for me."

I forced a laugh. "I'd have to be dead not to have felt something. Not to inflate your ego, but you're one hell of a kisser, Cade."

He shook his head. "No. It's more than that." He pushed himself up to a sitting position. "It's more than that, and that scares you to death."

"Second base and you think you know me inside out?" I folded my arms. "Sorry. It was a nice…kiss…"

Liar, liar, pants on fire! That was so much better than nice. And it was way *more than a kiss…*

But the spark in his eyes told me he wasn't going to let this go. He believed my bullshit about as much as I did. "Fine. Not that it matters, but yes. I like you! More than I should, considering the badly timed circumstances. I like you and I know that we could be something, Cade. If you'd been born here, if we'd had a real shot, we would have been amazing, I think. But if we get the cuff off and I survive this, then you and Noah will leave. You'll have to follow Dylan across dimensions and leave me here alone. Alone and knowing that I should have had an obnoxious, smart-ass brother. Knowing that somewhere out there, other Koris have a brilliant mother. Knowing that they have a *you*. Is that what you wanted to hear?" I saw in his eyes. I'd struck a nerve. He felt the injustice of it all, too. The unfairness over the fact that somewhere out there, hundreds of Cades had their Koris, but he had lost his, and I had never gotten mine.

He opened his mouth to argue — I could tell — but a soft beep from the door told us Noah had returned. He juggled several bags and closed the door behind him. When his gaze fell to us, sitting as far apart as possible on Cade's now rumpled bed, he frowned. "Am I, uh, interrupting something?"

I swung my legs over the edge and stalked toward him, refusing to look Cade in the eye. I grabbed the plastic bag with the dye and headed for the bathroom. "Depends on who you ask," I said over my shoulder, then slammed the door, furious at Cade for dredging up all the emotions I had worked so hard to suppress.

Chapter Twenty-Four

I wiped a smear of steam from the mirror with the palm of my hand. It immediately fogged back up. A second swipe, this time with a thin hotel towel, did the trick. There was a strange girl looking back at me. Her hair was black as night, and there was a profound sadness in her eyes.

I didn't have the faith Cade had in this plan. It was going on ten p.m., and Dylan's deadline was now just two hours away. The boys would bring *Ava* and Dylan would bring Dad and, hopefully, the last key. An exchange would be made, and everyone would be on their merry little way.

But the plan hinged on far too many variables. The disguise would fool Dylan only until he saw my face. And lot could go wrong before that even happened. Still, I was determined to make a go of it. I zipped up the dark blue hoodie Noah bought and slipped my feet into a new pair of black boots. When I was finished I stepped in front of the full-length mirror to inspect the finished product. Noah had purchased my entire outfit—minus the underwear.

Oh my God... How embarrassing would that have been?

My new clothes were all dark, lifeless colors—blacks and navy blues with the hoodie rimmed in dark gray. Apparently Ava liked her darkness, which in my opinion explained a lot about her attraction to Dylan and spoke volumes about her personality. I, on the other hand, loved color. Then again, most artists did. Give me vivid and thriving over graveyards and darkness, and I could live happily. I hated the thought that I might die like this. Take my last breath on this Earth swathed in colors that sadly represented my life. Lonely and uninspired.

I leaned into the mirror and tapped it twice, right between my reflection's eyes. "If I get through this, I promise to do something about it. I swear I'll live my life like my art. Take chances. *Live in vivid color.*"

Smoothing out the hoodie, I took a deep breath and pulled open the bathroom door. Cade and Noah were waiting on the other side of the room, and we were officially out of time. It was now or never. "Let's do this."

We arrived at the park thirty minutes early. Cade insisted on scouting the area beforehand. He wanted to have alternate escape plans and know every possible way Dylan could get close to us without coming from the most direct route. Once he was satisfied he had it all mapped out, we returned to the rendezvous point to wait.

Cade knelt in front of me. For the longest moment, he said nothing. Only watched me as though trying to memorize every last line of my face. Commit every detail to memory. "Are you sure about this?"

I forced a laugh. It came out sounding like a nervous giggle. "What choice do I have, right?"

"We could find another way."

I shook my head, not trusting myself to speak. He didn't believe that. There was no other way. This was the bonus shot. An absolute last-ditch attempt.

"This is the only way," I said.

He nodded sadly, then said, "You have the key?"

Dylan's self-imposed timeline was creeping up on us. If he stayed true to his original word, then he would skip within the next two hours. That left less than sixty minutes to lure him in, take him down, and steal the other key—if a second one even existed—and get Dad back. We were cutting it close. Too close in so many ways. I needed insurance.

I dipped my hand into my pocket, my fingers brushing the steely disc, then let my mouth fall open.

"What?" he said, taking a step toward me. "What's wrong?"

I fumbled with the small disk, tucking it into the small hole in the bottom of my pocket. "It's not here." Taking a shaky breath, I turned out both pockets and forced a whimper. "I think I lost it, Cade. In the commotion, it must have fallen."

I think at first he didn't believe me, because all he

did was stare. No expression and no words. However, it didn't last long. "You...*lost* it? How could you lose the only thing capable of saving your life, Kori? Do you realize what this means?" I could hear the anger building in his voice, buried just beneath the disbelief, so I interrupted him before he could blow up.

"This isn't about me. It's not about revenge or getting back what you lost. It's about stopping Dylan. Keeping him from doing this over someplace else." Taking his hands, I squeezed tight, then let go and started for the bench across the walkway. It took all my willpower not to turn around and face the pain I'd caused. Hopefully I'd get a chance to make it up to him.

The plan was for me to sit on the bench far from the boys, facing away. It would simply look like I was waiting for him. Cade would meet his brother—hopefully with Dad in tow—and bring him across the field. There was a single light a few feet from the bench. It would be just enough to see me sitting there, but not enough of a glow to show major details. Once they got close, we'd overpower him. I doubted it would go down that simply. Surely Dylan would come prepared, but as I told Cade—it was the only way. I was hoping for the best but preparing for the worst. That's what good soldiers did. And while I wasn't one, in the technical sense, I was beginning to realize I was a soldier at heart.

I took my seat and leaned back, pushing the dark strands of my newly dyed hair behind my ears. Provided he was telling the truth about the second key, it would all be over tonight. My cuff, as well as Dad's, would be off, and Noah and Cade would finally take Dylan down. Then they could go home. Back to their Earth.

Back to their Earth...

It was a shame, really. That the universe had cheated me out of meeting him here. He was strong and sweet and honorable. The world—any world—would be a better place with him in it. And that's how I soothed the sting of him leaving. At least he'd be out there. Someplace. Standing up for the little people. Doing the right thing. What hurt the most was wondering what might have been had he been born here. Had we been given a chance.

And Noah...combative, irritating Noah. Despite all his snapping and snarling, I'd miss him, too. His shrugging and sighing. His attitude and ravenous appetite. But he was just one more piece of a puzzle I'd never fit into. He'd taken a seat beside me, silently slipping his hand into mine. Every once in a while he'd squeeze, and I wasn't clear if it was for my benefit—or for his.

And that was how I spent the next fifteen or so minutes. Just sitting on that bench, lamenting about the life I'd never have. Sitting next to the brother who died so long ago. Pining for the love I would never get. Until I heard them. First it was the crack of a twig. The crunch of leaves underfoot. That was followed by the sound of soft voices.

"There she is," I heard Cade say. "That was the deal. Now give me the general and the key."

"You got what you wanted, son."

I tensed. Dad. That was Dad's voice! He was okay, and he was here. That was one huge step in the right direction. Maybe this was possible after all...

Dylan laughed. "I know you don't think I'm that

stupid, little brother. You get the key and the old man as soon as I get Ava."

Noah's hand in mine tightened. "He's coming toward us. You ready?"

"No." My lips split with a grin. "But what the hell."

He snickered and stood, tugging me gently off the bench, but keeping me faced away. My pulse pounded so hard, I was sure it would shatter me. Each breath was an effort. A war between the bravery I wanted so badly to feel and normal human instinct. Dylan could see me shaking. Despite the dark, he had to have been able to see the absolute terror in my stance. There was no way to hide it.

"Ava?" Dylan said tentatively. He was behind me, only a few feet away.

At the sound of her name, I picked up my head as I imagined any other person would have done. There was so much hope in his voice. So much fear. It was almost enough to make me feel sorry for him. He'd lost her, and it'd driven him nuts. He'd committed multiple atrocities and fought the universe itself to try to get her back. Was that what love did to you? Made you crazy enough to lose yourself? Maybe I was doing myself a favor keeping my heart walled up. I never wanted to be where he was. Never wanted to be torn open like that with no possible way to get stitched back up.

"I know this whole thing is weird, but trust me, Ava. I can explain everything." Material rustled, and he said, "Just get out of the way and let me talk to her."

Noah let go of a breath and released my hand. He made a move to start around the bench, but something stopped him.

"Where's Kori?" The taint of suspicion vibrated through Dylan's voice. The hairs at the nape of my neck jumped to attention as he came a step closer.

When no one said anything, he cursed.

The rest happened so fast. Something latched onto my shoulder and spun me around. I teetered off-balance, crashing into the bench and jarring my knee hard enough to bring involuntary tears to my eyes, before rolling off the edge and to the ground.

Noah dove forward, but it was too late. Dylan threaded his fingers into a handful of my hair and dragged me around to his side of the bench. "Where is she?" he demanded, giving a violent shake.

"She's not here," I said, breathless. "Like you and Cade, she was never born in this world. She never existed."

He let go of an anguished howl, and I cringed as his grip on my hair pulled just a little tighter. "You're lying."

Cade approached slowly, flanked by Noah. Dad, who seemed to have his hands bound behind his back, brought up the rear. Even trussed like a Thanksgiving Day turkey he looked imposing. "She's not lying, Dylan. Ava wasn't born in this reality. Neither were we. You had to know that was a possibility. You've seen it before."

Dylan didn't answer. He maneuvered us farther from the bench, deeper into the park. I struggled, unwilling to go gently into that good night, but he was stronger. Brute force wouldn't win this. Had to think smart and wait for my chance.

"Fine," he said finally. "Ava's not here. But Kori is." He inclined his head toward Dad. "*He* is."

"Neither my daughter nor I have ever wronged you,

son." Dad shouldered his way past Cade and Noah, stopping a few feet from us. "What happened to your friend wasn't our doing."

"Maybe not," Dylan spat. "But I made my brother a promise and, until I get my Ava back, I intend to keep it."

"You're an idiot," I spat, struggling against his grip just a bit harder. "*Your* Ava is gone. You can't get her back."

He leaned down, breath hot against my ear, and said, "Then I guess I'll just keep killing you. Over and over, I'll watch you die. And as the light fades from your eyes, I'll know that Cade is just as miserable as me."

It was just loud enough for the others to hear. Dad roared, and Cade lunged forward. Dylan jerked us to the right, out of his path. It was just the opportunity I needed. I threw myself forward with all my strength. He didn't let go, but his balance was disturbed. I inhaled deeply and brought my elbow back, into his gut. He let out a grunt, but still held tight.

I straightened and pushed, digging the toes of my brand-new boots into the mud. We flew backward, crashing into a large pine tree with tooth-cracking force. He let out a roar and pushed off the trunk, flinging me away as though I weighed nothing more than a feather. For a moment everything spun. A whirling kaleidoscope of nature's colors whizzing by at a vomit-inducing speed.

I hit the ground hard and tasted the foulness of copper as Cade crashed into his brother. They tumbled to the right of me, trading blows. For a moment it was all a blur. A flurry of tangled limbs and pounding fists mixed with feral grunts. It was hard to tell where one Granger ended and the other began. Noah hauled me upward, dragging me back to where Dad was as Cade got the upper hand.

"This ends now!" He landed a violent right hook, and Dylan's head rocked to the side, eyes rolling back. Without missing a beat, he wrapped his fingers around his brother's neck and began to squeeze.

Dylan came to life. He kicked and struggled, grasping and scratching at Cade's fingers in desperation. Still Cade didn't relent. Much longer and he would kill him. Dylan would be dead, and no one else would have to die. The whole thing would be over.

That's not who Cade is. He's not a murderer...

"Cade," I said, stepping past Noah. "Stop."

In an instant, Noah was beside me. I assumed it was to cheer his friend on, but he surprised me. "Cade, man. Enough. He doesn't deserve to live, but he can't go down this way. Not by your hand."

"He took everything from me," Cade said with a snarl. His eyes were dark with a gleam of madness. The kind of look someone gets right before they trip right off the deep end and start drowning in their own demons.

Dylan continued to paw at his fingers. "And someday we'll be—even," he choked out.

"You're not a killer." Noah took another step toward them. There was a distinct ring of panic in his voice. "I want him dead just as much as you do, but not at the cost of your sanity. You want it—I understand that—but you'll never be able to live with yourself. Do the right thing. Turn him in."

I could see the fight fade from Cade's eyes. The tension in his body drained away. The desire was still there, mingled with an inner darkness that made me wonder if he wasn't like his brother, at least in some small way. But reason and logic won out. His fingers loosened, and he leaned back. Dylan gasped and coughed, doubling over in a struggle to fill his lungs.

Cade took Noah's outstretched hand and stood. "Dylan Granger, by order of the United States Military under the direction of the Fort Hannity Tribunal, you are to be remanded into custody until the time you are able to stand trial and be judged for your crimes."

Chapter Twenty-Five

Once Dylan caught his breath he began to laugh. "You made a mistake, little brother." He wiped a streak of mud from his face. "You should have killed me. I would have."

"No you wouldn't," was Cade's response. But he didn't sound sure. He was looking at his brother differently now. Almost like he was seeing him for the first time—and he didn't like what he saw.

"I would," Dylan insisted. "I would take you out in a heartbeat if I thought it would make up for what you did. But death is too easy. Too fast. No." He shook his head, fingers balling so tightly that his knuckles turned white. "No. You need to suffer for what you did to Ava. The same way I'm suffering."

Cade stood a little straighter. "What happened was an accident. For a long time I blamed myself, but it's not my fault. I wasn't drinking."

"You *chose* Ava. They were both in the backseat and

you swerved right instead of left."

Cade's mouth fell open. "I chose? Do you hear yourself? I cut the wheel, Dylan. It was a split-second decision. I didn't consciously pick a side. Kori could have just as easily been sitting where Ava was. It just happened. It's time to let it go!"

Dylan laughed. He dug into his pocket, and for a second I was afraid he'd pull out a weapon. He didn't, though. At first I wasn't sure what he'd removed. Lint? Gum? It wasn't until he held up his hand, the second key between his thumb and pointer fingers, that I realized what was happening.

I launched myself forward, but I was too far away. Dylan whirled to face the trunk of the huge pine tree and smashed his hand flat against the uneven bark. I reached him as he lifted it away, the small bits of the key slipping through his fingers and falling to the grass.

"No!" I skidded to a stop and dropped to the ground, dredging up the tiny, now useless, parts.

I looked up to see him staring down at me. The expression on his face was one of pure hatred. "You're lucky." He shook his head. Lips turned downward, he said, "By doing it this way, I'm giving you something Ava and I never had. A chance to say good-bye."

"It's not that easy," Noah growled. He stepped forward and hauled me off the ground. "Cade couldn't do it, but I sure as hell can. If you think you're leaving this park in one piece, you're fucking delusional. I kill you and Kori's and the general's cuffs—as well as ours—come off. Everybody wins."

Dylan smiled. "I believe you. You always were the violent one. My brother had the wicked temper, but you...you lacked scruples and restraint. So do I think you'd kill me without a second thought? Totally. Will you? Not a chance."

Noah laughed and took another step forward. "Can't wait to prove you wrong, you smug fuck."

"Well, at least wait until you have all the facts." His grin grew wider. "See, if you don't let me leave, skip off this rock free and clear, I won't tell you where the bomb is. You might manage to save her, and yourselves, but you'll kill hundreds of others."

"Bullshit," Noah yelled. I could tell he believed it, though. His voice lacked conviction. His entire form deflated.

Dylan's expression was smug. "I'm a lot of things, but a liar has never been one of them, Noah." He glanced over at Cade and flashed him a toothy grin. "I think you both know that."

Noah's gaze met mine, and I suddenly understood why he'd been such a bastard to me. He didn't hate me. It was the opposite. He'd been afraid to get attached. To find his sister again only to lose her just like multiple times before. "And what if I said I didn't care? That the only thing that mattered was her?"

He threw up his hands. "I'd believe you about that, too." Dylan leaned forward and winked. He gestured between Dad and Cade. "We both know your moral compass doesn't point north, Noah. It's one of the things I've always loved about you. But do you really think they'd go for it?"

I glanced back, almost afraid of what I'd see. Obviously a part of me wanted them to do it. End his life and save us all. The nightmare would be over, and so many people on so many other worlds would be safe. But it wouldn't be the right thing. I couldn't let them sacrifice so many others for a single person, even if that person was me.

Dad's expression contorted, a mask of agony and rage. His little girl—the only part of his family that remained—versus hundreds of innocent lives. As a dad, his choice would have been easy. I knew that, and I loved him for it. But as a general, he had to make the tough call. And for that, I loved him even more.

Cade, so much like Dad in so many ways, seemed less conflicted. The struggle was there in his eyes, but the spark of resistance was so much less. He'd lost me already. Multiple times. And even though I wasn't *his* Kori, I was still Kori. He'd failed countless times and didn't want it to happen again.

"Enough," I said, pushing Noah aside. I looked from Dad to Cade and shook my head slowly. When I turned back to Dylan, I felt an ember spark deep in my gut. I'd never known true hatred until now. Until this moment. In a way, it was a good thing this was the end of my story. The last few days had shown me what hate could do to a person. How it could twist and turn and create monsters from saints if given a chance to fester. "You can go. Tell me where the bomb is."

"Aren't you the selfless one? I guess I should have seen that. I mean, I gave you the other key and you didn't use it to unlock your cuff. Guessing you won't now, either. Daddy's life will come first?"

"The key you gave me is gone," I said, resisting the urge to dive for his throat. "Lost in all the running."

He let out a hoot and slapped his hand against his knee. "Are you serious? Wow." He waggled a finger between Dad and me. "You really are screwed."

"Just cut the shit," I snapped. "You got what you wanted. Tell me where it is."

He grinned and pulled a handful of zip ties from his pocket. "Secure the three of them and the location is all yours, princess."

I took the small plastic strips from him, doing my best to keep both hands from shaking, and moved to Noah.

He stared at me like I'd lost my mind. "You seriously think I'm going to stand here and let you commit suicide? Because that's what this is. Letting him walk—"

I rose onto my toes and planted the softest kiss on his cheek. The action stunned him, and I used the opportunity to take his hands. "I'm glad we had a chance to meet. I know I'm not your sister, but as far as I'm concerned, you're the best brother a girl could hope for. She was incredibly lucky, and I'd be lying if I said I wasn't jealous." I wrapped the tie around his wrist and pulled it tight before he realized what I was doing. He opened his mouth—probably to tell me what an idiot I was—but I turned away and moved to Cade.

"Please don't fight me on this," I whispered, and took his hands. Tears stung my eyes. "We lost both keys. I'm a goner anyway... It's the right thing to do. For once, I want to do the responsible thing."

He was quiet for a moment, his eyes meeting mine with so much conflicting emotion. I studied the lines of his face. The subtle scarring and high cheekbones and lips too often twisted into a scowl. Cade smiled far too little. I hoped wherever he went after this, whatever he did, he found happiness.

"You're wrong." He took a breath, held it, and released it through pursed lips. "About me."

"Oh?" I wrapped the tie around his wrists and let the edge linger at the loop. "How so?"

"Earlier, you misunderstood the situation. You misunderstood me when I started to apologize. It wasn't because I felt like I'd been using you to reconnect with her." His jaw tightened, and I wasn't sure he'd continue. With a quick glance at Noah, he said, "I don't see her when I look at you. I might have in the beginning, but not anymore. I need to know you understand that. I was sorry because I felt guilty. What I felt for her doesn't touch on what I feel when I look at you." He leaned his head forward, resting his forehead against mine.

I inhaled deeply, committing the scent of pine and leather to memory, though it would be a short one.

"I see strength and bravery and talent that leaves me in awe. I loved her, but you…we could have been something cosmic if we'd been given the chance."

Hot tears spilled over, rolling downward and pooling at my chin in a fiery puddle before falling down the front of his shirt. I slipped the strap through the loop and slowly pulled it tight. "I think so, too." It was the worst kind of truth. A profound, yet small admission that might have changed my life. A relationship with Cade—with Noah—wouldn't have been impossible. It would have been amazing. Something that could have led me to open up again. To be a part of someone else's life without erecting fifty-foot walls.

I bit down hard on my tongue and turned to the last of them. To the hardest. Dad's face was like stone, his lips set in a grim line. His hands were already bound, and that was a good thing. I wasn't sure I could have done it.

"You don't have to do this, Kori." His voice held the taint of regret and a whole lot of pain, but also pride. "We can make calls. Get the police department involved. The base. You don't know that we won't find it—if there even is a bomb."

"I assure you, General Anderson," Dylan said. "There is. And if you don't move things along, princess, I'm going to skip, and you'll be out of luck."

I ignored him and focused on Dad. I didn't want to die. There was still so much I wanted to do. So many things I thought I'd had all the time in the world to experience. I'd had a taste of life, and I desperately wanted more. But how selfish would that be? How many people would have to die so that I could go on?

"We both know there's a good chance they wouldn't find it in time."

"You're my daughter." His voice cracked, and for the first time since Mom got sick, I saw the man beneath the hardened shell. The emotion and sadness he kept boxed away from the world.

"I know. And that's why I have to do this. Because you taught me better." I threw my arms around him and squeezed as tight as I could. When I finally forced myself to let go and back away, I slipped my hand into my pocket, fingers dipping into the small hole in the lining where I'd stashed the key away. "I love you, Daddy."

Before any of them realized what I was doing, I jammed the key I'd told Cade I lost into Dad's cuff. There was a loud snap, and it fell to the ground.

Dad let out an anguished howl and struggled against

the zip ties. I'd never seen his face so pale. So surprised and pained. "You—what have you done?"

"I didn't lose it," I admitted, turning to glare at Dylan. "*He* needed to think I did. I couldn't take a chance that he'd try to take it back. Then we both would have died."

Dad made a choking sound, giving his bindings one final test before deflating. I hated seeing him like this, so defeated and helpless, but it was for the best.

Clapping filled the night, and Dylan let out a whistle. "I gotta hand it to you, Kori. You are *not* like the others. So unpredictable..."

I turned to the boys. While Noah looked pale and hurt, Cade was downright furious. "You lied to me... How could you—"

"I had to." It was the only explanation I had. From the moment I had the key in my hand, I knew which one of us I'd use it on. The world needed Dad. He would go on to do good for a lot of people. This was my contribution. I had the opportunity to save hundreds of lives, plus ensure Dad went on to do all the amazing things he was destined to. As far as leaving a legacy behind, it wasn't great art like I'd wanted, but it was one I could be proud of.

One worthy of a soldier.

Dylan cleared his throat. "Time's up, Kori."

I whirled around and stalked forward, doing my best to ignore Cade's and Noah's furious protests. "Where is it? Where did you put the bomb?"

"Ya know," he said, flashing me a wicked grin and a wink. He slipped out of his jacket and dropped it to the ground beside him. "You're the best one yet. I'm impressed—and trust me, that doesn't happen easily.

That's why I just gave you a fighting chance."

A chance? He was insane. I'd never had a chance. He knew right from the start that we'd end up here. "Quit stalling. Where the hell is the bomb, Dylan?"

"It's in the loading dock at the mall. You have an hour and a half. Plenty of time to get the authorities there." Pausing, he sighed. There was a flicker of something less angry, almost a twinge of regret, in his eyes. "You know, I did what I had to do. I didn't want to hurt them, all those innocent people." He stood a little taller, and the flicker passed. "But I would have. Without a second thought—because it's what I *had* to do to see her again. To get her back."

He turned away from me and pressed his index finger to the back of the cuff, and just like that, in front of our eyes, shimmered, then vanished.

I dug into my pocket and pulled out the blue keychain knife Dad had given me on my sixteenth birthday. It was small, and the blade was on the dull side, but after a few minutes of sawing, I managed to cut his ties. He in turn, cut Cade's and Noah's.

"How much time do we have?" he asked Cade. I knew that tone. Determination. He still thought he could save me.

Cade frowned. He refused to look either of us in the eye. "Not much, sir. Without the keys, she's—"

I tuned him out. I tuned all of them out, actually. Cade was yelling at me—Dad had joined him—while Noah paced back and forth with his hands threaded through his hair, for the first time since we'd met, stunned into silence. Their words were there in the background, but they became nothing more than incoherent sounds and static. I surveyed the area, taking in my last look at what had been my moment. That single, life-defining action that changes you forever—however long that might be. That's when I noticed Dylan's jacket, sitting on the ground in the mud not far from me. He'd left it behind, for some reason. But really, it wasn't the jacket that caught my eye, but the small plastic thing poking out from one of the front pockets. Without a word, I sprinted for the leather, plunging my hand inside and pulling out a small syringe.

"He did it on purpose," I said, mainly to myself. "He took off the jacket and left it behind…" The others would disagree, but Dylan was smart. He wouldn't have left the jacket sitting there if he hadn't wanted me to find it. To have a chance to survive.

I wrapped my fingers around the syringe and stood. Dad and Cade, who'd finally realized I wasn't standing there listening to them yell at me, started over.

Cade swiped the syringe from my hand. His eyes were wide, a dangerous spark of hope igniting. "Is that—"

"Only one way to find out." I snatched it back, turning it over several times in my hand. I'd always hated needles, but as I popped off the protective plastic cap and rolled up my sleeve, I'd never been so happy to be stuck with a pointy object. I jammed the needle into my skin, cringing as it broke the surface, and pressed down on the plunger. My arm was instantly on fire, followed by an all over, tooth-chattering chill.

It passed quickly, though, and left me with one very important question. "How long do we have? Is there enough time for it to do what it needs to?"

"Already done," Noah said. He was grinning from ear to ear like I'd never seen before. "The effects of the quick prep are instant. You're packed and ready to go."

"Hadn't planned on a trip, but I'll take it." I turned to Dad, who was still staring at me with a mix of anger and horror. "Dad, I need to know about Mom. Why didn't you guys tell me?"

"She was recruited right out of high school," Dad said softly. His eyes sparkled, and he gave a small laugh. "I was there the first time they approached her. Her theories—her ideas—landed her at the top of their most wanted list. But she wanted no part of government work—or me."

That was almost too impossible to fathom. My parents had been so in love. The government thing, though... That I understood. While Mom had supported Dad and his career, I always got the feeling that she never trusted his superiors. "Obviously she caved."

He nodded. "She finally relented and I was assigned to her security team. She hated me, but I was a goner from the first time I set eyes on her. Each day I'd watch her work, and with every passing moment, I knew that there was only ever going to be her."

I smiled as his eyes sparked with memory.

"Persistence paid off. For me, anyway. I won the girl, but the military, well they didn't. Your mom confided in me. She said her work couldn't be trusted in the hands of the government. In anyone's hands, really. She said she knew without a shadow of a doubt that the world was not ready. She'd been working at the lab, but purposely not progressing." He forced a smile. "I was torn. Duty to my country, or loyalty to the woman I loved."

A chill raced up my back. Infinity existed here. Did that mean he...

"Cora was, and always will be, my life. It was her. Always her. I kept her secret and not once regretted the decision."

I shook my head. "I don't understand. Then how did Infinity—"

His expression darkened, and the fondness in his eyes morphed into something bleak. "I got sick. There was no name for it. No cure. I was dying, and there was nothing we could do."

Now it made sense. "Mom pushed ahead with the project..."

"She threw herself into it. Night and day, she stayed in the lab, desperate to find a way to make it all work."

"She thought another Earth would have a cure," Cade said, nodding.

Dad smiled. "That was what she believed. She was pregnant with Noah at the time. She always blamed herself for losing him. Convinced it was the stress that did it..."

"But this Earth's Infinity Project isn't functional." Noah glanced around, then refocused on Dad. He was trying hard to make it seem like he was unaffected by Dad's admission, but I could see it in his eyes. Sadness. "You're still alive. They found a cure?"

"They didn't. I was nearly gone. Days away from dying. Cora never gave up, but something was missing. She insisted the project wasn't progressing. I remember her coming to my room one night. It was late, and I was barely conscious. She kissed my forehead and told me how much she loved me. It should have been good-bye." He shrugged. "The next day, I opened my eyes and walked from the hospital, an inexplicably healthy man."

"She lied," I said in awe. "About the project not progressing. She figured it out, didn't she? Found a cure on some other Earth…"

Dad smiled at me. He pulled me close and placed the softest kiss atop my head. "She never confessed, but yes. I believe she figured it out. Found a way to make it work. She sought help, and saved me just as she'd promised."

"But she didn't tell the government," Cade said with a nod. There was a small smile on his face, and so much respect in his eyes. "She believed until the end that they couldn't be trusted with her work."

Dad nodded. "When she found out she was pregnant again… She still continued her research, but backed off. She was so afraid to overdo it… Then, when you were born, she ended up delegating much of the work to her team, determined to raise you. She made sure to steer them in the wrong directions, I imagine. To ensure the Infinity project never came to fruition."

A lump formed in my throat. "And then she got sick." I wasn't bitter that she'd saved my dad, but why hadn't she saved herself? Surely one of the Earth's out there had cured cancer.

"She wouldn't have wanted this for you."

He was wrong. While not exactly the way she'd meant it, Mom wanted me to live my life. Find adventure, love, and happiness. She wanted me to do great things. By skipping with Cade and Noah, I could accomplish that tenfold. I could help them track a dangerous criminal, and I could save lives. I could see not one world, but many. And if I had any say in it, no Kori Anderson on any world would lose her mother to illness. I would scour realities if need be. I would save her like she'd saved Dad.

"I love you, Dad. And I promise I'll be back. As soon as we find Dylan and get these cuffs off, I'll come home to you. I swear."

He straightened and gave me a sharp nod. There was nothing he could do and he knew it. Without another key, I was leaving whether I wanted to or not. "I'm proud of you, Kori. I always have been. She would be, too."

I couldn't help the candy-eating grin I knew was plastered across my face in that moment. Dad loved me. I knew that. But he'd always been disappointed at my lack of initiative. Of drive. To have these be his last words to me—at least for a little while—was more than I could have ever asked for.

To Noah, he said, "I am honored to have gotten the chance to see the man you would have become. I know your father is proud, because I am."

I couldn't be sure, but I thought I saw a shimmer in Noah's eyes. He straightened his back and offered Dad a firm salute.

I took his hand in my left, and Cade's in my right. I didn't know if skipping hurt, and I didn't want to admit that I was scared. Terrified, actually. As the tingling started, and my vision grew watery, I realized I was being given not only a second chance at life, but an extraordinary opportunity. I now had the chance to do real good by helping get a killer out of circulation, all while getting to know the brother I'd never had.

And then there was Cade. We were bound together now. Linked by Dylan and the cuffs. By what some might call fate… I didn't know where any of this would take us, but I was looking forward to finding out. To getting to know him better.

But aside from all that, and probably the most important—I had a chance to see my mom again. I knew it wouldn't be real, and any encounter I had with her couldn't last as long as I wanted. Cora Anderson was the heart, mind, and soul behind the Infinity project. Even if I was able to have just one more conversation with her, I would get my closure.

I had no doubt that I would make it home one day. We would find Dylan. For now, though, I had a feeling I was in for the adventure of a lifetime. I was going to keep my promise.

I was going to live my life in vivid color.

Cade

"And he didn't say a word?" Noah replaced the gas cap on the jeep, then popped the last chocolate chip cookie into his mouth whole. Wadding up the small package, he tossed it into the trash beside the pump and rounded the vehicle. How the guy didn't weigh eight hundred pounds was a medical miracle.

I tossed him the keys. "He kind of glared at me, then left."

More crunching. "That's not like him…"

He was right. My brother had never been a turn-the-other-cheek kind of guy. Cursing, threats—dramatics—Dylan didn't do anything silently. And after what I'd done to him… It wasn't every day that your own brother turned you in and set you on the path to execution. "Tell me I did the right thing."

Noah shook his head. He slid behind the wheel as I

settled into the passenger's seat. "Can't do that."

"Because you think I made a mistake." And I had. I'd made a huge mistake. I'd broken the law, something I'd sworn on my life that I would uphold and protect. I'd let him go.

"Because it's not my place, man." The engine sputtered, then roared to life. One of these days the ancient jeep was going to give out. It was on borrowed time. But, Noah loved the thing. Named it and polished its rusted body every damn Saturday. "You did what you had to do. I'll back you no matter what. You know that. Just be careful. If Dad finds out it was you…"

I let my head fall back and squeezed my eyes closed. "Yeah." His father—General Anderson—was not only my superior, but the closest thing to a father I'd ever known. If he found out how I'd betrayed him…

"I get it, you know. If that was Kori, I wouldn't have thought twice about it."

"Kori would have never done anything to get herself sentenced to death." Then again, even if she had, her brother wouldn't have turned her in like I had. "Speaking of—head to your place. She texted me while I was inside paying for the gas. Said she had some big news to share."

Noah mumbled something that sounded like "okay," then rummaged around in the center console until he found an open bag of chips. The jeep veered onto the road. We were only a few blocks away, so it took five minutes. Maybe ten because we hit every damn traffic light on Broadway. The entire way, all I could do was go over things in my head. Dylan had committed a crime. A crime against the military. The punishment was a death sentence. I'd known that, yet I'd still turned him in. Then, I'd changed my mind…

We pulled into the driveway, and Noah grunted. He pulled the key from the ignition and jabbed me in the arm with it. "What's done is done. Let it go. Your blood pressure is going to shoot through the roof. Not to mention your—"

I rolled my eyes and clamped my hand across his mouth. "Thank you, Doctor Anderson."

He snorted and got out of the car. I did the same. "All I'm saying is, you made a choice. You acted and now you gotta live with it. If we're lucky, he's two states over by now and is smart enough never to set foot near law enforcement again." He moved to unlock the front door, pausing a moment to scowl at me. "And seriously, is there a reason you're wearing your blacks? Do you need to do everything in that stupid uniform?"

I was damn proud of this uniform. Noah didn't quite understand it. He'd grown up taking the establishment for granted, but not me. Unlike the Anderson family, whose trust and friendship had been given freely, the army was the only thing in my life that I ever truly cared about. That I'd ever truly wanted. It meant something to wear this uniform.

When I wore this uniform, *I* meant something.

I waggled my eyebrows and shouldered him aside as he pulled the key from the lock. "Your sister *loves* my blacks—so yes." Over the threshold and into the living room. The Anderson house was someplace I knew better than my own home. I'd practically lived here since I was six. "Kori?"

"You sure she told you to meet her here? I thought

she was headed to the park to sketch." I pulled out my cell to double-check the text. "Yep. Says the house."

We searched the entire place and came up empty. It wasn't until we came back down to the living room that I noticed the basement door was open a crack. "Kori?"

"She's not down there, man. She hates the basement." Noah snickered. "I might have locked her in there when she was nine and told her an evil version of the Easter Bunny was going to eat her…"

I snorted. "You're such an ass…"

He was right, though. I knew she wouldn't be down there. But I started down the steps anyway, aware of an odd feeling settling in my gut. The lights were all off, so I couldn't see a thing, and when I got to the bottom and stepped onto the last stair, my foot slid in something slick, and my leg gave out. I ended up in a heap on the carpet while Noah snickered and groped for the light.

"The army must be desperate…" Light filled the stairwell and Noah's face turned ashen. "Is that *blood*?"

I'd started to pick myself up and froze, the air in my lungs all but turning to stone. It was blood. The entire bottom step was coated in it. It dripped to the floor, a thin trail of the stuff leading down the hall and around the corner toward the laundry room.

"She's a klutz, too," he said. He was shaking his head slowly, but there was panic in his eyes. "Just like you. She cut herself. Banged her head. Head wounds bleed like motherfu—"

I was up and running in an instant. Noah was right on my heels. He was yelling. He might have been cursing—the guy had a mouth worse than any trucker I'd ever seen—or he could have been calling out for

Kori. It was all just white noise though. There was so much blood.

Too much.

For a few seconds I convinced myself it wasn't her. We barreled into the laundry room, and at the far end, handcuffed and hanging from the pipes, was a girl. But she wasn't my girl. She couldn't be.

I threw myself forward, falling on my knees and slipping in the growing pool of blood. Noah had pushed ahead of me. He had his shirt off and was ripping it in half. When it was separated, he was beside the girl, tying the pieces over her wrists in violent, jerky motions.

"Here," he snapped. He grabbed my hand and wrapped the bandage tightly around her arm. "Pressure point. Inside fold of her elbow. Hold as firm as you can."

I did as I was told, never taking my eyes off her. Vaguely I was aware that Noah was on the phone. I heard the word ambulance, and bits and pieces of the address, then nothing. The sound of my own pulse, ramped and thundering in my ears, drowned it all out. "Don't do this, Kori. Stay with us. Stay with *me*."

"He got the vein. Nicked the artery but didn't slice through…" Noah was beside me, putting pressure on the inside of her other arm. Somehow he'd gotten her down. She wasn't attached to the pipe anymore. "It's been too long, though. She's lost too much."

That snapped my attention back. He wasn't looking at me. I didn't think he was even talking to me. He had a habit of talking to himself when things got bad. Entire conversations and arguments fought and won all by himself. "Noah…"

He looked up, and I knew. I could see it in his eyes,

in his expression. I could tell from the lack of life in his eyes. The way he shook his head was almost surreal. Once to the left, and then once to the right. Like the effort was almost too much. "They're coming, but they won't get here in time, Cade. It was too late when we got here."

I stared at him, sure I'd heard wrong. He couldn't possibly be suggesting...

He got the vein...

His words finally settled, and something rumbled in the back of my mind. Something dark and violent. "He *who*?" When Noah didn't answer, I lost it. "He who? Who did this?"

He didn't answer, but turned, his fingers still stroking the edge of her hair. I followed his gaze to the mirror above the dump sink. Written in what looked like lipstick was, *How does it feel?*

"No..." Though really, I'd already known.

I looked down. She was gone. It was strange, but I could tell by the air in the room. The lack of life, of spark. Kori had an energy that was almost electric. I felt it whenever she entered a room. She had a way of breathing light into darkness, into *my* darkness. Now, there was nothing. The space around me was a void and my insides were just...gone. I was hollow.

The room faded away. Brick and mortar, plaster and paint, none of it existed anymore. Nothing existed except for her.

And the rage.

I shifted so that I could lay her gently on the floor. After that I was moving. Noah called after me, but I ignored him. He wanted me to stay with her. To wait...

But there was no one left to stay with. Nothing left to wait for. No. I didn't need to wait.

I needed to act. Fast.

I didn't remember the walk outside, or getting behind the wheel of the jeep. I came back to myself only when I realized Noah had the keys.

Keys he was holding out to me. "He needs to fucking pay."

I didn't respond. I couldn't. If I opened my mouth, all that would come out was blackness and rage. It was in my blood, the anger. Dylan and I, we worked so hard to combat it. Took so much care in keeping it tucked away beneath the skin. Our father's legacy had been a constant cloud over both our heads. He'd unleashed his today.

I wasn't far behind.

The car ride from the house to Cora's lab normally took fifteen minutes. I blew every light and got us there in six. On the way I called the general. Told him he needed to meet me at the lab. That my brother had escaped. That he was heading there to break in, to steal tech.

To skip…

He'd started to question where I'd heard the term— Infinity was highly classified—but I hung up on him. The fewer questions he asked, the better. We could hash it out after this was over. After we'd made my brother pay for what he'd done. If I had to take us both out, Dylan wasn't leaving this place. At least not while there was breath in his lungs.

When we pulled up in front of Cora's lab, I didn't even bother killing the engine. Noah and I were out of the jeep and into the building in a flash. I flew past the elevator and burst through the stairwell door, taking the steps three, sometimes four at a time. By the time I hit the bottom landing, the pounding of my pulse and the itch in my fingers to tear into Dylan was all-consuming.

I rounded the corner and charged through the door to find him bent over a small box. I didn't think. I didn't hesitate or second guess my actions. I launched myself at him with every ounce of pain and rage over what he'd done fueling the attack.

"How could you!" I roared, grabbing him by the neck and throwing him sideways. I'd caught him off guard, so he tumbled to the left, but caught himself before going down completely.

Dylan opened his mouth, but I wasn't interested. There was nothing he could say, no excuse he could possibly concoct, that would justify what he'd done. I balled my fists tight and hit him in the face as hard as I could.

"She was innocent!" I hit him again.

"You knew what she meant to me." Another blow.

"She was your friend!" I swung again. That time, though, Dylan pivoted and ducked. The blow sailed harmlessly by, the momentum of it sending me off-balance. I crashed into a workstation as Noah propelled himself at my brother, a fury-filled roar on his lips.

"You sick fuck," he spat as his fists pummeled Dylan. One to the gut, another to the side of the head.

Dylan went down, crashing into a small metal cart a few feet away.

I started toward him, but Noah beat me to it. He fell to his knees and began whaling on him. One. Two. Three.

Four… He was lost in the rage. So lost that he didn't see Dylan's hand groping for the broken leg of the cart.

I called out a warning, but it was too late. Dylan brought the metal thing up with brutal force. It connected with the side of Noah's head and sent him sprawling sideways.

"Now you know how I feel," Dylan bellowed as he climbed to his feet. He snatched something off the table beside him—one of the project's cuffs—and clicked it into place around his wrist. "Now you have to live my nightmare."

The fury in his voice stopped me from throwing myself at him again. In that moment, the overwhelming reality of what had happened hit me, crushing my body like a fifty-ton weight. "It's not the same." There was anger in my voice, but something else as well. Something defeated. "I didn't kill Ava. What you did to—"

The general burst in, rushing forward. But Dylan was smart. He would have anticipated trouble. In a blurring move, he reached behind him and whipped out a pistol, pointing it at the general. "Stop."

Karl froze, the expression on his face a mix of fury and horror. "Take it easy." He held up both hands. "You're making this worse for yourself."

"You…" Dylan spat the word like the vilest of curses. "You deserve this as much as he does." He jabbed a finger at me. "He took her from me, but you're keeping her from me."

"Cade," the general said. Noah was stumbling upright a few feet away, the both of us covered in blood. His eyes flickered from Dylan to me, widening. "That's a lot of blood. You boys all right?"

"It's not—"

"They got their asses kicked, but most of that blood doesn't belong to them. Its Kori's," Dylan said smugly.

The general's expression twisted, almost as though he didn't believe it. A second later, he started forward.

Dylan popped off the safety. "Not kidding, old man. Stop." He held up his arm and gave it a shake. "I'm leaving. You won't stop me from finding Ava—or getting my revenge. You both kept me from the person I loved; now I'm going to return the favor. Everywhere I go, every place I skip to, I'm going to *kill her*. I won't stop until every single Kori Anderson is wiped from the face of this planet."

"You're not leaving this lab," the general said. His voice was low, dangerous. I'd heard that tone from him only once before, when I was little and Kori had had an issue with someone bullying her at school.

Dylan sighed and readjusted the weapon. "Wrong. You're the one who isn't leaving this—"

I kicked out and knocked the gun from his hand. Dylan cursed and dove for the table and Noah and the general rushed forward. They weren't fast enough, though. He pressed his fingers to the inside of the cuff and, as I lunged for him, he grinned. His boot came at me, lightning fast, and everything swam. My forehead kissed the edge of a metal table, and when the world stopped spinning, Noah, the general, and I were the only ones in the lab.

Noah helped me off the tile floor. "We have to move fast," he said. "We have to—"

"She's gone?" He shook his head. "Tell me I'm wrong. That I misunderstood." His gaze dropped to my blood-soaked shirt. "That it's not hers…"

I'd never seen the general, the man who'd raised me, a man whose strength and fortitude helped shape the person I'd grown into, look so broken. I understood it. A part of me was already rotting away. Dead and decaying beyond hope of revival. But I couldn't call up sympathy. Not in that moment. All I had was anger.

I dove for the table and grabbed the last two remaining cuffs. Dylan had taken three of the cuffs in the set with him, but that was fine. I only needed two. I tossed one to Noah. "Find the prep serum."

He nodded and took off for the set of cabinets on the far wall.

"No," the general said, shaking his head. The dazed look in his eyes faded, replaced by something violent. Almost animal like. "He won't get away with this. I'll send a team—"

"No team, sir." I held up the last remaining cuff. "Two left. That's it. Noah and me."

"You're just out of basic, and Noah is a civilian. You cannot possibly expect me to allow you use of a top secret military project—one you should know nothing about—to exact vengeance."

"What I expect," I said, using a tone I'd never used with him before. "Is for you to allow your son, Kori's brother, and the guy who loved her more than his own life, to go after her killer."

Noah returned with two syringes. They were filled with a pale pink liquid. "I think this is it."

"You *think*?"

He shrugged, and without hesitating, popped off the cap and plunged the needle into his skin.

The general's face contorted. "What are you—"

"Dad, Cade is right. There's no one on this Earth who will do more to find Dylan than us. There's no one who will be more motivated."

He shook his head. I could see he was torn. Ripped in half—loving father and loyal general.

"No one knows him like we do, sir."

He squeezed his eyes closed for a minute. When he opened them again, there was a spark of determination there. "Go. Bring that bastard back so I can watch him die. But be warned, you do this at your own risk. I cannot officially give you my permission. If you take this action, you accept full responsibility for the consequences. You're subjecting yourself to the possibility of the death penalty for a crime against the military."

I nodded as Noah sank the needle into my upper arm, then slapped the cuff around my ankle. It was just in time. A moment later, everything grew hazy. My stomach roiled, and a wave of nausea hit hard. One minute we were standing in front of the general, his grim expression a warning. The next we were standing outside the lab, alone.

On another version of Earth.

If you loved *INFINITY*,
don't miss Jus Accardo's *TOUCH*

Available now!

A Denazen Novel

Touch

Chapter One

I couldn't see them, but I knew they were there, waiting at the bottom. Bloodthirsty little shits—they were probably *praying* for this to go badly. "What do you think—about a fifteen-foot drop?"

"Easily," Brandt said. He grabbed my arm as a blast of wind whipped around us. Once I was steady on my skateboard, he tipped back his beer and downed what was left.

Together, we peered over the edge of the barn roof. The party was in full swing below us. Fifteen of our closest—and craziest—friends.

Brandt sighed. "Can you really do this?"

I handed him my own empty bottle. "They don't call me Queen of Crazy Shit for nothing." Gilman was poised on his skateboard to my left. Even in the dark, I could see the moonlight glisten off the sweat beading his brow. Pansy. "You ready?"

He swallowed and nodded.

Brandt laughed and tossed the bottles toward the woods. There were several seconds of silence, then a muted crash, followed by hoots and hysterical laughter from our friends below. Only drunk people would find shattering bottles an epic source of amusement.

"I dunno about this, Dez," he said. "You can't see anything down there. How do you know where you're gonna land?"

"It'll be fine. I've done this, like, a million times."

Brandt's words were clipped. "Into a pool. From a ten-foot-high garage roof. This is at least fifteen feet. Last thing I want to do is drag your ass all the way home."

I ignored him—the usual response to my cousin's chiding—and bent my knees. Turning back to Gilman, I smiled. "Ready, *Mr. Badass*?"

Someone below turned up one of the car stereos. A thumping techno beat drifted up. Hands on the sill behind me, drunken shouts of encouragement rising from below, I let go.

Hair lashed like a thousand tiny whips all along my face. The rough and rumbling texture of the barn roof beneath my board. Then nothing.

Flying. It was like flying.

For a few blissful moments, I was weightless. A feather suspended in midair right before it fluttered gracefully to the ground. Adrenalin surged through my system, driving my buzz higher.

The crappy thing about adrenalin highs, though? They never last long enough.

Mine lasted what felt like five seconds—the time it took to go from the barn roof to the not-so-cushy pile of hay below.

I landed with a jar—nothing serious—a bruised tailbone and some black and blues, maybe. Hardly the worst I'd ever walked away with. Stretching out the kink in my back, I brushed the hay from my jeans. A quick inspection revealed a smudge above my right knee and a few splotches of mud up the left side. All things the washing machine could fix.

Somewhere behind me, a loud wail filled the air. Gilman.

Never mix tequila and peach schnapps with warm Bud Light. It makes you do stupid things. Things like staying too long at a party you were told not to go to or making out in the bushes with someone like Mark Geller.

Things like skateboarding off the roof of a rickety barn...

Well, that's not entirely true. I tended to do these things without the buzz. Except kissing Mark Geller. That was *all* alcohol.

"You okay?" Brandt called from the rooftop.

I gave him a thumbs-up and went to check on Gilman. He was surrounded by a gaggle of girls, which made me wonder if he wasn't faking it—at least a little. A scrawny guy like Gilman didn't warrant much in the way of female attention, so I'd bet all ten toes he'd run his mouth tonight to attract some.

"You are one crazy ass, Chica," he mumbled, climbing to his feet.

I pointed to the pile of hay I'd landed in—several yards farther than where he'd crashed. "*I'm* crazy? At least I aimed for the hay."

"Wooooo!" came Brandt's distinctive cry. A moment

later, he was running around the side of the barn, fist pumping. He stopped at my side and stuck his tongue out at Gilman, who smiled and flipped him off. He punched me in the arm. "That's my girl!"

"A girl who needs to bail. Ten minutes of kissy face in the bushes and Mark Geller thinks we're soul mates. So don't need a stalker."

Brandt frowned. "But the party's just getting started. You don't want to miss the Jell-O shots!"

Jell-O shots? Those were my favorite. Maybe it was worth…no. "I'm willing to risk it."

"Fine, then I'll walk with ya."

"No way," I told him. "You're waiting for Her Hotness to show, remember?" He'd been trying to hook up with Cara Finley for two weeks now. She'd finally agreed to meet him at the party tonight, and I wasn't ruining his chances by having him bail to play guard dog.

He glanced over his shoulder. In the field under the moonlight, people were beginning to dance. "You sure you're okay to go alone?"

"Of course." I gestured to my feet. "No license needed to drive these babies."

He was hesitant, but in the end, Cara won out. We said good-bye, and I started into the dark.

Home was only a few minutes away—through the field, across a narrow stream, and over a small hill. I knew these woods so well, I could find home with my eyes closed. In fact, I practically had on more than one occasion.

Pulling my cell from my back pocket, I groaned. One a.m. If luck was with me, I'd have enough time to stumble home and tuck myself in before Dad got there. I hadn't meant to stay so late this time. Or drink so much. I'd only agreed to go as moral support for Brandt, but when Gilman started running his mouth... Well, I'd had no choice but stay and put up so he'd *shut* up. I had a rep to worry about, after all.

By the time I hit the halfway point between the field and the house—a shallow, muddy stream I used to play in as a child—I had to stop for a minute. Thumping beats and distant laughter echoed from the party, and for a moment I regretted not taking Brandt up on his offer to walk home with me. Apparently, that last beer had been a mistake.

I stumbled to the water's edge and forced the humid air in and out of my lungs. Locking my jaw and holding my breath, I mentally repeated, *I will not throw up*.

After a few minutes, the nausea passed. Thank God. No way did I want to walk home smelling like puke. I shuffled back from the water, ready to make my way home, when I heard a commotion and froze.

Crap. The music had been too loud and someone must have called the cops. Perfect. Another middle-of-the-night call from the local PD wasn't something Dad would be happy about. On second thought, bring on the cops. The look on his face would be so worth the aggravation.

I held my breath and listened. Not sounds coming from the party—men yelling.

Heavy footsteps stomping and thrashing through the brush.

The yelling came again—this time closer.

I crammed the cell back into my pocket, about to begin what was sure to be a messy climb up the embankment, when movement in the brush behind me caught my attention. I whirled in time to see someone stumble down the hill and land a few feet from the stream.

"Jesus!" I jumped back and tripped over an exposed root, landing on my butt in the mud. The guy didn't move as I fumbled upright and took several wobbly steps forward. He'd landed at an odd angle, feet bare and covered in several nasty looking slices. I squinted in the dark and saw he was bleeding through his thin white T-shirt in several places as well as from a small gash on the side of his head. The guy looked like he'd gone ten rounds with a weed whacker.

Somewhere between eighteen and nineteen, he didn't look familiar. No way he went to my high school. I knew pretty much everyone. He couldn't have been at the party—he was cute. I would have remembered. I doubted he was even local. His hair was too long, and he was missing the signature Parkview T-shirt tan. Plus, even in the dark it was easy to make out well-defined arms and broad shoulders. This guy obviously hit the gym—something the local boys could've used.

I bent down to check the gash on the side of his head, but he jerked away and staggered to his feet as the yelling came again.

"Your shoes!" he growled, pointing to my feet. His voice was deep and sent tiny shivers dancing up and down my spine. "Give me your shoes!"

Buzzed or not, I was still pretty sharp. Whoever those guys yelling in the woods were, they were after him. Drug deal gone south? Maybe he'd gotten caught playing naked footsie with someone else's girlfriend?

"Why—?"

"Now!" he hissed.

I wouldn't have even considered giving up my favorite pair of red Vans if he hadn't looked so seriously freaked. He was being chased. He thought having my shoes would somehow help? Fine. Maybe as a weapon? Rocks would have worked better in my opinion, but to each his own.

Against my better judgment, I took several steps back and, without turning away from him, pulled them off. Stepping up, I tossed him the sneakers—and teetered forward. Instead of trying to catch me, he took a wide step back, allowing me to fall into the mud.

My frickin' hero!

I struggled upright and flicked a glob of mud from my jeans as he bent down to snatch the shoes—without moving his gaze from mine. His eyes were beautiful—ice blue and intense—and I found it hard to look away. He set the sneakers on the ground and poised his right foot over the first one. A giggle rose in my throat. No way he'd be jamming his bigass feet into them.

He proved me wrong. Cramming his toes in, heels poking obscenely over the edges, he wobbled with an odd sort of grace to the embankment and wedged himself between a partially uprooted tree and a hollowed-out log. He teetered slightly as he walked, and I remembered the nasty gashes on his foot. Great. Now on top of *borrowing* my kicks, he was going to bleed all over them.

My gaze dropped to the spot he'd been standing. It was dark and the moon had tucked itself behind the clouds so I couldn't see very well, but something about the ground didn't look quite right. The color seemed off—darker than it should be.

I squinted, bending to brush my fingers along the dark spot, but more rustling in the woods had my gaze swinging hard left, heartbeat kicking into high gear. The next thing I knew, a group of four men exploded from the brush and came storming down the embankment like ravers on crack. Dressed in dark blue, skintight body suits that covered them from fingertips to toes, little was left to the imagination. Mimes. They reminded me of mimes.

Mimes with what looked a lot like Tasers.

"You!" The one in the front called out as he skidded to a stop. Looking at the ground, he surveyed the trail leading to the shallow water. "Has anyone been past here?"

From the corner of my eye I saw the boy, face pale, watching us. All the men would have had to do was turn to the right and they'd surely see him.

"Some punk came barreling through a few minutes ago." I stomped my sock-clad foot. Mud sloshed through the material and oozed between my toes. Ick! "Stole my damn shoes!"

"Which way did he go?"

Was he serious? I was about to make a joke about not being allowed to talk to strangers, but the look on his face made me think twice. Mr. Mime didn't seem like he was rocking a sense of humor. I threw my hands up in surrender and pointed in the direction opposite the one I planned on going.

Without another word, the men split into two groups. Half of them heading the way I'd directed, the other half taking off opposite. Huh. Guess they didn't trust a semi-drunk chick with a nose ring and no shoes.

I waited till they were out of sight before making my way over to where the boy crouched, still hidden behind the brush. "They're gone. I think it's safe to come out and play now."

He held my gaze and maneuvered out of the hiding spot. When he made no move to remove my sneakers, I nodded to his feet. "Planning to give my kicks back anytime soon?"

He shook his head and folded his arms. "I can't give them back to you."

"Why the hell not? Because seriously, dude, red is *not* your color."

He looked at the ground for a moment, then let his gaze wander over the path he'd traveled earlier. "I'm hungry." He was staring again. "Do you have any food?"

He gets my shoes then asks for food? The guy had some serious nerve.

The gash on his head still oozed a little and the faint bluish-purple of a bruise was beginning to surface across his left cheek, but it was the haunted look in his eyes that stood out above everything else like a flashing neon sign. He kept flicking his fingers, one at a time. Pointer, middle, ring, and pinky—over and over.

An owl hooted and I remembered the time. Dad would be home soon. This might work to my advantage. I knew bringing the guy home would royally piss him off. He'd have puppies if he found a stranger in the house. Hell, he might even have a llama.

But while the thought of pushing Dad closer to the edge gave me warm tingles, it wasn't my only motivation.

I kind of wanted a little more time with the guy. Those arms... Those *eyes*. We were all alone out in the middle of the woods. If he'd wanted to go serial killer on me, he would have made a move by now. I didn't believe he was dangerous. "My house isn't far from here—Dad went to the grocery store the other day. Lots of junk food if that's your thing."

The look in his eyes made me think he didn't trust me—which I didn't get. I'd given him my *shoes* for crap's sake. "I don't know who your friends were, but they might double back. You'll be safe at my place for a while. Maybe they'll give up."

He looked downstream and shook his head. "They are not the type of men who give up."

Acknowledgments

I wrote the first few pages of Infinity in 2012, then set it aside. Not uncommon. I have a large folder of first chapters, all sitting there waiting for me to return. Some I go back to—like Infinity—while others just sit there and collect virtual mold.

The basis of the story at the time was a girl who had lost her mother to cancer finds a way to travel to parallel Earths, where she sees her again. I picked it up in early 2014 after pitching the idea to my amazing agent and it sold. We got everything set and rolling, and the book was set to tentatively release in fall of 2015. Obviously since we're sitting in the 2016 calendar year, that didn't happen.

Almost exactly a month before Infinity sold, my own mother was diagnosed with stage 4 cancer. Unlike Kori though, I didn't lose her. Treatment was rough, and very, very long, but she is currently cancer free and doing well.

In a lot of ways, this book has been one of the hardest I've ever worked on—but also the closest to my heart. I can pretty much remember where I was at every stage of its life. 99% of Infinity was done in oncology wards, doctor's offices, hospital rooms, and chemo treatment sessions. During the course of Infinity's early life, I watched my mom struggle and fight despite a bleak prognosis, and remain in a state of awe over her fortitude.

There is not a thank you big enough for my mom. She showed me what true strength is. She is a warrior, and far braver than I could ever hope to be.

And to my husband, Kevin, who is probably the most amazing man on the planet... I would have drowned ten thousand times over if not for him. I would spend days at the hospital, and he would be there with me, after exceedingly long days at work, despite being ready to drop. Always there, always holding my hand.

Thank you to my editor, Liz Pelletier, for believing in me once again, and also being so patient and allowing me the time I needed to deal with things. I remain convinced that Entangled was one of the best decisions of my life and am eternally grateful for everything you've done for me over the years. Also, virtual hugs to Stacy Abrams, Christine Chhun, and Nancy Cantor for helping bring this book out into the world, and also to Lynn and Gia for being amazing crit partners.

Hugs and kisses to my agent, Nicole Resciniti, who came into my life just months before it fell apart. This is our first book (of many, many more) together and I am honored to have someone like you in my corner.

And thank you to LJ Anderson for the breathtaking cover. The colors, the simplicity... I was truly giddy when I first saw it!

And finally, to all of you. Thank you just isn't quite enough. For your patience and continued support, for your understanding and kind words. It's taken me much longer than anticipated to bounce back from all of this, and I truly appreciate everyone sticking with me. Hugs, kisses, and cookies for everyone!

GRAB THE ENTANGLED TEEN RELEASES READERS ARE TALKING ABOUT!

FORGET ME ALWAYS
BY SARA WOLF

All warfare is deception. Even in high school.

It's been nineteen days since Isis Blake forgot about him. The boy she can't quite remember. She's stuck in the hospital with a turban-size bandage on her head, more Jell-o than a human being should ever face, and a tiny bit of localized amnesia. Her only goal? To get out of this place before she becomes a complete nutjob herself.

But as Isis's memories start to return, she realizes there's something important there at the edges of her mind. Something that may mean the difference between life and death. Something about Sophia, Jack's girlfriend.

Jack Hunter—the "Ice Prince"—remembers everything. Remembers Isis's purple hair and her smart-ass mouth. Remembers that for a little while, Isis made him feel human. She made him feel. She burned a hole in the ice…and it's time to freeze back up. Boys like him don't deserve girls like her. Because Jack is dangerous. And that danger might be the only thing protecting her from something far more threatening.

Her past.

Opposition
by Jennifer L. Armentrout

Katy knows the world changed the night the Luxen came. She can't believe Daemon stood by as his kind threatened to obliterate every last human and hybrid on Earth. But the lines between good and bad have blurred.

Daemon will do anything to save those he loves, even if it means betrayal. But when it quickly becomes impossible to tell friend from foe, and the world is crumbling around them, they may lose everything to ensure the survival of their friends…and mankind.

Remember Yesterday
by Pintip Dunn

Sixteen-year-old Jessa Stone is the most valuable citizen in Eden City. Her psychic abilities could lead to significant scientific discoveries, if only she'd let TechRA study her. But ten years ago, the scientists kidnapped and experimented on her, leading to severe ramifications for her sister, Callie. She'd much rather break into their labs and sabotage their research—starting with Tanner Callahan, budding scientist and the boy she loathes most at school.

The past isn't what she assumed, though—and neither is Tanner. He's not the arrogant jerk she thought he was. And his research opens the door to the possibility that Jessa can rectify a fatal mistake made ten years earlier. She'll do anything to change the past and save her sister—even if it means teaming up with the enemy she swore to defeat.

SPINDLE
BY SHONNA SLAYTON

In a world where fairies lurk and curses linger, love can bleed like the prick of a finger... Briar Rose knows her life will never be a fairy tale. Most days it feels like her best friend, Henry Prince, is the only one in her corner. But then a mysterious peddler offers her a "magic" spindle that could save her job at the spinning mill. When her fellow spinner girls start coming down with the mysterious sleeping sickness, Briar will have to start believing in fairy tales...and in the power of a prince's kiss.

OLIVIA DECODED
BY VIVI BARNES

This isn't my Jack, who once looked at me like I was his world. The guy who's occupied the better part of my mind for eight months.

This is Z, criminal hacker with a twisted agenda and an arsenal full of anger.

I've spent the past year trying to get my life on track. New school. New friends. New attitude. But old flames die hard, and one look at Jack—the hacker who enlisted me into his life and his hacking ring, stole my heart, and then left me—and every memory, every moment, every feeling comes rushing back. But Jack's not the only one who's resurfaced in my life. And if I can't break through Z's defenses and reach the old Jack, someone will get hurt...or worse.